TATTERED PORTRAIT

By

Jef Huntsman

Published by Belray Books, LLC

This book, and all characters contained herein are fiction. Any resemblance to actual people or real events is unintended.

Tattered Portrait / Jef Huntsman – First Edition
ISBN # 978-0-9975748-0-7 (pb)
ISBN # 978-0-9975748-1-4 (ebook)

Cover designed by Harry Baldwin

Dedication

This book is dedicated to a feisty, amazing lady who sat for hours under a small lamp with spell-bound eyes sliding across many a written word—my mom, Clara Huntsman.

TATTERED
PORTRAIT

Tattered Portrait

By Jef Huntsman

Chapter 1

I don't mind planes. I'm not afraid of bumps and drops, and never have thoughts about everyone screaming as the plane nosedives or of oxygen masks dropping down in front of passengers like dangling vessels of doom. But today I watched the dark clouds gather to the east as discomfort hardened down deep in my gut, radiating from my belly button to my shoulder blades—my own Bermuda triangle. Simultaneous sensations skittered up my throat, slamming the top of my head, radiating into my skull.

Don't get me wrong, I hadn't developed a sudden fear of flying. I just wasn't all that ecstatic to be going to the place I once called home. Sure, I loved Aunt Velora and my sister, but disconcerting thoughts of my dad unraveled me.

Dad almost sounds like a swear word the way I use it. *Daaahd!*

My father was a jovial man who greeted people with scatological jokes and offensive alcohol breath from his early-morning to late-night binges. He was trained in the law and dressed the part; the only distraction was the bottles clacking together in his suit pockets when he stood up to address the court.

Early mornings, when his head was almost clear, he would pour liquor into opaque, empty bottles of fancy mouthwash, cough syrup, Bayer aspirin, and even an old bottle of Coppertone suntan lotion. At night, the bottles prattled in the dishwasher as he enjoyed his nightcap in the study, a room of dusty books and a desk pocked with highball-glass rings. Regardless, the doors were shut and locked most of the time.

The tiny room outside the study was our living room, though not much living ever happened there. It held two uncomfortable oak chairs with a lamp between them that I remember my mom referring to as a "whore's lamp." Sometimes we brought down toys and played on the hardwood floor, just outside our dad's study.

Fear always shrouded me when I entered my father's study and saw him at his desk. I would stand cowering, silencing even the sound of my breath. Sometimes I would wait forever to ask whatever I came in for. Other times I would back out of the room without a sound, then scamper quietly up the stairs to my room. He always knew I was there; making me wait was his sword. Dad ignored me as he sipped from his coffee cup, with the inscription "Best Dad," supposedly my sister Jen had given it to him. The two of us knew it was really from Aunt Velora. The thought of it always made me laugh at the irony. Inches from his cup sat an uncapped bottle—scotch if it was morning, whiskey if it was after noon.

My body sagged in the seat as I eyed the home's worn look from my rented blue Hyundai. I didn't go up to the porch and knock on the door. In fact, I kept the engine running for a fast getaway in case anybody appeared at a window.

I spent my grade school to high school years at Aunt Velora's. She was the reason I was here at all. I received the invitation, written in a red pencil scribble, telling me to get here before she dies. Yes, it was a little dramatic, but it worked—I came as ordered. She was the one adult from my childhood who I knew possessed humanity and a good set of running legs when she chased me.

I turned off the car, but left the keys at the ready in the ignition. My mind changed and I turned the key, giving enough gas to hear the soothing roar. I'd need a paper bag if my breathing didn't slow down. Even as an infant, I felt the volatility behind the broad smile of the man I called "Dad." It's amazing how much sperm can affect a child. Because here I am, as pathetic a human as there ever was, waiting for my father to walk out the door while I keep the gear shift lever partially depressed.

The house was silent, but stories echoed from its unpainted front porch. The once-pristine sidewalk to the porch steps appeared reshaped by the environment. The cement lifted up in places as though an earthquake had knocked it about. Each section was separately jilted by the old, front yard trees that grew until Dad's "water conservation" turned our once-green shade trees into grey monuments. It would have been better to impose the conservation on his liquor cabinet. But that wasn't happening.

I never really thought about going in the house. I just wanted to see it in the light. Whenever I dreamt of this house, it always appeared at night; sometimes it was raining and often it was windy. Even when I was five years old, my house felt like a claustrophobic closet. On the few days when my self-absorbed father actually left the house to meet a client, I would turn my face towards a sunny window and breathe in the freshness of sunlight. The rest of the time, the blinds were shut. He scolded me many times after I forgot to pull them closed. Sometimes Mom would take the blame.

My father told me, so often I could quote him verbatim, that we were born of king's blood. He was proud of that tidbit and would work it into conversations without any setup. His story was grand; he claimed we descended from King Louis, complete with his carriages and courtesans. Or, as my dad would put it, "He had a way with the ladies, and would ride behind the finest horses in one of five carriages." Supposedly, the wonderful King Louis dispensed food at the fountains and churches to the peasants of his kingdom. He was generous, loved, and as handsome as a prince in a Disney movie.

About a decade ago, I searched for our genealogy and found Louis. He was French—not Welsh, as my dad imagined. That's not all: Louis was nothing more than a feudal landowner who (local stories say) resided with Satan after his hanging. When I told my father about my research, he brushed me off with a dismissive wave. "You don't have the years to understand history, like a fully schooled gentleman," he said.

He was deliberately blind to the fact that by then his child possessed his master's degree. I answered wryly, "Perhaps not. But then, I don't understand drinking like a fully primed alcoholic, either."

He scooted me off with another of his hand waves. Even his inebriated posture seldom wavered from erect and perfect; his suited body almost always stood framed against the window, while the summer's evening sun spotlighted a galaxy of book dust—but there was always the wave of the hand shoving away unresolved issues. It meant the conversation was over and the door was shut again.

I was my dad's designated driver, starting four years before I received my driver's license until my departure east to the University of Tampa. Once I left, my sister drove the king's liquored blood from royal palace to royal pub.

I remember my mom sitting on the porch on a bentwood chair, watching me and my sister play on uncut, verdant grass. She moved between moods of contentment and silent exasperation. Mom may have occasionally smiled; I just don't recall any of those times. I do remember her lovely voice.

On good days, she used to call us to dinner with a sing-song lilt, "Ben, Bennie . . . Benjamin." After a pause of a couple of breaths, there was "Jen, Jennie . . . Jennifer . . . dinnertime." I remember that not only because of its rarity, but because she always sounded pleasant and loving. I'm pretty sure she suffered from a solid case of depression, but she never tried to drown it with alcohol. Her escape through my infant years was downing coffee by the tank and staring blankly into nowhere.

When I was five, Mom disappeared. Dad used to say, "She took off with half a man, because she couldn't handle a whole one." She went off with a slender man with thick, dark hair who wanted to be an actor, or so Aunt Velora told me and my sister. She also mentioned, "He ended up being nothing more than fizzled ambition." Remembering her old comments, I assume that my aunt and Mom must have at least talked occasionally during those early years.

There was also a rumor from my Grandma Parch that Mom

and the skinny man were living in a mining camp in Montana. Each time she talked about it, Grandma always snickered, as though she knew more. Grandma outlived Grandpa by fifty-one years. She died at eighty-eight from a heart attack while taking a shower. She was more of a holiday grandma—we saw her only on Christmas, Thanksgiving, and Veterans Day, the three cold holidays.

***

A mixed breed of dog, with hair matted and spiked from congealed filth and burrs, barked at me from the sidewalk. I threw him a couple of Ranch Doritos to quiet him. He waited for more. I threw the whole damn bag out. He nuzzled in it, shook it several times, then glanced up and walked away. I guess I was trying to be inconspicuous, though I'm not sure I accomplished it. I knew I wasn't ready to talk to Dad. Wasn't sure I ever would be.

A couple of times, I thought the doorknob turned. I gulped air, then realized the mirage was probably the heat. I waited.

The curtain moved. My heart began beating hard, trying to escape through my throat. My foot involuntarily pressed on the gas pedal. The engine roared in park. The house lay still.

Chapter 2

My sister and I were raised mostly by my Uncle Keith and Aunt Velora. They were a fastidious couple who were more acquaintances than friends or lovers. They always walked around each other without conversation or acknowledgement. Of course, there was the talk of food or the weather that broke up the clatter of silverware at the dining table. "I'm going to the store" was spoken more to the house in general than to anyone in particular, as if addressing a chair or a lamp. They both pursued separate, inanimate loves that ridiculously held them together. Though they ignored each other, they adored us with more attention than we deserved.

Uncle Keith was a shoe store owner at an insignificant strip mall. My New Shoes, it was called. As far as I knew, he only owned two pairs of shoes—his day shoes and his night shoes. The day pair was polished to a high black shine. The night pair were more moccasins than shoes, tinted brown with age.

He spent most of his time off collecting magazines about guns, hunting, and fishing. They were stacked everywhere in the half-basement, leaving only a winding path to his aged, cheap desk. I never saw him go hunting, never even remember him visiting a forest or a lake. His closet was filled with white dress shirts and blue pants—no camouflage, no bright orange vests. As far as I knew, he owned only one gun, a 22-caliber Smith and Wesson handgun that was mounted in a glass case, centered perfectly on the fireplace mantle. It always seemed alone and out of place with the other ancient, grand-room décor. It was a small, feminine weapon that became lost and insignificant when my uncle held it in his soft palms.

The handgun was retrieved from its case with the twist of a cabinet lock at the back every evening after dinner, before Uncle Keith hid himself away in his basement. He would rub it down with an oil cloth after several minutes of caressing his weapon. I always wondered if the thing would grow legs and dart for the door if anyone ever put a bullet in it. The pistol was a piece of metal art and seemingly the love of my uncle's life. As a child, I watched him beam a smile at it whenever he walked by that fireplace.

***

I checked my watch and thought about getting something substantial in my belly. The flavored chips left a taste on my teeth with a little orange dusting that I kept trying to rub off with my tongue. It lingered. I held off on the hotel check-in, as though I was waiting for an invite into my father's house. I knew I couldn't handle being behind his closed door more than a millisecond. The thought of walking through the area where the gate used to be brought internal feelings of constricted breathing and lightheadedness. Dad wouldn't ask me to stay anyway. He might ask me to drive him to the store for a fine bottle of wine or to a local pub to savor the heat of Johnnie Walker Red sliding down. He romanticized drinking like an elite skill.

I knew the house wasn't moving and the door wouldn't open, but I stared nevertheless. I anticipated life where there wasn't any. I waited for color but saw only shades of grey. It never felt like my house. I just borrowed a piece of it until I was six, then I was shuttled over to my aunt and uncle's, returning only for brief periods. The memory of those short visits left distaste in my throat and tightness in my shoulders.

I put my hand to the ignition and rattled the keys, willing myself to start it up and drive away. I hated Dad. Why was I having such a hard time breaking frail bonds? Why the hell was I here?

I couldn't help glaring at the house and wondering what the magnet was. It never was that great of a house. Many in the neighborhood were much better and hopefully held brighter memories. They, at least, had open curtains. Other people on the street did family things. They went to movies and out for ice cream. On rare occasions we went to restaurants that mixed and stirred and poured colored concoctions.

The yard was small. A single garage was buried down two paths of concrete to the back right of the house. If I remember correctly, weeds were always the plants of choice in the backyard. The house held three small bedrooms, two up, one down; a kitchen with a back door no one opened; a front room that was used only for walking through; and my dad's study with aged bookcases behind closed doors. I recall Mom heavily watering the front yard and surrendering to Dad anything behind the four-foot fence that separated the front from the back.

I lay back against the door and popped a mint in my mouth as silence gathered around me. I was almost relaxed and content. I thought about Aunt Velora and her message. I held it on my outstretched tongue and giggled a bit. Is she really sick, or was this a ploy to get me back to town?

***

Aunt Velora was pretty without makeup, her face was full with a narrow nose and flower-stem-green eyes. She could barely do math, and she stumbled to read the newspaper with her lips moving. I loved that lady more than anyone else in my family, except maybe my sister, Jennifer. All of her eccentricities and plainness created pure beauty. Our bedroom would light up when she walked in at night to read us a story. Even her cooking didn't discourage my love for her.

She possessed her idiosyncrasies, like her husband. She was a less-than-average-to-terrible cook who spent a good part of her day cutting recipes out of magazines. Between the two of them subscribing to magazines, the mailman used two hands to deliver the mail. When he drove away, the mailbox post bowed slightly, waiting patiently for someone to remove the afternoon delivery.

Her closet was double-stacked with shoes, half of which were bought at stores other than My New Shoes. Uncle Keith pretended not to know, but he raved about the ones from his store and ignored it when she wore one of the mutts.

Aunt Velora was a collector like her husband. She filled shoe boxes with recipes, meticulously, each bulging a bit at the seams, with lids that would never fit again. She wrote the date the box was filled with a black Sharpie, taking her time with each number. Then she walked them ceremoniously down the hall, placing them in one of her chest of drawers.

A whole room was designated as her recipe room. It was a small room with a touch of madness written all over it. It was loaded with various garage-sale chests of drawers, stacked one on top of another around all four walls, leaving a gap for the door to open 90 degrees. Several small chests ran back to back in two aisles forming the library of the absurd, as I called it in high school. A nailed-shut window blocked the light, leaving a lone sixty-watt light bulb eerily lighting the whole arrangement with shadows. Each square in every box listed mixes with sprinkles of cinnamon, parts of plucked chicken, parsley, cream, one-half cube of butter, whites of eggs, salt and pepper, tablespoons of this and that, two pounds of some chopped-up animal/fish/bird, ovens set at precise degrees for a precise time. Desserts, appetizers, broiled meats, and main entrees were all crammed together with no other designation than the date they went into the recipe room. There were still several empty chests, even though Aunt Velora had been collecting her recipes long before I went to live there.

Aunt Velora loved the idea and exotic nature of cooking. She just wasn't that good at it. Her baked potatoes were like dust in leather pouches. Her meats were charred with the black haphazardly scraped off into the kitchen wastebasket, mixing with the remains of previous meals. Vegetables were cooked in blackened butter with spices that didn't blend, and they were never stirred, creating a soft underbelly and over-spiced raw topside. I can still smell the smoked flavor of her kitchen, my nostrils wishing for the day it might disappear. The place settings were white-tablecloth, restaurant perfect, fork and knife spaced exactly on a fancy folded paper towel.

If it wasn't for school lunch, I probably would have starved. I always wondered how Uncle Keith ate each meal as if it where

Thanksgiving.

I recall my dad saying, "Velora is the only person I know who can dirty up ten pots and five skillets and still not come up with a decent meal."

***

The house still wasn't changing. My inner sense told me he was home. My fingers swatted the keys again. I wiped the sweat from my forehead and the back of my neck with a drive-through napkin from the glove box. The heat shimmered above the sidewalk and scattered loose papers and tiny tumbleweeds in stop-and-go currents of air. A couple of teens walked hastily by and eyed me as if I were some degenerate pervert. Lawn sprinklers in some neighbors' yards appeared to be turning summer-parched soil into patchy green lawns; some were mowed; some held shoots of seeds around chain-link fences. My father's was the only rectangular house with flaking paint among the rows of semi-identical boxes with asphalt roofs. The neighborhood was quieter and more desolate than I remembered.

I startled. Did I imagine it, or had the curtain moved? I kept a steady beam on the big front room window, Dad's extended study. It was lifeless. Perhaps heat waves or my hunger were creating delusions. I downed the last warm spurt of a dollar bottle of water. The taste made my eyes scrunch up. I shook my head awake, wiped my face with the same napkin, and started the car again. Something ground, just as I remembered the car was still idling. I wanted to leave, but there was something else I wanted that kept me from putting the car in drive. The air conditioner blew loud, hot air into the car. I ignored it, my eyes still locked on the house.

How long have I been here?

My neck was getting stiff, so I leaned the seat back a couple of notches. I knew I should go, but I kept giving myself a few more minutes. I was oblivious to the time, let alone the car pulling up behind me. A quick burst of siren and the flutter of red and blue lights caught my attention. I turned. A dark uniform came around the back of my car. I was still trying to figure it out when a policeman, with one hand on his holster, cleared his throat. I sat forward and tried to bend my head to look out at the officer. He said, "Got business here?"

"Uhhh, this is my house."

"This car or a particular home?" He glanced around the neighborhood.

Worry centered in my chest. *Did I break some law?* I could feel my stomach gurgling, acid rising to my chest and wondered if the officer could hear it. I turned to see another officer at the other side. My stomach rumbled again. I muttered, "No, I grew up here. Well, kind of here, but mostly at my aunt's house. It's over on Tarragon and 43rd." I knew I was babbling.

"Please step out of the car."

"What?"

The other officer gazed in with his gun drawn. He stared at me as if I were deranged. His nose was smashed, with a large mole on the left side. His uniform was tight over muscle and broad shoulders. The first officer knocked on the door to get my attention, saying, "Slowly get out of the car."

Stress seized my throat. I looked down as sweat from my forehead spotted my shirt in two drips. I decided I was overreacting. I hadn't broken any laws. My sweaty palm reached for the handle and carefully opened the door, thinking all the time, *please don't blow my head off.*

I wasn't used to this. This was only my second situation with the police; the other was when Eddie Freeman and I toilet-papered Donna's house. That time, Eddie took off and I was left stuck in the crotch of a tree with a cop's flashlight on my face. I spent two hours cleaning papered bushes and enduring the humiliation of asking forgiveness from Donna's rough-looking parents. They called me an "asshole delinquent" about twenty times.

The police didn't show any signs of grabbing their weapons back then, though. I stared at the nightstick and the black holster as I moved in slow motion out of the car. My hands raised in front of me, open palms out. I tried to act casual, but that wasn't working.

As I started to say something, the one officer spun my body into the car. The other officer hustled around the car, as if they were apprehending one of those ungodly people pictured on the nightly news. My hands trembled. Yeah, I was a bit of a coward, but I possessed enough sense to let bullies be bullies. I was cuffed and pocket-searched. I tried to breathe without making a sound, something I learned growing up with Dad. My pockets were turned inside out. My wallet, hotel keys, a wadded-up Kleenex, and the plane stub sat on the trunk of my rental car. Smashed-Nose began searching through the rental.

"What have you been doing here," he asked, studying my open wallet, "Mr. Parch, for the past four-plus hours? Are you stalking someone?"

"Four hours? No, I barely arrived. My father lives over there." My head gestured in the general direction. *Had I really been here that long?*

"Your father? You park in the street for several hours and stare at your parent's house."

"Well, yeah, that sounds a little . . . ."

"We have information that you never went to the door. What's your father's name?"

For a moment, I drew blanks, then I remembered, "Lawrence Parch," my voice sounded hollow.

The first officer signaled with his head to Smashed-Nose; Smashed-Nose went up to the house and rang the bell. As if it ever worked. After a few minutes of pushing the doorbell, he looked through the side window, then knocked on the door. A few seconds later, my dad opened the door. After a brief conversation, Dad looked over at me and smiled with a twisted grin.

As the two came within a few feet of me, Dad said, "So, this is the kid who is stalking me? He doesn't look like much."

"Dad," I hated the pleading tone. It hurt as his name came out. The last thing I wanted was to have to ask Dad for anything.

"Probably a pervert. I've been told I'm quite a handsome older man."

"Dad, tell them who I am!" I tried to sound exasperated, but with handcuffs on and rising embarrassment, my words still came out like a street beggar.

"The voice is familiar, and I've seen that face somewhere." He rubbed his chin, "You know; I think I've seen his picture in the newspaper or on TV with the other derelicts. What was that store that was just robbed? Oh, yeah, it was a Burger King." Dad nodded and winked at the first officer. "He sure does look familiar."

My face was turning red.

"Is his name One-Eyed Lefty?" He chuckled and waited a few beats, "Nah, he's a Parch. Been so long, I just wasn't sure. We better check his ID to be positive."

I was ready to punch him in the mouth and risk being arrested for real. The officers caught on, as another patrol car pulled in behind the first. The second set of officers got out and walked over.

I should have known visiting Dad's house was a bad idea.

"Dad, will you tell them to get the handcuffs off?"

"Why does he keep calling me Dad?" He glanced over at the officers, as if confused. "It sounds so foreign, so out of character."

The four officers began to laugh. The first officer asked, "Do you want to press charges?"

My father eyed me over with a skeptical look, all lip biting and squinty eyes.

"Daaaaad!" I burned holes through him with my eyes.

"Yeah, I suppose I had something to do with the birth of this fish tender."

"Fish tender?" Smashed-Nose asked.

"He watches fish for a living. Can you imagine getting a paycheck for that? It's baffling."

My face flushed, and I twisted around so I could glower straight at him. "Some fathers are proud of their kid's accomplishments. Can you imagine that?"

"Let him go." He ignored my comment and stood smug and nonchalant about the whole thing.

After the police pulled away, all I could choke out was, "I gotta go."

"Expected nothing more." He began to walk away, then stopped and turned. "Next time you want to stalk me, use the door. It's cooler inside."

I roared the engine in neutral, trying to drown out his laughter.

An enormous stomach groan startled me. I put the car in gear, pulled away from the curb, and glanced at my cell phone. No calls, and almost five hours had elapsed since I pulled into the neighborhood. As I drove, I tried not to think about what had happened. The houses I passed turned to an industrial area, then more houses, then a business section near the hotel.

The hotel restaurant was elegant with all those extra forks, white tablecloths, and portions so small a mouse would pass them by. I kept rubbing the red rings around my wrists. After a final cup of coffee, I stopped at the hotel store for expensive snacks and then headed to my room to gulp down over-sweetened, over-salted goodies.

I knew I should have gone to Aunt Velora's or Jen's house instead of Dad's. Sorrow lumped in my throat, and a silly tear formed in the corner of my eye. I wiped it quickly with my sleeve, as if someone was watching. I hadn't even called either of them since arriving in town. I glanced at the phone, but didn't pick it up.

Chapter 3

Lying back and almost touching sleep, I was halfway through an hour's rest when an alarming song played on my cell phone. An upload of *Who Let the Dogs Out,* a joke from my girlfriend Amy, announced my aunt's call. The phone danced on the table. Annoyed, I touched the screen to answer. I heard, "Are you sleeping through the best time of the day?" The voice was cheerful. It felt like home and someone who cared. I took a sip of water, trying to clear my throat.

"Benjamin Parch! There are rules when you come to town. One is that you call your loving aunt immediately. Two is that you stop by my house. Three is that I need a cheek kiss from my favorite nephew. Where are you?"

"Oh, I just checked in and was about to call," I lied.

"You were going to call me from your dream? Sorry, dear, but that phone doesn't ring."

I never could put anything over on her. "Ok. I fell asleep, and I've been in town for a little bit."

"How far out is your nose growing now? Your plane arrived at 8:20 this morning. You think I don't know these things? Wake up and get over here before the cancer takes me."

"Okay, Okay. I'm on my way. Do you need anything? Food? Soda? Coffee and a donut?"

"Just get here. If you want food, pick some up on the way over. And you don't have to be afraid of me cooking you something. I've learned how to cook since you've been gone. It's called takeout. I've gained ten pounds in the wrong places. I would've been 400 pounds by now if the cancer wasn't keeping me trim. Now hurry up." Aunt Velora had turned into a live wire, a changed woman since Uncle Keith passed away eight years ago.

I pulled behind several cars just south of Aunt Velora's house. It seemed mine was not the only invitation. The house didn't appear the same. The front door was red. The trim was burgundy. Someone fairy-dusted flowers all over the front yard. There were stepping stones, short trees, and a natural looking fountain. Water cascaded off flat rocks before settling in a pool of odd, blue-tinted water.

Music from old show tunes was blaring out the front windows. I gazed down, noticing my foot was keeping time with the music. *How silly is that?* I thought. I almost wanted to smoke before I went in. I actually touched my shirt pocket before realizing I'd kicked that habit years ago. I was uncomfortable, not knowing how to react as I walked to the door. *Oh, my God, a lipstick red front door. It looks like the door of a whorehouse*, I thought, *not my little old aunt's residence.*

A grin fell over my face that wouldn't leave.

The stones laid a wavy path to the stained cement porch, another change. The air along the path was fragrant and feminine. The smells slowed my heart down. Before I could knock, my aunt flung the door open, putting a lot of stress on old hinges. She was radiant. Before I could say hello, she pulled me into a tight hug, a long scan, and another hug with a girlish yelp. Then she led me by the arm into a room I didn't recognize.

The old grey-toned walls were now bright yellows, sizzling pinks, and lime greens. Every wall was different. All of her old-world wood and paisley-fabric furniture had been replaced with something out of IKEA—glass, chrome, mirrors, and more colors than any room should have. I couldn't help blinking, putting my nose and forehead into it. Her 73-year-old body danced me around the floor, introducing me with machine-gun names and one-sentence biographies. I was smiley and polite, echoing laughter whenever needed. I peered over shoulders at all the room changes. Too much colored-data input was giving me a headache. I pasted on a grin, letting her guide me by the elbow.

Saying that my aunt had changed was an understatement. It

was 180 degrees into a whole new dimension. She was effervescent and used words like *prodigious*. What alien planet did she visit?

I was force-fed new people until I finally grabbed her by the shoulders, turned her to face me, and told her I wanted to talk. My fingers lightly tapped her cheek. I smiled and pointed down the hall, then followed her as the obedient son.

Opening a door, she signaled for me to walk in first. Three bright mustard walls and a screaming blue wall made me squint involuntarily. It was carnival bright, but at least it didn't match. Three card tables were folded at the far blue wall to the side of a white framed window. I glanced at her. She smiled and bowed her head.

"What happened," I said, "to the recipe room?" I held my arms out, flapping them slightly in a gesture of confusion. "Wasn't this the infamous recipe room? It's empty and so damn bright. And a window? And a three-bulb light fixture. Are you in some odd cult? Are you doing drugs? Who decorated this—Chucky Cheese?"

I peered closer, feigning to see if she was even my Aunt Velora. She gave me a quick grin.

"Calm your cookies. About five years ago a couple of friends and I hauled the whole room out to the back yard and threw the best bonfire. I'm told it could be seen for miles. The worry warts in the neighborhood—three of them anyway, the ones with their curtains closed, except for a slight gap so they can spend their days waiting for something like this to happen—called the fire department. I sent Alice out for hot dogs and cheap boxed wine. You remember Alice, the one with the hair . . . ?"

"Yeah, the hair that made a four-foot, eight-inch woman appear to be a full six foot. Of course, I remember."

"Anyway, the fire trucks came in with sirens and those hot outfits and conquistador hats. I met head on with a couple of them, while two others were ready to hook up at the hydrant in front of old man Macleod's house."

"Isn't he about your age?"

"Never mind. He has always looked the same age . . . old. I don't have any resemblance to his age. Let's see, where was I?"

"The firemen."

"Right, right. I invited the firefighters and most of the neighbors over to the greatest weenie roast in all history. We used hangers taped to a length of pipe to not burn our noses. I mentioned calling the Guinness people, but no one knew the number. Fred, from up the road, took pictures and said he would put them on Facebook. Can you believe I have a Facebook page? I feel like such a snoop after five minutes of reading about people's lives. Most people, or I should say 'friends', are odd or despicable and the rest are plain boring."

I thought, *this from a woman who stored hundreds of thousands of recipes?*

"The room is great," I lied. "We talk on the phone once a week. You never mentioned any of this," I motioned with my hands in big circles, "extravagance."

"It's unimportant."

I moved over and gave her a light loving hug. "You look great." A scent of perfume and something else triggered my nose. It was a faint odor of marijuana. I shook it off as my senses playing tricks on me.

Her body possessed the spirit and jumpiness of a teenager with gray hair and the fans of deep creviced temples. She felt fragile as my arm wrapped around her. I sensed her thinness. I decided that the signs of cancer must come and go, or else she does better with pain meds than I ever could.

"It feels good to have you home."

I stepped back to admire her. "It is definitely great to see you. This is so much nicer than the phone. You are better than I imagine."

"Have you seen your dad?" she said.

Her question took the wind out of me. It seemed so abrupt. My head jangled timidly. My mouth felt dry all of a sudden.

"He misses you."

"The only thing he misses is my driving him to the liquor store," I said, a little too meanly.

Her head jounced and she narrowed her eyes. "You truly don't know? Have you talked to him in the last couple of years?"

"We exchange insincere Christmas cards once a year. And

sometimes I get mine by Christmas." My voice was way too sarcastic. I could see it hurt my aunt. "I'm sorry. We just don't get along that well. I'm not sure I want to see him."

"You stopped by his house when you got into town, didn't you?"

It hit me like an accusation. To give me time for a reply, my feet slid a couple of steps back. I didn't want to lie to my aunt. I thought of changing the subject. Her house, her hair, something. Nothing came into focus.

"Sorry, you took too long; did you stop and visit?"

"Kind of. I drove by the old neighborhood. It still gives me anxiety."

"Shabby house, huh?" She stared directly at me. I remember her giving me those same eyes when I came home from school late reeking of cigarettes. I used to get the glare of her face and the disapproval in her tiny high voice back then. Things don't change much.

"He's a Mormon," she said.

"A what?"

"A Mormon. He no longer drinks or smokes those nasty cigars, rarely swears, and he goes to church every Sunday. He volunteers for things he wouldn't have done if they paid him five years ago. He is always carrying scriptures as though he's Moses coming down from the mountains. Remember his yellow, tan, and blue shirts? Now he wears only white, starched shirts. He's changed."

"My dad, the well-dressed drunk, is a—"

"A sober Mormon. Yep, it rearranged inside me for a while before I was able to absorb the thought, too."

"He hated Mormons. He hated Catholics, Jews, Muslims, and Baptists. All organized religions and all liberals. When—when did he become a Mormon?"

"A few years back. His appearance is different. He still has red cheeks and practiced posture, but the egocentric stick has fallen out of his butt. He's more . . . casual."

"I remember him talking about church people with spittle spraying and expletives beginning and ending every sentence. He sent complete terror through the eyes of those nicely suited young men who knocked on our door. They barely got a few words out before he roared at them about their cult disguised as an actual religion. He used a whole pre-scripted tirade. It was his closing argument. 'Joseph Smith was sent by the devil to destroy all Catholics.' He would bellow as though he cared about Catholics at all. And his final argument as he leaned his face close to those poor boys, was, 'Brigham Young was a hippie pervert marrying women for deviant sexual favors.' I'm shocked. I don't get it."

"Oh, the Mormons were skeptical too, the first couple of years. You need to see him. He prays like a saint and pays money out of his own wallet to his new church."

"He fully disrespected people trying to be saved by God. I'll have to remind him about his lectures: 'Stand up on your own two feet, you God-fearing people,' he would say, then take a strong belt of the amber liquid of the day. I have to see this."

She walked over and held my hand. "He'll be here tomorrow. You two need to talk."

We walked out into the growing, mingling crowd. After a lot of "remember me?"s and "you were this high," I silently slipped away.

The hotel room gave me safety. I lay wide awake on the bed, gazing out at the sky through partially open drapes. The wind slowly pushed the spotty clouds to the north. I had taken in a lot for one day. My mind skipped over unknown facts about my new dad. "Unbelievable" and "holy shit" were the words that kept popping up. I was rattled, but kept giggling every now and then. It wasn't even my own giggle. It was one borrowed from a crazy in a rehab center. Even that didn't bother me. I fluttered my head as if to clear it of the looseness inside.

My psychologist girlfriend, Amy, says I have unresolved issues. It's a nice way of saying your parents screwed you up. Don't most parents alter us in some pathetic way? Mine were just better at it.

Somewhere between recollections and new musings, I fell asleep.

Chapter 4

Someone pounded on my door. My mind absorbed it for a while, then tried to decipher whether it was real or a dream. "Coming, coming," I said, as my bare feet touched the carpet.

The pounding became louder and more obnoxious. I didn't do the peephole; I just opened the door quickly, as if I would punch the person on the other side.

"Hey, brother, you sleep like you're passed out. Are you following in Dad's footsteps?"

"Yuk, yuk. Come on in. Let me throw some water on my face."

"No!" she stated. "A hug and a *how are you* would be appropriate."

I held my arms open. She came at me like a football tackle. I put one foot back to brace the onslaught and gave her a kiss on each cheek. She nuzzled her nose into my shoulder affectionately.

"You Okay?" I whispered.

She pulled away. "Damn, it's good to see you." I momentarily lost my breath as she punched me in the gut. "I stood out in the hall for twenty minutes. You come into town and sleep?"

I stepped back. I could see her clenching her fist again. "Hi, Sis. You're still beautiful, and your arm strength is as good as ever."

"I should pummel you. I know you've been here all day. And drop the pathetic droopy eyes. I haven't fallen for that puppy-dog expression since I was five." She swallowed a breath and glared at me. "And I'm not beautiful. The proper term is gracefully aged.

21

Check this out." Her hands pulled back at her temples. "I have
crow's feet." Her hands shifted to her belly. "And this, I don't even
know what this is or where it came from, but it's there and it won't
go away. I go to the gym, I eat fruits and vegetables; I've tried
talking to it; but, no, it just stays."

I thought about something sarcastic to say. I held on to it.
"It's really . . . really good to see your face. I'm not that great of a
brother, but I do miss you."

"Have you heard about Dad?"

"The Mormon thing? And the sober thing? Dad thinks he
quits drinking every time he passes out. Now you and Aunt Velora
believe him? Jen, you forget how many times he quit before. It's a
revolving door. Every few years he quits for a few weeks, goes
through the tremors, then rips the house apart to find a stock we
haven't tossed. You really believe him?"

"I have my doubts, but it's been years. I never wanted to tell
you. I wanted you to see for yourself. I'm still struggling. He wants
the daughter he tossed out at three years old."

"You're over it, and all is forgiven?" I said with a harsh
laugh.

"Not by a long shot. Plus, he keeps sending Mormon
missionaries to my house. He forgets he's the one that taught me
everything I need to know about religion. I'm so sick of trying to
have Christian behavior with satanic thoughts," she responded.

"You should join him. They're probably serving bourbon in
those tiny Dixie cups on Sunday. Otherwise, why would he go to
any church?"

"You may be right."

"So, Sis, what do you think of Aunt Velora's pre-funeral
party? After the invitation, I couldn't wait to raise my glass."

"You still have that sarcasm." Jen bit her lip and rattled her
head like a dog emerging from a lake. Her eyes held mine. "I think
the whole thing is morbid . . . and ghastly. It hits me right here."
She put two fists to her chest. "All I really want to do is cry."

I moved over, giving her a hug. Tears started. Jen was always
tough, unless it involved Aunt Velora; then her girly emotions
erupt and the façade is shed, leaving her loving little girl-self
exposed. After a few minutes, the hardened lady came back and

she pushed me away. Her hands went to her hips, her red-stained cheeks fading back into her backyard tan.

"Can you believe the formal invitation? I read it three times before it sank in. It was decorated like a doily, for God's sake. All frilly. I think she even added a drop of perfume."

"She did. I got the same thing. I smelled it several times. I thought it was a mistake until now. I assumed she accidently dropped some on mine. Old lady, lavender perfume . . . very theatrical."

"The whole letter was dramatic, hand-written in her loopy penmanship"

"Yes. It. Was."

"'Please join me for my pre-funeral party,'" Jen said mockingly, her voice inflecting as my aunt's would, with adjoining hand gestures. "'As most of you know, I will be leaving this earth shortly. It is nothing to fret about,'" she paused, biting her lip.

"'A long vacation from this bodily rag,'" I said.

"She did say 'bodily rag,' didn't she?" Jen began laughing.

I shook my head with a smirk that puffed up my cheeks and made me feel young again.

"'This is my gathering of fun and song before I miss out on all the parties to come,'" she recited, holding on to a fake necklace as my aunt does whenever describing something she's fond of. "'It will leave all future parties sucking dust. No RSVP. Just be there.' I had to read the date and time three times before I figured it out. I called her anyway just to make sure. Is she the silliest, most wonderful, crazy woman you've ever met?"

"Yes, yes, and yes."

I escorted my beautiful sister down the sidewalk not far from the hotel. Like a contagious yawn, she giggled and I followed. It went that way for a block and a half. I knew we were thinking the same things without telling each other. It used to happen all the time. Anyone watching would think we were out on a pass from a hidden mansion of shock therapy and psychological drugs. And perhaps we were, with that mix of genetics and parental abandonment. We bobbed our heads as if listening to rock and roll and laughed from down deep within our stomachs in contorted waves. She snorted and I grabbed her hand, trying to stifle myself.

We found humor in all our shared memories and newly developed ones.

Sliding into a booth at a seafood restaurant and bar, Jen asked, "You're buying, right?"

"We'll just charge it to the royal family on Brook Stone Drive where the great descendent of King Louis raised us from poverty to whatever it is we are now."

"Yeah, what are we now?"

"Two kids formed by a brandy-loving father, a disappearing mother, a great hunter of an uncle, and the best blackened cook this side of our wonderful Aunt Velora's stove."

"I didn't know Dad liked brandy. I didn't know he picked a favorite."

"Sorry, Sis, I'm embellishing."

We burst into another series of giggles. The waitress came and stood patiently. I held my hand up to her, trying to gain control of the person I hadn't been in a long time—probably since Herbert Hoover Junior High. I signaled to my sister to go first.

"I'll have a ginger ale and an ice water."

"And I'll have a Seven-Up or whatever you have that's clear and bubbly. Do you have some kind of mixed seafood appetizers?"

The waitress was a thin female—thin face, thin nose, thin legs, and the chest of a fifteen-year-old boy. She canted from the hips slightly to the left. Her sleepless eyes raised as the tumblers in her brain tried to lock on the menu. "We have crab-stuffed mushrooms and clam chowder, and there's a large prawn cup with cocktail sauce and fried calamari." She looked pleased to remember that much.

I gazed at my sister for approval of the order. "Everything you mentioned but the fried calamari. Sounds wonderful?"

Jen nodded with a wink and a thumbs-up signal, her curls bouncing and settling back as if on cue. She was always flipping her blonde locks, even when there wasn't a hair out of place.

My sister always possessed a womanly sturdiness. She walked like a model, but her right arm should have belonged to a boxer. She wasn't thin or fat, more perfectly proportioned and curvy. She made the girls jealous and the boys intimidated.

We talked about past indulgences and fatuous mistakes. The

laughter gave a break between each old story. For my sake she stayed away from anything about our less-than-loving father. She probably skipped it as a favor to herself also.

"How's Albert?" I asked. She married the man 12 years ago. He was shorted on sperm count, so to this date there were no children. He was an odd arrangement of scientific brains, low self-esteem, and a thin mouth that rarely talked. He was handsome in a plain way and dressed to show off the common man within.

"Still boring."

"Anything new with him?"

"No. He still stands with chalk making marks on the board, talking directly to the wall, and putting high school students to sleep. I'm told they hardly remember ever seeing his face. Even now, I hear his monotone voice, and I wish strangling wasn't against the law."

We chuckled.

She started on him again. "And that bowed walk, like he's trying to break through thick air with his nose. It's so infuriating, I gotta love him."

"His question mark stance still bothers you? Remember, Miss Posture, not all of us can be like you—erect, with effortless grace. Actually, you and Dad. Sorry for the comparison."

"Being overly nice will not make me pick up the check, and lumping me with Mr. Posture doesn't help."

"What's that flattery cliché?"

"It will still get you nowhere with me."

We gazed at each other, smiling. She is not just my sister. She is my best friend. We talk so seldom anymore; I sometimes lose track. She has that glow about her that lets me absorb just enough to relight a happiness I forget family can hold. *Life is not a series of lunches with you, Sister; it is way too busy for that, and I regret it.*

"What are you thinking about? You went somewhere for a few minutes."

"I'm thinking . . . about you."

"Whatever. Did you bring your psycho girlfriend along?" She sucked her lips in.

"She's a clinical psychologist, not a psycho."

"So, is she up in your room, waiting to put you on the couch and straighten out your wrinkles?

"Really, Jen, I don't haul her around for a booty call. She is a busy doctor and we date. That's it."

"Ooooh. Dr. Psycho. You have been dating for quite some time. Four-plus years, right? I think this is more than dating. I assume you have sleepovers?"

"That is not something I talk to my sister about. We need to change the subject, or I'll start asking you about Albert and your sex life."

"This is a very touchy subject with you. You either have a great nightlife with her or she's ready to dump you," she paused, "and Albert and my sex life can be totaled up in one word: infrequent and insipid. Well, two words."

"She's not ready to dump—"

"That good, huh?

"Was it seven o'clock at Aunt Velora's?"

"You're trying to change the subject. Enquiring minds need to know."

"Can we please change the subject?" I knew as soon as I asked she wouldn't let up. She can be relentless if she wants something.

"Spill the beans on your psycho dream girl."

I noticed her elbows planted firmly on the table and her chin resting patiently on her fists. We stared at each other for a moment. "My girlfriend and I have an exclusive arrangement. We go to concerts and movies and parties together. I care about her, and I think she likes me as well. We've been seeing each other for more than four years so, of course, we have 'sleepovers,' and they've been frequent over the last year. FYI. She stays at my place quite a bit because it's closer to her work, so it makes sense."

Jen pointed her index at me. "It would make much better sense if it were closer to her work." She was mocking me in that sarcastic voice she is so good at.

"Actually, I'm not sure she even likes my place. She's always rearranging things and asking me how long I've owned 'that,' as she scrunches up her nose like sniffing distasteful air."

"Trust me, she doesn't like your place. She must love you a

TATTERED PORTRAIT

lot."

"Okay. That's it. No more."

"Marriage?"

She waited almost a full minute for me to answer. "You know I will wait you out." She waited several seconds more then punched me in the arm.

"You forget I've asked three girls to marry me over the years. Each one turned me down as though it was a stupid question." I tilted my head. I'm not sure any of them ever came through the front door.

"You were surprised they turned you down? You asked those three more as the next step of long-term dating than love. This is different. I think you actually love psycho girl."

"We've talked about it. No time frame or anything. We both have deep-seated reservations. We've both seen our country's divorce rates. Hell, think about dear old Mom and Pop."

"Well, get over it and get her a ring."

"So we can have a perfect marriage, like you and Albert?" I joked.

"Never. I have seen this lady. She is talkative and interesting, full of self-respect, and she has good posture. Both of you have a settled ease when you're together. You're a match."

After three hours and many refills on water, the waitresses were giving us the release-the-table eye. I paid the bill she had left on the corner of our table about an hour before. Outside, the shadows were darker; wind-swept debris from one side of the street now lay huddled at car tires on the other side. We walked arm in arm down the sidewalk, skipping every third step just like we did as kids.

Chapter 5

As I walked back to my hotel, the traffic thickened and the sun became nothing more than a thin, gold line following the ridge of mountains. Cirrus clouds reflected the same gold ink. As we walked, Jen jabbered about all the things she wanted to do and hadn't. She needed to let life's frustrations out, and I was available. As a man, I did my best to curb myself from fixing her problems and just let her chatter. It went against the grain.

She wanted to go to France or Italy, to enjoy a seashore resort, to sail on the ocean, to find the planets through a telescope, and she wanted to meet Bruce Willis, for God's sake. I nodded and shook my head in all the right places.

From across the street I heard "Bennie . . . Bennie?" We both turned and saw one of my old mistakes, Klarisa. She was waving frantically while waiting impatiently for a break in traffic to join our conversation. I wasn't thrilled, though she always took my breath away. Her sensual femaleness spilled out whenever I saw her. She was the first girl in grade school to wear a bra, and made sure everyone knew it.

Her womanly figure and sensual puffy lips came jogging across the two-lane road, jumping over the median strip. She seemed oblivious to any traffic. Cars stopped with everything the brake pedal would allow, but no one honked. Faces peered out of truck windows as they watched her move. White pants, black stilettos, and a blouse and belt matching the shoes hit the sidewalk like a deer over a fence. No one makes an entrance like K-pop. Few can sprint gracefully in heels.

TATTERED PORTRAIT

In school, she went by the name K-pop, short for Klarisa Potenza. Nowadays K-pop sounds like a rapper. (I imagine she shed that name long ago.) Seeing her now conjured up pressed grass on moonlit nights at the park and twisted cowboy hat sheets when Aunt Velora was out.

I was embraced with force. I saw it coming and put one foot behind me as a buttress. My arms wrapped around her. We danced in a circle for a minute. She led; I followed. Jen stepped back as Klarisa's feet left the ground and folded up. Her long hair waved behind her. I stopped spinning and said "K-pop, you're the same brat in your mid-thirties as you were at fourteen." Jen stood by with her arms folded.

Mischievous green eyes met mine. "Who's in their thirties?"

Her glare told me not to answer. I smiled. She held the allure of a soccer mom and a burlesque queen wrapped into one package.

"I haven't seen you in eight . . . ten years," Klarisa said.

"It's been eight. You look the same, if not better."

She giggled. It was a forced giggle for my benefit. She was always good at that. I'm fairly sure she hadn't noticed my sister at all. Jen stood behind her, shaking her head no and waving her finger as though I was destined to do something wrong.

"You remember my sister Jen?"

She barely glanced in Jen's direction. "Why, of course." She reached over and held my hand. "Are you staying at your aunt's or your dad's place?"

"Neither. I'm at the Marriott." Jen stared over Klarisa's shoulder and curled her nose up, giving a smile that presented more like indigestion.

"The Marriott, huh? I'll have to stop over." The wind seemed to shift.

My heart rate was up. Jen moved in close behind me, poking hard into my ribs. "I'm not staying there much," I said as Jen's eyes bore holes in the back of my skull. "My aunt has this whole party thing going on. I have a lot to do for that. I'm just using the hotel as a base for naps and things." I was talking too much, and I felt my sister's glare from the periphery. I remembered the years of dating K-pop and our two brief affairs. It had all been a catastrophe.

Jef Huntsman

***

In high school, Klarisa was a good Catholic girl who wouldn't have sex until marriage. Well, not exactly no sex—we kissed and hit every base but home plate. She was fluent in things young boys only have dreams about.

I remember when we first met. She leaned over close to me in our junior high pre-algebra class and asked about some math question as though I seemed wise enough to know. I wasn't sure about her and I knew I wasn't sure about pre-algebra. I always wondered about pre-algebra; it was like pre-swimming. You either swim or you sink. Klarisa was like that. We swam. There was no awkward learning about each other. We were complete friends from that first moment.

She embodied girl smells, short skirts, a voice like a song, and clean fingernails. I'm not sure what the algebra question was. I just shrugged my shoulders and uttered, "I'm still stuck on division." She laughed, I took a breath, and within a few weeks we began eating lunch together.

By the middle of high school, she asked, "Are you Catholic?"

"Undeclared," I answered. It was something I heard my father say.

"This isn't a college major. It's an important lifetime commitment." She glared at me as if I was completely stupid. "How can you marry me if you're not Catholic? I assumed you were Catholic but didn't go to church because of your dad."

"Marriage? We're sixteen years old!" I was shouting in breathy, hushed tones. Her eyes got big. Her chest heaved. She was biting her lip so hard I expected blood. "What's this about marriage? I can barely finish my homework; I don't have a car. I have an old worn-out motorcycle that rarely works. Marriage?"

She began walking around me in circles, pointing a small manicured finger at me, pink polish waving. She started to say something several times, but just kept biting her lip instead. She stopped, then put her hands on her hips and said, "I thought you loved me. If you did, you would declare a church, my church." She froze, waiting for my answer with that attitude only girls have mastered.

"I love you," I paused, "of course. I don't know anything about being a Catholic or any religion for that matter. I haven't even figured out what I want to do after high school or whether I'm going to be an astronaut or a fireman. I don't know what college I may or may not attend. I've never given a second thought to a religion or marriage. I just want to hang out with you." We were in front of her locker.

She kept her hands on her hips, staring for a time then abruptly walking away without another word. I watched the sway of her skirt and thought about chasing her and declaring my new devotion to Catholicism. Instead, I slammed her locker shut with a closed fist and walked the other way. Our friendship lasted, but with a gap—well, more of a chasm between us.

***

Years later when I came home after my undergrad college, Klarisa was married to a nice virgin Catholic boy, Raymond, from an upstanding banking family. He ran a thriving dental practice. I saw them on the street as she walked three steps ahead of him. I could almost see the ring and chain on his nose. She held out her chest and gave me a dismissive, yet interested, wave. I pasted on a smile but noticed her legs. I wondered if she wore a halo of contentment.

She phoned me at my aunt's house later that night. She knew I was back from college. I heard my aunt's disapproving voice from high school as she told me who was on the phone. The womanly sound of songbirds came through the line as Klarisa said, "Can we get coffee? Are you free?"

"Just a minute," I hesitated. "No . . . no messages from graduate schools or employers wanting me to call back as soon as possible. I'm free." I wanted to see her. I didn't want it to be too easy. "What time and where?"

"How about Earl's on 2nd and Vine at nine."

"That's a way out."

"Yes, it is."

"Okay." It sounded so clandestine, a lump formed in my chest. I felt guilty as Aunt Velora asked me reprovingly about leaving at this hour, but she barely left the house as far as I knew. It really wasn't that late.

Klarisa was there in a booth with steaming coffee in front of her, hands wrapped firmly around the white cup. I tried not to think about how beautiful she was. I sat down. We both eyed each other over. I was almost afraid to speak.

Finally, she said, "You're still handsome. Are you any smarter since college?"

"First, handsome is a hard push. And if you mean by smarter, have I become Catholic? No, I'm still a heathen, but I'm much better at algebra."

"I don't care about being Catholic anymore."

"You're not Catholic?"

"Oh, I'm still a full-bore Catholic. Go to church every Sunday. Help with poverty and cake sales. I believe in the Bible and God. I just don't care anymore. I'm more realistic."

"Is that why you can talk to me again?" I said, chuckling.

"Okay, enough church talk. I want to know about you. How was school? How are you doing? What's your girlfriend's name?" She paused and smiled. "How's Aunt Velora? How's your dad? What are your plans?"

"It would be easier if you wrote all your questions down on a yellow pad and numbered them. Was the first question about my politics or genetics?"

"You know exactly what I asked. You forget I know you. Probably better than anyone. You remember everything."

The waitress came by, filled my coffee cup, and went to get me a slice of the squash pie I saw when I first came in. Within 30 seconds, she came back with a slice. She said she forgot to ask about á la mode. I declined and sipped my coffee. Klarisa's perfume mixed with the salty odor of French fries. The place was empty except for the two of us and a foursome of booming teens.

"School was a busy time of tests and beer. I'm feeling great. My girlfriend left me for a tuba-playing environmentalist, and I was the idiot that introduced them. Velora is sweet and overly attentive. I can't do anything on my own without her getting a motherly hand in. I have nightmares of her washing my back while I shower. She's the same sweet Velora. My dad is probably drunk with a slight chance of being upright. I was told he went to a three-day rehab center and was booted out on the second day for threatening to file suit over corned-beef hash. My plans are in limbo. I want to get into graduate school, so I'm waiting to hear back on a couple of scholarships. I would also consider taking a job as a waiter here if things don't develop quickly." I waited a beep. "And you?" The air stilled.

Klarisa said, "Wow. That's quite a response."

We shared reckless sex in her back yard the next afternoon. I remember being apprehensive, but distractedly involved. The grass was slightly damp and it didn't seem to matter. When I finally left and went back a few weeks later for my master's, I began having nightmares about a mad dentist chasing me with horrid-sounding drills. I was 22 years old at the time, and my memory of it is still vivid. Guilt does that once you're away from the seduction.

***

Jen nudged me slightly. The traffic noise seemed to evolve from nowhere. I glanced towards her, and the sun reflected painfully off a windshield. In a condescending voice she said, "We have to get going." Klarisa paid her no mind. I felt Jen's infuriation as I lingered, squinting.

I found myself staring into Klarisa's round green eyes. Damn, those were weapons. They were the worst part of her charm. They pulled you in without an escape. They stimulated juices way down in the primitive brain. I tried to peek down at her neck, thinking that was neutral ground. Her neck was womanly soft and contoured. Even at thirty-six, her skin was smooth with no wrinkles. *Perhaps elective surgery?* No, her skin held just the right tension and cushion. The knife and stretch makes the skin unnatural because the dermal layers still fold at the collarbone.

Her voice broke into my mind wanderings. "I'm thinking about divorce. My soon-to-be-ex, Raymond, will pay me well after my lawyer and a private detective get their jaws on him. He's been sliding cash payments from his dental practice into a hidden safe behind the furnace in our home. Hundreds of thousands stacked neatly where he thought neither the IRS nor his loving wife—me of course— wouldn't find it. He told me way too often that he needed to check on files in the basement. I told the detective. A few electronic pictures and he'll cower down. When I have the safe and its contents, I'll hold the whole thing over his head and he'll give me the cash payments."

"How shifty of you. A good Catholic girl like you going after blood? And thinking about divorce? Isn't there some kind of taboo about that?"

I was more afraid of her now than I'd ever been.

"Ray was a good Catholic boy. It is the eye-for-an-eye sort of thing. Men are not supposed to hide things from their wives. It is God's will."

Jen kicked me in the shin. "I have to go now."

I rubbed just above my ankle. "Oh, okay. I'll get with you later."

"I thought 'you' needed to do those things you were talking about. Maybe 'you' should get back to it, psychologically speaking."

Yes, I know I should call Amy.

I knew she was trying to pull me away from Klarisa, and with good reason. My brain never worked right around Klarisa. I played dumb and Jen knew it. "I can put that off for a few minutes. You go ahead. I just want to talk to my old friend for a minute."

Jen leaned in close to my ear. "The talking I'm not so worried about. It's more of what it leads to." She smacked me in the shoulder.

"I'll let him go unscathed," said Klarisa. "You needn't worry," she glowed with a large fake smile.

Jen's cheeks puffed and flushed as a scowl held firm on her earlier cute face. I imagined her giving Klarisa a solid right hook to the jaw. She held her ground between us.

"Jen don't worry; I know I have a fiancée."

"You do?" Klarisa spat out. My face reddened.

I changed the subject. "What is your ex-Ray, up to now?" I remembered him from school, a year older and twenty years more boring. "Oh, wait a minute. I just realized that your husband is now X-Ray." I couldn't hold back a mouth-covered chuckle.

"You find that funny? You still have simple ways. Infantile

humor."

"I'm just here to please myself. Lessons from the father."

"You have always blamed your father for things you do."

That hurt and broke any sexual tension that was building up. I must have stood up straighter, though I don't remember.

"Sorry," she said. "I didn't mean that as an insult. I know that joking about your father is a release."

"That's what my shrink girlfriend says. I've got two opinions now; it must be true."

Jen's eyes burned through me as if I was something from a dog park she just stepped in. She turned with a moan and headed down the street.

Klarisa and I went to the restaurant Jen and I had just left. The waitress gave me a double take. Her face adjusted into a glare. We seated ourselves.

I signaled to the waitress for more coffee. She had left us alone for some time and the cream in my cup was separating. She nodded and scooted behind the counter for a fresh pot. The traffic outside became louder as did the clinking of forks on plates. The restaurant filled as the night closed in on daylight. Five booths and three bar stools were full. I glanced out the window.

"Tell me about this shrink girlfriend," Klarisa said with new interest in her voice, less seductive, more inquisitive.

The waitress poured coffee and asked if we needed menus. Both of us shook our heads no.

Tip disappointment plowed across her face. We weren't going to win with her.

I waited a long beat after the waitress left, returning my eyes to the window. "Amy's fantastic. We see each other regularly and enjoy most of the same things—movies, walks, concerts, being together. We met at a conference in Boston. She was at a lecture on new personality-arranging drugs. I was in the same hotel lecturing to a group of twenty-year-olds about octopods and sea grass. We talked in the lobby for some time then went out on a dinner date. We found out her office and my apartment were a few blocks away. Things progressed. Now I think we're somewhat in love."

"You think you're 'somewhat in love?' Ben, you either know

you're in love or not. You don't think it. And there is no such thing as 'somewhat in love.' Do you even like this girl or do you think"

"I am pretty sure I love her," I said harshly, "but I'm trying to figure it all out. We are great together. I want to be with her whenever I'm not. She makes me smile and laugh. She makes me feel better about myself. I love the fragrance of her and the softness of her voice. Jen tells me I have never been in love. I think her words were 'Ben, you are in need . . . not in love.' She tells me I won't know when I actually fall in love. Jen also tells me I'm definitely in love with my psycho girlfriend. 'Psycho,' that's what she calls her. Jen can't make up her mind either."

"Cute. I always thought one would know when one was in love."

"Me too."

I glanced back at her. She took a sip of coffee. Red lipstick peppered the rim.

"When I married Ray, I knew I didn't love him. I loved what he brought to the table—sustainability. He was Catholic, he paid attention to the leash I held him by, and he came from a good family. But, he was b-o-r-i-n-g. I made up events just to get a breath of fresh air. I looked for my fun in affairs."

"Yes, I can attest to that."

She ignored me. "I thought I would fall in love with him over time. Let me tell you, love will never happen after listening to someone drone on about an unusual molar or fascinating gums. If I didn't have books, friends, TV, drunken affairs, and family, they would have locked me up long ago. I guess all I know is what love isn't."

"We both have that working for us." I said.

"We are pathetic, aren't we?"

I gave her a thumbs-up and a smile. We left feeling a bit sorry for ourselves and rightly so. I promised to call her after the party. She mentioned that she was invited and may just drop by. A tentative hug and we were off. I forgot everyone was invited. Walking back, I wasn't sure I wanted her there, especially since Amy couldn't make it. I had no faith in myself.

Aunt Velora's party was tomorrow night. I grabbed the rental keys off the counter and decided to see if she needed any help.

TATTERED PORTRAIT

On the way over, I decided to call Amy. As I dialed, I thought about whether this was a feeling-guilty call or a regular call. I lied to myself and decided it was a regular call. My head nodded slowly, listening to the first ring and waiting for Amy to pick up.

Later, adrenalin pumped as I held tight to the wheel, dropping the phone, turning to the left with my foot hard on the brake, and barely missing the blur of something with a ball cap on and a white dog attached to a leash. I heard my carry-on bag punch into the back of the passenger seat as the wheels squealed and came to a sudden stop angled across the road.

A redhead girl with a ponytail waterfalling out the back of her cap flipped me off. Her dog hunched down and barked. My heart raced as I glared at the faces of the gawkers; each one said *stupid-ass*. The cars began honking behind me. I eased through the intersection, took a left, and pulled over to the side of the road. When my heartbeat slowed, I found my phone. It had hung itself up. I pulled back out into the traffic.

Dad was helping Jen string lights in the trees in the backyard. He was up on a ladder, so I wandered over to make sure he wasn't drinking. He caught me staring and blew out a stream of air.

"I haven't been drinking," he said.

Jen smiled.

"Oh, I didn't think—"

"Yes, you did."

Jen laughed, "He's sober. I know it's hard to get used to."

I handed up a string of lights.

Dad smirked. "It helps if you untangle them first. You been drinkin'?"

"Clever, Dad."

Jen smiled, "Dad tells me you've been stalking him."

"Almost got arrested, too, if not for his father bailing him out." He shook his head. "Disgraceful."

"I'm going in to find Aunt Velora."

"Try not to ruin the Parch name while you're in there," Jen giggled.

I waved my hands and walked away.

Finding my little aunt in the kitchen pointing and giving

orders from a stool made me glad I came. Her voice was feathery, yet demanding. She was wearing a lacy thin skirt and a dark blue blouse with the collar up. She was spectacular.

I was starting to wonder if she actually had cancer when she spotted me and squealed out my name. We hugged. She stood back with her arms extended, observing with proud eyes. We hugged again.

"I'm here to help."

"Chairs."

"Chairs?"

"Yeah, they're out front in the panel truck. Set most of them over to the side of the house, then take a few and set them up around the backyard. I want them in conversation clumps."

We hugged again and I headed out the front door.

My mind drifted. I kept thinking about a dream I'd dreamt of Klarisa. She was a bulldozer in heels with one extra button undone on her blouse. She kept pushing that beautiful dirt into me. I was backing up, but it wasn't fast enough.

***

The last time I saw Klarisa she was still married to Raymond. I was home working on my doctorate. It was seven years ago or so, a couple of years before I met Amy. Klarisa spotted me pulling in front of my aunt's house and she stopped. As usual my heart paced faster and faster.

I didn't even see my aunt or uncle before I was having lunch with Klarisa. Studying those well-built eyes. She kept asking about my apartment in Tampa, Florida, and teasing about how much she'd love to visit. I ignored the implied question. She was married. I tried to hold onto good morals, but I was in that period of peak manhood. It created nervousness in me, a stumbling at my end of the conversation.

We had a lovely time with the heat turned up. She rubbed the back of my hand with one finger in little circles. With exasperation and reluctance, I pulled my hand back, pretending to need a drink of water. As a fatuous heart-pumped male, I tipped the water over and flipped the fork facing the next booth. Klarisa was helpful as I changed colors in waves across my face.

After soaking my cloth napkin, I caught the waiter's attention signaling for the check with a silly motion of my hand. The waiter began searching through receipts. On the only corner of the table not soaked by water, he set the bill down with a tip-me-good, I-have-to-clean-this-up look. Klarisa quickly retrieved it, saying, "Let Raymond get this; I have his business card." She tilted her head back and let out a contagious giggle. I could tell this was making her feel better about herself. I tried to get it from her, but she held it to her breast, a territory I wasn't about to be grabbing.

I watched her add a 50 percent tip to the bill with a smile. She grabbed me by the arm and walked me to my car. I said nothing though my mind was spinning. She bent forward to kiss me on the lips. I twisted so it landed on my cheek. Nothing was appropriate about Klarisa.

She said, "See you later." in a soft voice.

I replied, "I'll let you know when I'm back in town."

She wasn't deterred. "Or maybe sooner."

As she walked away, I sucked in a long, meaningful breath trying to calm that deep ancient brain. An affair with a married woman, especially Klarisa, was not a good idea under any circumstances. After he last time, I was sure I could not face the guilt again. I knew I would always have a desire for her. But it felt the way I imagined being a race horse put out to stud—more forced work than I needed.

The next day she wanted another lunch date. I thought about my dissertation. My mind said no in a hundred ways; my stupid mouth uttered the words "one o'clock."

My feeble brain battled with her words, "just friends having lunch." I set down my cell phone. The thought of her made my mouth dry and my lips all loose, the way it does when you leave the dentist's office. I sipped coffee and stared at the bare beginnings of my first draft. "Eight pages," I said out loud.

My aunt came around the corner. "You're a little grey. Are you getting enough sun?"

"I'm fine."

"Who was that you were talking to?"

"Do you remember Klarisa?"

"Of course. You two were always at the library studying. Isn't she married to that dentist without a chin?"

"Yes, but I think he has a chin."

"Well, I wouldn't go to a dentist without a chin. I go to Dr. Wells. He has a prominent chin. I trust him. What's Klarisa up to? She always possessed a bit of devil in her, as I recall."

"She wants to meet for lunch."

"Oh. That's so friendly. She is sweet. I haven't seen her in ages," Aunt Velora paused. She glanced up into a corner of her kitchen as though something was wrong. Then she watched me. "Probably wants to have lunch with a man with a chin for a change."

It was settled. I was having lunch with Klarisa because of my chin. The absurdity of it actually made me feel better.

I spent that night back at my aunt's house, then moved into Jake's two-room cabin with my notepads and computer. It was one of the reasons I came home to work on my thesis. Jake was in Europe for four whole months. At my aunt's I couldn't walk around in my boxers or relax and read a book. She was everywhere. She set so much food around me while I was working that I thought I was at a Home Town Buffet. I rarely saw my uncle, but my aunt was a mother hen. When I picked up the keys the next morning, I let out an audible sigh.

Jake's cabin was at the edge of Cottonwood Canyon, nestled in thick trees about 60 yards from the main road. I carried all my stuff down a dirt path, across a bridge, and into a quiet, peaceful cabin. I was in awe. Perfect.

After three consecutive dates in safe restaurants with tablecloths, white plates, and Raymond's credit card, she slipped in a change on the fourth date.

The phone rang. I didn't even say hello, before Klarisa's voice came through; it was more of a command than a question. "I'm picking something up. I'll meet you at Jake's cabin." My mind was shaking between maybe and no. She hung up before I could form an answer, but I was obedient. My throat was getting that thing that happens when you know you haven't done anything wrong, but you know you might. I thought seriously about leaving, opting for a beer and a sit on the couch with notepads spread out on the coffee table in front of me.

I was a standard male of our species with no inherent willpower when it came to women. Females can lead us, and we follow like the dumb beasts we are.

I paced, locked the door. Paced some more and unlocked it. I turned off the lights. It did no good; it was still daylight. I wore out the carpet and the lock on the door by the time the doorbell rang. I opened the door so slowly and carefully that she pushed it to make sure someone was behind it.

She entered, glancing around as she handed me two sacks. I set the sacks down with the smells of female and food rejuvenating the house. Her perfume lingered as she pushed past me. Stepping to the side, I placed myself opposite the counter from her.

"It's definitely a man's place." I took that as a compliment. Brown leather sofa, no pictures, industrial bar stools, a coffee table from a Viking pub, a lamp out of some type of hole-infested wood—orderly, but undusted. "Men are so boring in their décor," she continued. "Jake needs to stretch out his feminine side a little."

"Okay." That's all I could come up with. I felt shorter somehow and it wasn't even my place.

She glanced in the bedroom. "A bed with a hand-me-down blanket, no comforter, exotic wood-carved heads on the floor, a painting waiting to be hung of sailboats, for God's sake, and an adjoining bathroom. So neat and tidy, it looks unused in a bomb shelter sort of way—men!"

Her voice was nice but with a hint of disgust in the tone. She always did say exactly what she thought. She glanced at the kitchen counter as though it needed Lysol. She puckered her lips at me and tossed me a kiss with those delicate fingers. She smiled, "Really, is this what you and Jake are like?" Her hands and eyes pointed around the place.

"It's me for two months until I finish my thesis. I take it you love what Jake's done with the place?"

"I'm not sure. What was it before it was pillaged?"

"Ha, Ha! I'll put in a good word for you when I leave. I'm sure I could get him to swing a lease for you on all this lavishness."

"That would be wonderful," she said. "May I keep the

raccoons?"

"Of course. I don't think I could fit them in the car when I haul all these priceless antiques back to Florida."

She swiveled and stopped, gleaming back at me. "I take it this is where you eat, on bar stools at the counter." She discarded her sarcasm. Klarisa pulled a napkin out of one of the sacks and brushed off the stool seat and sat down as if sitting on plutonium.

Back in high school she used to hike miles to a lake, set out a blanket, and picnic on the ground with all the forest bugs. Marriage and adulthood apparently destroyed the girlish adventurer she once was. I hadn't moved since she began her inspection.

Klarisa took in a forced inhale and a powerful exhale. "I'm sorry. Suburbia has taken such a hold on me. All the same houses with strategically placed furniture that can be envied through maid-cleaned windows. I forget there is such a wonderful air of actual living out in the world. Have I become completely Stepford?"

"Yes, but you hid it well until you entered my cabin of horrors. I don't think Jake will be offended. This place is functional. Why pretty it up, I say, when I'm just a guest on a short stay?"

She caught me staring at my project of notepads and books. She ignored it.

"Functional, that's a positive term I could use for this. I don't try to be mean. I guess I'm just as snotty as my neighbors."

"Let's eat," I said. We dug into the sacks. I was famished. After, we sat on the grotesque leather couch, our feet on the Viking table. We passed a cheap bottle of wine back and forth. I didn't have plates, cups, or coasters. After a time, we laughed like the teens we used to be.

The sun held an orange glaze across the room as the time shifted between day and night, painting the sky. I was full, happy, and relaxed.

Just when I thought she was about to leave she put her legs up on mine and leaned back into the couch. She began biting her lip and gazing at me. I turned my eyes from her, but noticed in the periphery she was still staring. We couldn't think of anything to say.

Finally, she opened her mouth asking, "Is it true you're

studying fish?"

"Marine biology. Fish and all the other aquatic creatures. My focus is on octopods. They are quite brilliant creatures."

She wasn't really asking to get an answer. She was trying to break the tension. She leaned up and gave me a soft mouth kiss. Then another. A stronger man would have asked her to leave.

It didn't take long to escalate. It became searching and sweaty and primal. We had gone through this phase before, but she clearly knew things now that I wasn't used to. My hands explored her spine and graceful contours. The feel of her under my hands melted what little resistance I possessed. I turned. She giggled. We rolled to the floor.

Hours later I woke up curled in her feminine softness, feeling her chest rise and sink with satisfied sleep. We were cradled between the couch and the coffee table. A table leg was imbedded into my shoulder. I twisted to get up.

"Aren't you supposed to be home?" Worry and guilt swept through my mind.

Sleepily, Klarisa tried to pull me back down. "I think I am."

I pulled away. "This isn't right. This can't happen ever again. You need to get up and go home. It's 1:15 in the morning."

She purred and closed her eyes. Sleep relaxed her.

"Klarisa, what about Raymond?" I was standing. She ran her hand up my leg. Irritation swelled in me. I knocked over the empty wine bottle as I turned to walk to the kitchen. Knowing this wasn't a good idea didn't seem to deter me. Klarisa had that way about her. I glanced back at my stack of work, squinted, and couldn't dig deep enough for the willpower.

I am so stupid. This is wrong in so many ways. Stupid. The end of my pen was a knurled mess as I spit blue plastic from the end of my tongue.

Coffee was brewing within a few minutes. As the water seeped through the filter of wet grounds, my eyes walked up and down her full beauty. Her hair billowed out on the rug as if blown by the wind. Her hips were prominent and flowing gently down smooth legs to purple manicured toenails. Through the first and second cup, I tried to look away in futile attempts. She finally stirred. *Stupid.*

"I smell coffee." She stretched. I handed her a new robe of mine. I had dressed behind the counter in last night's clothes. She tossed the robe to the side. "I need coffee and a shower."

I held out her coffee and pointed her in the direction of the bathroom. A moment later, I heard water running. I sipped my coffee wondering whether a love-crazed dentist would break down my door at any moment. I walked over and made sure the door was locked.

Dentists possess all sorts of tiny tools and pain knowledge. I asked again about Raymond as I poured her and me another cup. I didn't need the caffeine with all the anxiety.

"He's at a dental convention for five days. He left yesterday afternoon."

"You planned this. He's gone? This is worse. I'm not sure why. My damn brain shut down sometime last night. This is really wrong." I rubbed my temples, trying to abate the headache that was sure to come.

"I miss you!" she said. "I loved how we were together; I have been thinking about this for years. Raymond is a financial provider. That's it; he isn't you."

"I'm not me right now. I don't do these things. It's too clandestine and guilt-ridden." I needed to get back to college. I needed single girls. I needed less complication.

"I don't love him. I almost despise him when he comes home. Sometimes I want to smack his face with my fist." She punched the air with fake meanness.

"Aunt Velora says he has no chin."

Her hand went over her mouth, and she stifled a giggle. "She's right. He doesn't."

I led her to the door and slapped her on the rump as she left. I was the happiest, rottenest person ever. All the next day, I kept seeing her where the carpet was matted. *That's it. I've got it out of my system, and she's gotten it out of hers. We just won't see each other again.* I walked back to the bathroom and immediately saw the "I love you" written in lipstick on the mirror and her panties flung over the faucet. *She's not going to leave me alone.*

The next two days she was back again. I was uncomfortably obliging. After a week of on-and-off visits, I said "no" and meant it. I quit answering the phone and the doorbell. I studied up for grad school. Soon I would be back in a quiet dorm at the University of Tampa—back to my life of actually asking someone on a date without my hands sweating and those breathing problems. No more married women. No more Klarisa. I didn't see Klarisa once in the eight days before I left for school. The bad thing about it was I became bothered on the plane that she hadn't tried harder.

***

The chairs unloaded and the lights set up, we went inside to enjoy pizza and loud conversation. Dad was actually funny—and, except for the tales about me, fairly amusing. He put me at ease, though I wasn't sure I wanted to like him. Maybe this was the father I could have had if he hadn't found solitude and ambition in a bottle. A couple of times, I even caught myself laughing at his jokes.

Jen held her hands out with the palms up and whispered, "See?"

I leaned in, whispering into her ear. "It's a phase. He'll grow out of it."

"Admit it, you are actually having fun with this old guy. And check-it-out—he's drinking only water."

"That's what the bottle says. Have you smelled it? Never mind. I don't think Russian vodka has a smell." I grinned.

She gave me a hug and a peck on the cheek then backed away with a hard, long-lasting pinch on my tummy skin.

Chapter 6

I quickly stepped out of the shower as my cell phone sang its obnoxious tune. Wobbling through the room, I tried to pull my pants above the ankles. A bare toe grabbed the edge of a metal bed leg. An expletive formed in my mouth, but I was in too much pain to let it out. My face scrunched and my toe throbbed, I picked my cell off the table. Hurriedly rolling my thumb across the answer button and fingering the speaker icon, I squeezed out a breathy "Hello" and sat on the bed massaging my big toe. The words came out raspy over the roof of my mouth.

"Are you in the middle of something?" asked Amy. "You sound as if you're running?"

"I think I'm practicing ballet and judo at the same time. I just have to watch out for those moving bedposts."

"What?" Amy sounded perturbed. She seldom understood my efforts at humor.

"I stubbed my toe."

"Oh, I get it. How are things going?"

"I went to a childhood-bashing lunch with my sister. She raves on and on about you by the way. She thinks I should kneel at your feet and save the air you breathe in jars to be released for my pleasure when you're away." I walked back in the bathroom and toweled the steamed mirror. I had shaved in the shower and done a pretty good job without a mirror. My toe throbbed as I stepped gingerly on the tiles.

"She is brilliant. I'm so glad one of you received the brains. You tell her I miss her. It was so nice when she visited. We have to have her back to the city." Amy gave emphasis to "the city".

"You realize she does live in a city—an inconsequential one, but a city just the same."

"Ben, I wasn't trying to be condescending. I'm sure her Salt Lake City is a lovely city."

I really didn't want to be annoyed at Amy. I missed her. In a way, I almost wanted her with me but not enough to actually ask her to come. I grew up with misguided, misinformed relationships, and I hadn't gained much from the child I was.

"How about your father? Have you seen him?"

"My father. What a joke. He released himself from that responsibility years ago. I'm not quite sure what to call him. He always made me call him 'Sir.' Isn't that absurd? Sir is a term of respect. I've always felt it was a joke for him to have me call him something he didn't deserve. Even when I say 'Father' or 'Dad,' and it disrespects fathers all over the world." I was complaining again.

Amy is patient. It comes with her job, but to hear the same whiney talk from her boyfriend must be tiring. "I'm sorry," I said. "I'm sure down deep I respect and love him. Boys are supposed to love their fathers. Right? He actually has been as close to pleasant as I've ever seen him. It drives me nuts."

"It is rough being in the same town as he is. Isn't it?"

"Sorry. You know how I sometimes get. I'm just babbling."

"But you actually care about the man. You may not respect him, but you yearn for his respect," she said.

"I am not on your couch, doctor. You are trying to psycho-babble me about feelings I neither need nor want." There was a pause in our conversation. I took in a deep breath then exhaled loud and long. "I'm sorry. I know you care. You are working on 36 years of inbred father disease. It is hard to heal." I knew my face was as tight as a pulled rope. I was glad we were just on the phone. I tried to change the subject. "How's Anvil?" Anvil is her earthy-smelling pet frog at her office.

"Did you see him?" she said softly.

I realized she held the steering wheel in this conversation. "I was much too pathetic for that when I arrived. I waited out in front of his house to watch him not walk out. He never did. I waited for hours trying to not talk to him. I did see him. He is aging and I drove off. Oh, and he almost got me arrested. See, you have a loser for a boyfriend."

"Who is never self-deprecating, so knock that stuff off. You always get into a funk when you are in the same town as him. You always do stupid things there too. That's why you never visit your aunt or sister."

"Probably true . . . no, it's completely true. Oh, there is one tidbit of gossip I've heard from Aunt Velora and Jen. My so-called father has become a Christian—a Mormon, to be exact." I waited for Amy to take that in.

"A Mormon? I thought they didn't believe in alcohol?
"What?"

"My reaction exactly. He quit drinking several years ago, as the rumor goes. I haven't verified any of this yet, but my sources are reliable. And he supposedly carries scriptures with him everywhere and goes to church every Sunday."

"You have to talk to him," she said. "You need to see this for yourself and let me know all the details. This is huge. Do you realize how hard this must have been for him?"

"I never realized how much you savor rumors. My psychologist girlfriend loves gossip. No wonder you can talk to people all day."

"I guess a lot of it is like gossip. You make my profession sound so Kravitz."

"Kravitz?"

"Yes. You know, the neighbor lady on Bewitched who always stared through the drapes at Samantha. Gladys Kravitz; it's an industry term. So, when are you going to talk with your father?"

"I thought we could glare at each other from across the room at Aunt Velora's party. No need for banter if we both store up contempt and focus it from our loving eyes. We save a lot of unnecessary words that way—mostly expletives, but words nevertheless."

Amy uttered a long "mmmm."

"Actually, I did see him at Aunt Velora's today. He was helping out. Can you believe him helping out? And he said things that could be construed as amiable."

"You really hung out in front of his house?"

"Don't try to find anything you can write a paper on. I was curious. I wanted to see if he still walked with his heavy foot forward as he usually does by mid-morning."

"What was that about getting arrested?"

"You are always listening even when I think you're not." I told her about my experience with the cops and my dad saving me from a life of crime. She laughed.

We said the "miss you"s, and I hung up feeling guilty. Deep down, I probably did want my dad's respect, but I hated myself for even wanting that. It seemed so unattainable and pitiful.

I dressed in a collared blue shirt; khaki, casual-Friday pants; and brown tennis shoes. *What does one wear to a funeral party?* I checked my shoes. *Good choice. I may need to run.*

Chapter 7

I arrived at Aunt Velora's house an hour and a half before her party. I wanted to see if she needed an ice run or some other chore done. I struggled to find a parking place. Cars were squeezed into her driveway and up and down the street. I checked my cell, wondering if I read the time wrong. I parked around the corner and two houses up.

As I jumped out, I stared at the house in front of me. It was a remodel catastrophe. Someone turned my old friend Jake's home into a southern plantation. It made all the other dated split-entries and ramblers seem out of place. I assumed a slow-talking contractor from the Carolinas changed the façade of the house to four white pillars, cascading roof, overdone trim, a porch with two rockers, and a grand, wide, white-cement staircase that dropped like overflowing water to a flower-trimmed walkway, then out to the sidewalk. White shiny stucco enclosed the outside walls. The house was small and overstated as a dollhouse for a child celebrity. I wondered what happened to Jake and his family. We hadn't talked in years. I gazed one more time then strolled to my aunt's house.

As I walked up to the door, kitchen smells drifted gently past me. I inhaled a deep breath. My aunt definitely wasn't cooking any of this.

Two men in their mid-seventies coughed and spit, making me glance their way. They were leaning against porch pillars, smoking with long, even breaths. The one in a blue jumpsuit smiled, saying, "You're Velora's kid?" His exhale covered me in a grey cloud and kicked away the kitchen fragrance. I grinned, noticing two mouthfuls of nicotine-stained teeth.

"Yeah, you've seen her?"

"Course we've seen her; it's her house. We're the greet'n committee. I'm Hal, and this younger version of me is Von."

Von spoke up with a cough and an exhale of more smoke. The hack went on for a full minute or more. I was patient on the outside, but ready to run through the door on the inside. His cough stopped and he thumped his chest a couple of times. "I'm only ten months younger, but I could always take my older brother."

"You never took anything but a beatin' and you know it."

"Von, Hal, it's been great meeting you both." I turned and bolted through the door before I needed a nebulizer.

The house inside was filled with early pre-funeral bash people; a lot of them. There was a vague familiarity with certain faces, but most were strangers taking over the house in which I was raised. I bobbed my neck a few times, trying to find a path through the front room herd. Following the smells to the kitchen, I found my aunt's best friend, Babs. I never knew if Babs was short for something or if it was her last name. She attacked me with a hug and a flat-footed kiss on the neck. I put my arm around her; she babbled about something that I couldn't make out through all the kitchen noise. She made the universal sign of drinking with thumb to lips then pointed to the back yard. I waved goodbye and made it through the overcrowded room like a bumper car in a chicken coop. I still couldn't find my aunt.

The backyard was filled with displaced prattle, though I could make out certain words. There were galvanized tubs filled with ice, beer, and soda in four places in the backyard. Two makeshift bars on each end of the yard were manned by four teenagers. They held drinking grins on their faces and were probably working for free as long as "free" was defined as sampling the wine and cases of cheap beer.

A fortyish girl with good makeup and a spring party dress waved at me from a few feet away. She seemed like someone I should know, but didn't. She came my way, so I stepped forward to greet her. My hand reached out to hers. She pushed my hand away and gave me a hardy hug, almost lifting me off the ground. I felt my lungs exhale the smoke Von and Hal had force-fed me on the porch.

"I haven't seen you since Mrs. Handy's Spanish class," She said.

"Hola," is all I could get out.

"Buenos dias, senor," she said, then noticed what I assume was a panicked face. "You don't recognize me?" She straightened her shoulders, putting her hands on a thin waist above ample hips. "Pam Sullivan?"

"Oh . . . Pam. Where are the glasses, straight hair, and no makeup?"

"Surgery is amazing these days, I found out what a curling iron is for, and I started using that silly stuff my mom used to put on. You're still the same."

"Well, I need surgery on this." I pinched my belly with both hands. "My dad got a full head of hair for life. My grandpa gave me a receding hairline, and I'm working on his belly roll. You look wonderful and healthy. Is your husband here?"

She ignored my question. "What are you up to? Someone told me you sold fish."

"Must have been my aunt or my sister. I'm a marine biologist, which essentially means I actually study octopodidae, not really any true pisces. We take notes on octopods in their environment and in large aquariums, and write down what we see. They are the most fascinating cephalopods, with unique abilities to adapt." I gazed at her expression and added, "Boring stuff, but it pays the bills."

"It sounds fascinating. Do you go on voyages with Jacques Cousteau?" She laughed with a very feminine rhythm. I waited for more.

"Wait, I think he died, so maybe you've gone with his son and travel to exotic locations with blue, see-through water." She sang that same laugh, and decided I adored this older version of the bottle-glassed girl with a sharp mind.

I remember talking in Spanish to Pam a lot. Our desks were adjoining, and she helped this illiterate Spanish student pass the class. She had that same laugh back then. It brought back the few good memories I have of high school.

TATTERED PORTRAIT

"The closest I've been to Jacques is a quote on the wall above my desk. It says, '*The sea, once it casts its spell, holds one in its net of wonder forever.*'" Her eyes raised skyward as if trying to figure out an algebra problem. "No, he hasn't taken me sailing, and neither has his son, Jean. I'm waiting to be asked on a voyage. I mostly hang out with my computer or in some distasteful, mosquito-infested marsh."

"That's an adventure I've never thought of having. You need a drink?"

"Sure, walk me over to a tub, and I'll grab a bottle of water."

"I thought you scientist types drank wine and smoked Cuban cigars in high-ceilinged rooms with other proper men."

I listened to her giggle for a moment. "Oh, and what do girls of your measure do?"

"We are proper." She reached into the tub and held up a can of beer. Pam displayed the can as if on a television commercial. I laughed. She followed suit with a much prettier tone.

The two of us sat on folding chairs swapping stories about how bad high school was. She told me about her marriage to a software salesman who travels the globe. She sees him every third week of the month. "It is a perfect marriage," she laughed.

I told Pam a little too much about Amy. I'm not sure why this girl from the past was so easy to unload life with. It was good therapy for both of us. The subject of my father hidden in a crevice in my brain, waiting to be brought out again. *I hope she doesn't ask.*

I heard my aunt's voice. She was storming towards us. I stood to receive her onslaught of kisses and hugs. She bragged about me to Pam, touching each finger on her hands as though she was counting my many virtues, of which I found none. I bowed my head, probably turning a shade of crimson. Aunt Velora held my elbow so I couldn't escape. She excused us and whisked me off to socialize.

Cordial gatherings have been the one thing I have never been good at.

I said hello and bobbed my head like a feeding chicken. I saw smiles all around as I searched for escape with each new huddled group. They all asked the same questions in various ways and told me how great Velora was. I tried to be gracious, but boredom crept in. The list of names hardly lasted seconds as my mind drifted them off to some hidden place. The Franks and Veronicas and Eds and Aprils floated away like leaves off an autumn wind. My palms are sweaty, and I feel the perspiration of anxiety bubble up across my forehead. By the third group I had unconsciously turned off the conversations, though I nodded in full agreement. Most of those people seemed to have been there since breakfast.

Aunt Velora stopped in front of one large man whose back is near us. She smacked him slightly in the arm. I quietly thought of Jen and grinned. His beer spilled and he turned around. I was introduced to Kragun, whom I remember as the school bully. We were sometimes friends, but mostly he gave me wedgies and elbow bumps in locker-lined halls. In our high school years, he exuded the genetics of a stout German immigrant. Kragun's father's build was that of a television wrestler; his mom looked like she could take his dad. After school, he went right into the Marines. I hadn't seen him since, but those eyes and that bulbous nose were unmistakable. Now, his body appeared more molded by beer and laziness. He looked as if he should be sitting in a Lazy Boy recliner; standing appeared difficult.

I saluted him, saying, "Hey, Kragun. How ya been?"

Round as he was, he still towered over me. If I stared straight ahead, I gazed into his now-hidden Adam's apple. "I'm okay," He said.

"What are you doing now?" I asked hesitantly.

"I'm the butcher over at Safeway. I heard you were a sea urchin or something."

"Yeah, something like that." I rolled my eyes to the side at my aunt, hoping to signal time for a getaway. My aunt smiled. "How're your parents? They still over on Claybourne?"

"No, they both died of heart attacks within a year. Dad first. I was still in the Marines, but they shipped me back for the funerals and such. I'm living in the Claybourne house now. My sister didn't want any part of it. She's in Nevada running a youth correctional facility. I think she loves bossing kids around."

"That's nice." *What else would I say?*

Kragun turned to my aunt. "Ben here always accepted my

stupid teenage shit and never once told on me. He was something."

Aunt Velora said, "All is forgiven since you brought those patties and wieners for the grill. It will calm the crowd until dinner is laid out."

"Velora, you're the only one in this neighborhood who doesn't treat me like the dumb ox I am. I appreciate it."

Kragun had somehow gained a heart. I was a bit disoriented by the feast. There was a moment of stares then the three of us said our good-byes. No hugging; I didn't want my underwear lifted.

I checked my watch, probably the only one who did, and noticed the party was about to start in fifteen minutes. Who would have known? With all this laughing, conversation, grilled meat, table loads of potato and noodle salads, heat, and alcohol, I assumed the party would end early. I would find out later how wrong I was.

A young lady whisked my aunt away with an upset party question about napkins, or plastic ware, or both. I noticed someone I actually wanted to talk with and darted towards her. My brother-in-law was downing handfuls of potato chips with one hand, washing them down with beer from the other. Jen was in rapid conversation with a lady in too-tight blue jeans, bearing the puffy hair of the fifties and childbirth hips. As I walked closer, I noticed Jen's friend's lips were the reddest I'd ever seen—all florescent, obscene, and showy. Jen was total smiles and hand movements. She didn't notice me until I grabbed her elbow. She hit me with an abrupt squeeze. Air escaped my lungs with an odd noise. Jen released me, beaming.

"Do you remember Andrea?" Jen said, holding her friend's hand. "She was my best-est friend. We've known each other since before grade school. Her parents gave her all the best toys, so we played at her house constantly." They both giggled and did a little foot movement back and forth as if pretending to be string puppets. "We were inseparable until she moved to California with her parents. What grade was that?"

"The end of ninth grade," her friend answered.

"Andrea, are you living back here?" I asked. I consciously told myself to quit staring at her stand-out lips.

"No, just visiting my mom. She moved back here after the

divorce two years ago. She brought me along to the funeral party to see Jennifer. Doesn't this seem just a titch morbid, to celebrate a death before it actually happens? Sorry, I tend to say whatever's on my mind and then regret it right after my mouth closes. Truly, no disrespect to your wonderful aunt. By the way, she looks too healthy to be ill."

"No problem, whatsoever," I said. "Jen and I are both a bit queasy about the whole beer drinking, party lights celebration. Morbid doesn't even begin to describe it. She wants me to give a toast during dinner. I'm thinking about running and hiding in my hotel until it's over."

"It's spooky," Jen said. "I'm not sure whether to break down and bawl or empty a bottle of wine."

Andrea gave Jen a hug. She nestled into the crevice between the neck and shoulder and cried. Her breath would catch ever so often between the tears. I was out of place. I hung back for a while then began patting my sister on the back. All around us, people were celebrating. I felt a tap on my shoulder and turned around. Aunt Velora stood there with wonder on her face and hands on her hips.

"What the hell's wrong with you three kids? I know you haven't seen each other for a long time, but you're changing the party mood something awful. You need to cut back on the alcohol."

I turned to my aunt, pulled my water bottle out of my back pocket, and waved it in her face. "It's Jen and her friend Andrea. They can't keep away from the two young boys tending bar. It's embarrassing."

Jen slugged me in the ribs. For a few seconds my breath was suspended and my mouth searched for air. Finally, it came in gasps. She was actually giggling, though with a bad case of red eyes.

"You two are the same. Growing older hasn't helped you grow up," Aunt Velora said. "Can you two make sure everyone's happy for a while? I need to lay down for a few. Parties are great, but they wear me out, and I suspect this will be a long night."

I grabbed her frail elbow. "Let me walk you upstairs."

"I'm not an invalid; I just have cancer. Now take care of the party. Make sure everyone has a good time; and if your dad shows up, keep him away from the drinks."

"I thought you said he's changed?"

"He has, but this is still a fox in a chicken coop thing. If it's too much temptation for him, whisk him out. My days of babysitting him are over."

"Okay. We'll take over as hosts, but I'm still walking you up to your room." I wasn't about to babysit my father either.

She held her forehead with both hands and grimaced. Probably a headache I couldn't even imagine. As I tucked her into bed, her arm reached up and patted me on the cheek. Fondness filled me when I closed the door slowly and softly. I followed the constant prattle through the hall and outside again, and felt the looks of "that-poor-child" on the back of my neck.

Chapter 8

Charcoal and lighter fluid odors flowed across the back lawn. My stomach growled with anticipation. It was the smell of comfort even though these parties never happened when I was growing up. People were huddled in groups around the bars and each barbeque. Laughter was dispensed, salting the air with happiness and friendship. I was out of place, actually enjoying my own solitude with all the pleasant action around me. It was a tribute to my aunt, who hopefully was resting soundly. I didn't even swat the fly buzzing my head as the insect tried to find a place to land. My sweet aunt was upstairs trying to regain the strength that age and disease were slowly stripping from her. When I checked on her, she lay helpless and stoic in sleep as her friends danced to her un-dug grave. I knew she would bounce out of bed for a second round. Her vitality would fill the backyard again.

A large group surrounded my sister. Giggles were ebbing and flowing as she entertained. Jen's small hands moved everywhere, pulling her arms with them as she excitedly spoke. As each new person entered the group, she exchanged personable hugs then went back to her routine. She received all the personality in our family. I'm not sure what I received—probably just smoldering hatred hidden in the back of my mind that resurfaces periodically, mostly when I return to taste the bitterness of my father's home town.

Just when I was feeling better, the fly returned and brought in a couple of recruits. Two of them landed—one on my ear the other on my nose. The third buzzed my neck. My relaxed mood changed quickly. I was a biologist. I knew what flies did. I began swatting them fiercely and gyrating my body. I tripped on a sprinkler and spun to the ground. I sat up to see Jen and her whole group headed for me with smiles of concern. *Oh shit!* I didn't want this. I lost my invisibility. Now the whole sympathetic yard came to my rescue. My eyes closed, wishing everyone away.

"I'm okay!" I shouted, but they kept coming. I stood up quickly as if nothing happened. Someone said, "He just had a seizure." My chin folded to my neck and my face flushed.

The questions flew like volleyballs. "What happened?" "Are you okay?" "Did you twist your ankle?" "The vet's here somewhere, should we get him?" "You dancing?"

I excused myself to get a drink, and the group retreated back to their positions. I breathed in, long and slow and deep. My hands tried to wipe the redness from my cheeks.

My heart rate slowed then peaked again as I saw my father come around the far side of the house. Chin out, neck straight, he paused with contempt as if sneering at the peasantry. I thought about the fantasy of his royal roots. A cool breeze rushed down the back of my collar.

Dad talked to someone who was grabbing water for him and a handful of Chex mix for himself. He couldn't even reach down and get one for himself, the damn highness. He was too far away for me to see his eyes, though I assumed they were hollow and red-webbed as always. I wasn't falling for his Mormon charade. I envisioned him stumbling or walking into a table. He didn't. He wore a grey fedora that he tapped whenever anyone walked by him. All the people talking to my father seemed to find him wonderful. Laughter carried in the air. It was disturbing.

Maybe he actually quit drinking. I couldn't get my mind around that. He was like a smoker who quits every time he douses a cigarette in an ashtray. I began wondering what it would be like to have a sober father. Sure, now he does it after I'm thousands of miles away and no longer need to toss a ball. It would have been nice when I was six or seven. Now I can't decide whether it would be a good or bad thing. I'd fallen over the soccer ball, struck out at bat, caught a football once running backwards to the sideline, and sucked at table tennis. I never was that great at sports. Why should

I be? I could always blame Dad.

Someone bumped me from behind. The jolt brought me out of my daydream. I turned. My old friend Jake, from around the corner, stood grinning. A pink shirt and a barrel torso embraced me. Jake always reminded me of someone who should be cutting down trees in the northwest. He squeezed me enough to squirt my lungs out of my ears. I dropped my water bottle. He stood back and shook my shoulders. I started to smile, then he came at me with another manly hug. I'm fairly sure I heard a popping sound like ribs breaking. Jake released again. Air flowed silently back to my lungs. I instinctively held my arms out in front of me in case he wanted more.

Jake held me at arm's length, repeating my name in different tones. I reciprocated, though a little winded. I was physically shaken as he laughed.

"How are you, old buddy?" he asked.

"I'm good," I said, "though my lungs are still slipping back into position."

"Have you crossbred any odd fish? I remember seeing a movie about that. Damn things ate most of a village."

"I don't believe I've wreaked havoc on any villages. I just observe and write details down. Actually, my students do most of that, but luckily I get the glory."

"If I do that with my home aquarium, can I get paid for it? I think I've noticed my tetras consorting with a snail. Maybe I should write it up in a journal of some kind."

"Maybe you should." Behind me I heard the ambient noise of people gathering and friendships renewed. The smell of lilacs and beer overpowered the meaty barbeque.

He stood as though he was contemplating it. "Can I use your name as a co-whatever-it-is? Thesis writer; no, it would be a study, wouldn't it? A co-study-er? No, that's not right, either. Co-author—yeah, that's it. Would you be my co-author?"

"Not in the least. So, Jake, what are you doing nowadays? You were making cabinets a while back." In high school, Jake was the best player on the team, and he seldom made a basket. But he could dribble and pass like a pro. The other thing going for him on court was size. His bulk was intimidating to the opposing team, so we always went to finals, but never won.

"I'm a contractor," he said, "mostly residential. I'm working on a small commercial job now, a remodel and an extension."

"Did you do your parents' old house?" I know my voice was accusatory.

The pre-funeral revelers were getting louder and more animated as I glanced around the yard. I could see my aunt toasting everyone without taking a sip from her wine glass. Her wine was probably ginger ale anyway. She appeared rested and her left cheek held a few crumpled blanket lines.

"Yes, isn't it lovely and atrocious? I call it the Southern Belle of the Desert."

"I kind of got that from the white pillars out front. I kept waiting for Rhett and Scarlet to walk out on the porch and argue a bit."

"That's exactly what I was going for." There was a pause. "I live in that one-sixteenth-acre Carolina estate with my boyfriend, Rick." He waited for my reaction.

Boyfriend . . . Rick? Never figured. Didn't care, but never figured.

He held a grin on me. "Surprised?"

"Yeah, a bit, though as it's sinking in . . . not so much. Where's Rick?"

"He'll be by later. He adores Velora. He works the afternoon shift on the force."

I gave him a puzzled expression.

"He's a cop—a detective, actually. He hates it when I refer to him as a cop. He has issues."

"Haven't we all," I said. Over Jake's shoulder, I spotted dear sweet Dad coming our way. He was zeroing in. I started doing those short, quick sips of air through pursed lips. Night seemed to be coming on way too early even though the sun was far from ready to set. I searched desperately for an escape, but he's a fast old man. His gait didn't seem impaired by alcohol.

"Well, if it isn't the building fairy and my fish market son." His attempt at humor. Even sober he was pretentious.

Jake said, "It's good to see you, Mr. Parch."

My face reddened. I knew, because I had felt those flushed

feeling so many times, years before. He hadn't changed. Didn't matter whether he was Mormon, Catholic, or agnostic, he was still the same. I bit my lip as my throat tightened. I tried to do more than open my mouth, but speaking seemed to be out of the question. After watching him smile at me, I finally got out a raspy barb. "And the town drunk crawls up from the floor." It was mean, and I regretted saying it as soon as it came out of my mouth. Jake's face turned stern, and he churned his head at me.

Dad gave me an amused stare. "You do have my sense of humor." He shook hands vigorously with Jake, then came at me for a hug.

I backed up. What was he trying to do? All the molecules of my body changed. I was being thrown completely off kilter. I could see from his face he found some pleasure in that. His arms finally lowered in rejection, and he scowled.

"Son, see the change that has become me? I just want you to know there are no hard feelings," he fidgeted.

I don't remember the last time we talked. I send him Christmas cards that I sign with only my name, no false hope of receiving one from him. Though, he has sent me one most years that I receive about the end of January.

There was anticipation as both of us watched each other, though not directly. We checked out each other's shoes then began staring at spots on our foreheads. No real eye contact. I finally broke through the dead air with, "Are you waiting for an apology from me? Well, okay, Dad, I'm so sorry you chased out Mom, sent Jen and me off to Velora's, and only called when you needed a ride from a bar stool."

I knew I was being mean again, but I couldn't seem to help myself. I start out with intentions of being civil. But, soon as I see him, I just want to twist the knife. And then afterwards, I'm quietly ashamed. Jen tells me I need to read a book she recommends about forgiveness. I usually reply with something about forgiving people all the time, but that Dad just hasn't made the list, yet.

Jake held out his palms and faded away with lightning speed, disappearing in a crowd of rowdies. The mood was party time, except in my uneasy propinquity. Dad appeared annoyed.

"I have risen from that coffin that entombed me. I have

stepped into the light." Dad seemed to be speaking at a point over my head at no one in particular. "God has shown me the truth of my old ways, and he has set me free." He was loud enough several people around the yard glared in our direction with questioning glances. His chest rose proudly as his lungs filled as if to complete his sermon. He held the most serious regard on his face, scraping the edge of intelligence. "I was empty . . . ."

I stifled a laugh, biting my lip, and then broke in quickly. "Dad, you sound like an evangelist. You are not in front of a waffling jury with me . . . or perhaps you are. All I see in front of me is the man from whom I hid bottles."

"See, even back then you were trying to save me."

"I was trying to save myself and Jen." My voice matched his.

I glanced around, noticing some of the groups had stopped their conversations and eyed us with concern. Our battles were well-known. There would be gossip and family innuendo for some time. I thought about walking away. In the distance behind Dad, my aunt turned a finger at me. I grabbed him by the arm and tugged him like a precocious child to the shady corner of the yard. We were as alone as we could be at a party of two or three hundred and growing. We found solitude between overgrown shrubs and a thick-barked pine. Blue birds fluttered above us, frightened by the intrusion.

I peered back through the needles and berries. Groups on the grass disregarded us as old news turning inward to bad jokes, old lies, and new gossip.

"Dad," I began. I needed water. My throat was dry, and I could feel my face flushing. "This is Aunt Velora's party. Your sister. You need to keep a low profile, meaning no drinking or passing out or empty sermons, and I'll be civil. We need to keep our voices and ourselves respectable. Maybe we could just text each other," I concluded, in a half-hearted attempt at humor.

"I don't text. I still send stamped letters, and don't friend me on Facebook. I have a reputation, you know." He smiled, waiting for my rebuttal. It was almost like a real conversation. A flush rolled up my face. Inside I giggled. My face started to form a smile, hidden behind a clenched fist. I shook my head.

"I'm still an alcoholic, Son, always will be. I am also a

reformed sober alcoholic with four years and three months under my belt. I intend to keep it that way. My church helps me a lot. So does chewing gum. I still sit down to read and reach for a tumbler that's not there. This is hard. It takes a lot of church and a lot of gum."

I grinned and nodded. Pain shot up my leg as a thorn spiked me on the ankle. I moved a step to the left. I felt a bit covert, hiding in the bushes. "Okay, I'll give you a slight benefit of the doubt. And quit calling me 'son.' It sounds like we're related." I smiled. "Sorry, my sarcasm is sometimes only funny to me. I'm not used to you being sober." I waited a few beats. "If that's truly what you are?"

He nodded and inspected the ground, appearing almost defeated. "I enjoy the humor. One has to laugh at himself from time to time. I understand I've not been the best father figure."

"Ya think?" I saw him, perhaps for the first time, as an old man trying to erase thirty-six years. He struck me as beaten. He rubbed his cheeks as if pushing away tears.

"All this time, you were being sarcastic, and I took it as a frontal assault." His eyes narrowed. His lips curled ever so slightly. "I almost find drinking repulsive. The smell of alcohol still pulls my leash with a fairly hard tug. Luckily, I have other interests to lead me on the straight and narrow."

"Obviously that doesn't include yard work." I said a little quickly. I thought, *sorry! I need to work on my inappropriate sarcasm,* but my lips remained shut.

"Oh, yes, you've been to the house? A stalker, as I recall? Almost needed to have you incarcerated?" He was charmed by this memory. He held a satisfied demeanor on his face, and he stood straighter, as if that could happen.

"It wasn't about you. I drove by and got a glimpse of the yard." My throat was dry as a sun-bleached cow skull. I shifted my weight back and forth to erase the lie. It didn't work. My eyes kept darting to the empty plastic bottle in my hand. He watched me intently in silence. He knew I was full of it. Anxiety moved in waves through my body, the type that comes from adjusting the truth. Guilty as charged. We stood uneasily as the air around us grew stagnant.

"Yeah, the outside is a little overdue and ancient," he said. The air finally moved. "I have the intention of fixing it up, but other wishes appear to rise above it on the list. I spend a lot of time with my church duties and such. They're my new addiction."

"Well, I've seen worse," my voice softened. The anxiety moved down my chest and pooled in my stomach. Tums, I thought. The rage of memories sat in the back seat, as I almost appreciated our conversation. These were uncharted waters. I had always talked to him with sarcastic meanness. He was the drunken overlord disciplining the child peasant. I understood that. I rolled the idea of this new dad around in my brain for a while. I wondered how long his new declared self would last.

He could sense my confusion. I think he even savored it a little. He began to laugh. Not a giggle, but an all-out laugh that made his throat wiggle. His eyes were happy, without the scarlet ripples I always used to see.

I hesitated to smile, knowing the absurdity of his changes. I bit softly on my lip; there were too many years of distrust to shake off from fifteen minutes of his being almost nice.

Jolted from my thoughts, I became aware of her voice. "It seems as though you're working on some changes in your life."

Her hands covered my eyes. With her distinct perfume and breasts pressed into my back, I knew instantly who it was. "Please, Klarisa."

Dad laughingly said, "Looks like nothing changes in your life."

I pulled Klarisa's hands down with force. "My father and I are having a private conversation." Her appearance dropped just a touch. I realized I came across a bit rough. She held up her palms and walked away. A branch swatted her on the cheek. I glanced at Dad. His features showed sympathy for me. I didn't like that at all.

"It is good to see you, Son." It came out of a humble enough face to make me think he may have even meant it. I don't recall him calling me "son" more than five times in my life. I had always been Benjamin to him, a formal name I hate to this day.

Why does he keep calling me "son"?

He started to reach out for a handshake. Partway through, he thought better of it, and his arm dropped to his side. My fingers danced on my thigh. I'm not sure I was ready for that intimacy. Even though my hand was thinking about it, my mind held fast to that scared child within.

We both nodded as if the conversation was a bit too much, overwhelmingly awkward. In unspoken agreement we moved out of the bush. With slight eye contact he slid over to a group barely around the corner. I galloped to the far side of the lawn. My breathing was uneasy. My nose crinkled as spilt beer and old-lady perfume followed the light breeze. I began gawking around like a hungry bird for my sister. I needed friendship that I understood. My dad left me dizzy and queasy.

Klarisa was leaning into the makeshift bar to the west, making the young bartender blush. I definitely knew I couldn't handle her right now. I moved, putting a loud prattling group as camouflage between the west bar and me. I began thinking about my dad and how hard it would be for him to be around all this liquor. *What was that about?* I mentally changed subjects, regretting my compassion for my dad.

As I was sneaking around the semi-drunk group, a toast was given that they all laughed at. A large-handed man reached from the group and grabbed my elbow. It was firm and almost demanding. "Ben, is that you?" he said.

"Yes?" I answered quickly, hoping he would ease up on the grip. My answer held the inflection of a question. His face was unfamiliar, but kind.

"You've put a little bulk in all the right places," the man stated. His entourage turned to face me as if I were a spotted celebrity. My shoulder was guided into position. My body followed. I was quickly engulfed within the circle of bad jokes, back pats, and stale beer breath. I was home.

"I'm Grant . . . Grant Jones." I glared up at him as he released me from his grip. I wanted to rub my elbow but decided to pretend manhood. "I was a couple of years older than you."

"Still are, I imagine," I joked.

Everyone laughed as if that was really funny. They all stared down waiting for more of my wisdom to shine. I knew that was all I was up to. I glanced back and forth between the two bars, thinking I could excuse myself with the need of a drink. The one at the east side appeared safe. No crazy married women that I've slept with there.

"I need a . . ." I was interrupted by a man that reminded me of my fourth-grade teacher. He looked like a stork with the biggest, roundest eyeglasses I'd ever seen. "Let me get you a drink. Beer or wine?"

I thought about water, but that wasn't on his menu. I gargled out "wine," trying to be one of the guys.

"White or red?" I heard as he walked away.

"Red." I held out a finger and thumb indicating a small amount. "Thank you."

The group held me captive.

Grant, my new friend, broke the short silence. "I remember you from junior high. At least I was in junior high. You would have been in elementary." He eyed me as if trying to get inspiration from the sky. "It was probably the summer between fourth or fifth grade." The circle moved in a half step. "Me, Poder, and crazy Mandelli found you and that freckled kid with the stand-up hair fishing at the river in the gully. You guys were perched on the cement bridge."

I instantly realized who he was. My face flushed, and I tightened my hands against my sides. Stork handed me an overflowing glass of wine. I spilled it on my shoe, stepped back, and emptied a third of it on the ground. Grant looked different to me now.

"We came by, harassing the two of you, and you went all nuts, swinging that fishing rod at us like a sword."

"Well, there was a little more to it than that," I said. I glanced behind me, seeing my dad sitting alone and upright on a folding chair. Two sides of me were pulling in different directions. I didn't want the humiliation of the past with Grant. Then there was my dad trying to be nice to me, him sober, and all in the same visit. *What a son-of-a-bitch.* I turned back to Grant

"Oh, yeah." He waved it off with his huge hands like it was nothing. "Crazy Mandelli did try to give Ben here a wedgie and thump the freckled kid on the head with his knuckles. Anyway, Ben was swinging his rod. He about tore Crazy Mandelli's ear off and caught me up in his fishing line. It must have been a hundred-pound line. I couldn't even break it. I finally grabbed a pocket knife from a tackle box and cut it." The circle gained a few new members as everyone stepped back a bit.

I glanced around for somewhere else to be. I was only half-listening and completely disinterested. Old feelings circled in my stomach.

He stopped for a minute, thinking. "Crazy Mandelli somehow yanked the fishing pole from Ben then stomped it in half and threw it in the deep part of the creek." He flicked his hands in the air making a tossing motion, forgetting about the beer in his hand. He soaked three startled men to his right. Laughter ensued. A guy across from me flicked his drink at Grant. More laughter. Grant pointed with a finger gun at the whole group. "Someone, get me a beer."

With giggles all around, a Bud was passed around the circle to Grant. He downed an impressive swig. With one hand firmly on his beer and the other gesturing, he started up again. "The freckled kid was so scared he threw his pole in the water himself. He would have thrown the tackle box in, too, if Ben hadn't wrestled it away. Finally, they lost their toughness, and both of them jumped off the bridge into the water, tackle box held high."

"I realized this was a fight I couldn't win. When I did, I was scared shitless, but I didn't let on," I said.

Giggles and small chatter filtered through the group.

"You two swam like scared ducks to the far side then just kept running. We three idiots laughed and laughed. There were pole scratches on Crazy Mandelli's face with blood oozing from them."

I remembered the whole thing but kept silent. At the time, it made me mad. I never ran from a fight, though there were only a few times I needed to, but I had heard about Crazy Mandelli and didn't want to find out if any of the rumors were true.

"Then later that night," Grant continued, "Ben and his uncle paid my dad a visit."

The story began pulling me in. I remembered sitting on a yellow-flowered couch, the ugliest thing I'd ever seen, and my uncle talking to them. Grant's dad appeared stern, with a peppered jowl. He kept pinching Grant's ear and asking, "Is that true?" I felt sorry for Grant. I heard his dad was a rough ex-Marine and a terror to other neighbor kids. Grant gradually crumpled down to half my height in the hardback chair, his earlier bravado sucked from him.

I turned and caught eyes with Klarisa. She flipped me off and grinned. Aunt Velora waved just behind her and threw me a kiss.

"My butt hurt for three days and I wasted my Spudnut money paying for their stupid poles. Crazy Mandelli's dad just paid his share, saying, 'Boys will be boys.' Mancelli laughed every time he saw me on my Spudnut run. That was by far the dumbest thing I ever did . . . well, besides marrying Pamela Chonsky."

"I was embarrassed to go to your house with my uncle," I said. "I felt like a snitch. He grilled me for an hour to find out who did it. I've never seen my uncle that way. He rarely left the house and always grinned as though a clown danced in his head. He came unglued on you and your dad. I don't think I ever used that new fishing pole. It's probably still in the plastic it was wrapped in years ago." I scratched my nose and thought back. "I bought two bags of donuts from you through Mrs. Anderton. You probably never knew I paid for part of my own fishing pole."

Dad still sat alone, glancing over at me every so often.

"You should've bought the whole basket, you little snitch," he said. "Back then I only got a quarter a bag. That's a lot of donuts to push."

The whole group laughed and patted me on the back. The whole scene made me miss my Uncle Keith. He was an odd duck, but I loved him just the same. I pinched tears as though they were tears of laughter. I'm not sure I'd ever thought about missing my uncle. I certainly didn't know him well. Talking wasn't a necessity for him. We just lived in the same house all those years. This too was new territory.

The group leaned in as a thin, high-necked man began telling his own story of stupidity. These stories went around the group with bonded laughter at the end of each one. I slipped out after about the fourth story, faking a laugh as I blended back to the party.

Chapter 9

I rubbed my temples. All these people trying to talk to me was giving me shortness of breath and a headache. My neck raised and twisted like a periscope through a sea of people. Where was Jen?

A few chatting groups parted, and I spotted her holding the attention of three girls. She was in her element as I watched her mouth moving and her hands dancing through the air. I felt comfortable and safe, as I stepped toward her. A hand grabbed me by the bicep. The grasp was forceful and spun me around. My eyes were inches away from Klarisa's. We stared at each other for almost half a minute. Breath sifted through clenched teeth faster and faster. I struggled to muster a smile, because I knew it was the proper thing to do. My mouth opened to speak, but no words formed.

Klarisa came at me with eyes of intent. *Oh shit!* Her lips plunged toward mine, but missed their target as I jerked my chin to the side. I felt the forbidden wetness of an open-mouth kiss. We gazed at each other in silence. I wiped her saliva from my cheek as nonchalantly as possible, pretending to fix my hair. Naughty eyes stared at me. Her lips pressed in a sneaky grin. Her hands cupped my neck and jaw. Target acquired. Her tongue probed my mouth. I didn't even remember opening it. My eyes were bulging, glancing around over Klarisa's shoulder for her husband or anyone else who might make my guilt peak. No one paid attention, but my throat tightened anyway. I pulled away, though with adolescent reluctance. My stomach tightened. My breath came in gasps.

TATTERED PORTRAIT

Klarisa pulled slowly back. I tried not to lean forward, but I'm pretty sure I did. "I've wanted to say hi all night," she said. My throat constricted, and I stared at everything but her. My feet uncontrollably kicked at the grass. "I've been searching for you. You're always with someone or flying around the yard like the social animal I know you're not. I think we should slip away for a while."

I stammered as my ribs seemed to constrict. I thought about Amy waiting for me back in Florida. That was a real relationship. We shared intelligent conversation, liked the same restaurants and take-outs, and we were a couple. Plus, we enjoyed healthy, fun, affectionate sex with neither one of us married to someone else.

"Well, I have to take care of my aunt." My mind was completely inept in this confrontation, especially the type Klarisa dealt. The grass was beaten up by my feet again.

We both glanced over at Aunt Velora as she received a fresh glass of water and gave back a smile that could cure disease. Velora held court with three gentlemen, who shared enough age between them to go back to biblical times, all waiting on her hand and foot. She loved the attention. I feared the three of them would need a ride home in an ambulance.

Klarisa raised her eyes in disgust. "She appears to be pretty well taken care of."

I grimaced.

Klarisa closed the distance between us again. She gave me a big hug, pressing her breasts into my chest. She was deliberately reminding me of what I could have. Her breath was fragrant. My nostrils flared as they inhaled sweetshop flavor. I shook off my male thoughts, gently pushing her back with my hands on her waist. She leaned in slowly, rubbing soft lips on my cheek. The temptation was strong, but I turned, stepping just out of striking range.

"I thought you were dentally married to good ol' Raymond," I said.

Her eyes narrowed on mine. "For now. It gives me a root canal just being reminded." She canted her feet and poked her hip out. My hold slipped. Her hip glanced off mine as her fingers held my neck.

71

I changed the subject and backed up a few inches, pushing her hands away. "Are you having fun at my aunt's party?" She gave me a glower of disgust as if I'd just committed treason. With fatuous gestures, I feigned indifference.

I knew it was a stupid change-of-subject question. But men become stupid and adolescent when faced with probable sex, even unwanted probable sex. The whole thing reeked of disaster and guilt. I was working hard at controlling any what-the-hell thoughts. I held my chest out as stoically as I could, trying to rule the rest of me.

"Ben, you seem panicked around me. There is no reason for that." She pulled me by the elbow. I followed, though I thought about standing my ground. I was led to one of the bars. The same kid was behind it, his eyes glassy, his movements overly slow and controlled. He probably should have been home by now. *Where were his parents?*

I gathered myself together, turned off the primal brain, and flapped my hand *no* to the young bartender. I tried to put on the most serious look I could as I faced Klarisa. I assumed from her reaction my face held the pallor and distortion of someone about to heave. I was going for strong.

"Are you all right? You look sick."

"I'm fine. I just didn't want any more wine. One glass is my limit. I have my father's genetics, remember? I'm actually not sure if he gave me the alcoholic gene or not, but I'm not tempting fate."

"How often do you drink?" she said in a concerned tone.

"Not often. A fifth a night. Sometimes two or three if I don't eat. It seems to soothe me."

"Smart ass."

"Honestly, a little at social events; you could barely fill a full bottle with all the wine I've drank over my lifetime. Mostly, I just carry the glass around." I rubbed sweat from my brow with a napkin embossed with "Velora's Pre-Funeral Party." I swallowed distaste on my tongue. Klarisa was eyeballing me with an expression of worry, her finely painted eyes squinting. It took me a minute to recall what we were talking about. "And my social calendar is filled with sporadic and few dates. I'm a water and ice person. Mostly I'm busy in my lab with Donald and Goofy. You know alcohol doesn't interest me. I can't imagine why." My hands templed as I raised my eyes.

"Who?" Klarisa's nose scrunched up.

"What?" I asked.

"Donald and Goofy?"

"They're just names for two of the octopuses I'm studying."

Her face told me she wanted nothing to do with shop talk. She reached down and caught my fingers in her hand.

Her features changed as her eyes blazed down on me as if I were prey. I decided to keep talking, moving back to our previous conversation. "Every time I see a bottle of booze; I think I need to hide it or dump it out. I'm a riot at cocktail parties; the booze always disappears down the drain."

"Well, let's get you water or a root beer from the kiddies' bucket." She laughed.

I followed my elbow as I was pulled the few feet to the tub of ice and beverage. I realized she wasn't about to let me go. She glanced back at me. I lowered my eyes. Her cleavage showed enough I turned my head, but not instantly. "A ginger ale," I said talking to no one in particular. The kid at the bar gave a glimmer of perplexed understanding, as if he knew something but the dots weren't connecting. I recalled watching my teenage friends in high school drink. It never ended well.

Klarisa stood up and grabbed my shoulder again. I flinched at the tightness of her grip. "I'll run you to an AA meeting right after you finish your soda." She laughed again.

As we turned around, Klarisa said, "Oh, God, here comes your bodyguard. She's in attack mode, isn't she?"

Jen headed our way with the movements of a bull, her horns down and charging. Her summer dress bunched up in front with the back flowing behind. The people she left were still talking and glancing at Jen's long strides. Judging from their expressions, she left abruptly.

She skidded on the lawn just in front of Klarisa and me. Her dress dropped into place. Jen nailed me with a hard fist to the arm. She glared at Klarisa.

"Klarisa, we just keep bumping into you. How is your husband?" Jennifer said. "I haven't seen him. I can't imagine him doing dental work at this hour." She eyed everything with avian posture, then glared at Klarisa.

I was being held by each arm with a firm grip and a slight tugging. I was between the two women as they dug fingers into opposite biceps. I winced, but stood steady with my teeth gritted. My ginger ale was shaking out in spurts.

"Jennifer, it's so nice to see you again," Klarisa said in that tone and inflection that means just the opposite. "I don't see your husband either. Albert, isn't it?"

Jen pointed her chin out. "Oh, he's here. Albert is melting into a lounger in the front room. But he's always with me."

"That must be satisfying for you."

Jen's eyes locked on mine. "I need you for a minute." Her head jerked to the side. Relief flooded through my body as if enjoying a fan on a summer day.

"Great, I'll send him over when we're done," said Klarisa.

My head swung back and forth between them, and I tried to change the subject. They almost snarled over my shoulders. Klarisa put her free hand on mine, knocking my drink to the ground. She locked fingers. I tried to shake it, but her grip was too solid. Anxiety raced blood to my cheeks. "This is such a great party," I said. "The weather's perfect." While I was babbling about one innocuous subject after another, Jen interlocked her whole arm through mine and literally yanked me off my feet. I caught myself from falling, quickly duck walking behind her. My arm was red where Klarisa had grabbed it. She stood with her mouth agape after a string of vulgar words sprayed in Jen's direction.

Jen stopped about ten feet out with her neck twisted as tightly as it would go. "Perhaps with luck we can visit again, Klar-is-a." Jen broke the last word into syllables, separated with spittle. I saw a smirk as she turned her face forward, yanking me around the corner of the house. I stared straight ahead, pretending not to notice Klarisa's flushed face.

Jen led me to the front yard in a prisoner's march. As we edged up on the sidewalk, Jen said, "Just getting you away from the sex witch while you're still intact and not boiling in her pot."

Kids were playing in the street, whooping and hollering, all energy and youth bouncing around in the road in front of us.

TATTERED PORTRAIT

Anyone close could hear my irritated breath, it was so loud. The lawn gave off that smell I always associate with the color green, a damp and living fragrance. Shaking my head, I laughed. "Thank you, but I could have excused myself at any time. You forget I'm a big boy now."

"With a tight zipper," she glowered. "Grown up has nothing to do with it. That skirt she has on was leading you around like a dog collar."

"No faith."

"I know your history," she paused, "and I understand how the male mind works—mindless males, as we girls call it."

"Yeah, you think anyone noticed? She was a bit aggressive," I said. "I started to worry about her telling her husband."

"Yes, people noticed. A couple of them were hooking up the hose to spray you two down when I rescued you."

"Funny."

Jen held her hands on hips, elbows out. "First of all, she wouldn't tell her husband. Second, if she did, he would disappear into a puddle like ice cream on a hot day. She rules the house. Probably tells him how long he needs to work and how she wants the kitchen polished."

I thought about that for a minute. Amy came to my mind, and I shuddered slightly. I needed to call her. "And what about you? Any handsome smooth talkers come your way?"

"Yeah, right. I'm what they call frumpy."

"No. You are a gorgeous lady with sexy curves you hide with house dresses."

"Excuse me; you're my brother. You are supposed to say nice things, but what's wrong with my dress?" Feral eyes and dark shadows filled her face, her stance rigid.

"Nothing, I just notice what guys notice. It doesn't mean I know anything about fashion. I see you as the pretty-faced, well-proportioned, smart girl you are . . . the one with the right hook from which I keep flinching."

We stood in silence for a while. Jen was smiling and thinking. I could tell she was feeling good about herself.

She blurted out, "Of course I like approval and appreciation. God knows I don't get it at home. But I'm not wearing a screw-me skirt and a top so tight and thin my areola show." She paused with that disgusted tight face I'd seen throughout childhood. "And, yes, I do like watching well-tailored men and six-pack men who hang tools around their waist, but I'm not leaning into them with a pouty 'Hello sailor'."

"And I do?" I asked. I knew the answer before her mouth opened.

"Like you said, you're a guy. With her, you lose all sense of reason, and your brain drops to your feet or some other appendage."

"Okay, okay!" I held my open palms up, exasperated. Jen always knew how to discipline her brother. Maybe I could blame this on my dad. No, not this time. "So, how's the weather been here?"

We both laughed. I gave her a brotherly hug then put my arm around her and gazed back to the street.

Several sprinklers were set up on the asphalt road with long ropes of hose shooting out from the neighbors' outdoor faucets. I hadn't noticed until now how loud the kids were. Fifteen or twenty of them happily dared each other to run through the downpour.

Jen and I walked down the sidewalk. She tried to shove me into the street. I began pulling her toward a sprinkler.

"Benjamin," she said loudly. There was that sister voice again. I stopped, but kept holding on to her. "Ben, I have to look presentable at our aunt's party."

"And I don't? You started it." I let go of her arm.

She lunged at me and I backed into the spray. "You were never presentable," she laughed. I started toward her. She screamed and ran into the house, trying to lock the door just as I arrived. I tried pushing my way in. She smacked me in the arm. "You need to stay outside. You're way too wet to come into the house." Her finger waved at me.

Man, I love my sister.

A few seconds later, she opened the door.

The crowd out back was yapping, laughing, gesturing, and downing cases of beer. Lights flickered above them as they enjoyed exaggerated stories. Jen pinched my neck. "You keep away from the sex witch." I nodded and meant it.

TATTERED PORTRAIT

Repeating clangs sounded from the back porch. My aunt emerged in a black evening dress. She seemed to glide and float across the small porch as she banged a metal ladle against a stewpot. I wondered where she grabbed the energy for all the festivities. She sparkled, beautiful and perfect. I didn't know my aunt bought anything but house dresses; I was impressed, and I'm sure I wasn't the only one. She was the queen as her ladle guided everyone to huddle in front of her. Groups broke up and moved forward, makeshift bars became empty, and her loyal friends and family gathered in subdued quiet.

Aunt Velora's cheeks reddened. I could tell she was a little in awe of herself, embarrassingly so. She took a short sip from a wine glass that I knew was filled with cranberry juice and toasted her crowd. There was a cheer as plastic cups and beer cans greeted her back.

She tried to speak, but for a while could only jab at her bright red lipstick with a dry tongue. She bowed her head for a moment as everyone watched her in anticipation. As her head slowly rose, she began in a powerful voice that I recalled hearing in this same neighborhood as she called me home. "First, I want to thank you all for visiting me on this wonderful occasion."

Wonderful occasion? This was her pre-funeral party as she so gracefully put it.

"My incredible neighbors who prepared the food. My friends who bought the liquor." A few cheers were heard echoing through the back yard. "My loving niece Jennifer has helped immensely. My nephew Benjamin traveled a great distance to be with me. Thanks to my brother, who let me share his two beautiful children." She began to cry, a little at first, morphing into heavy sobbing that hurts the chest. She turned away from the group.

I pushed my way through the crowd and bounced up the steps to my aunt. She nuzzled into my chest. I patted her back and turned, facing the group "She just called me a beautiful kid. It's a good thing memories change with age. I won't repeat what she used to call me back when I was this high." I held out my hand at waist height.

Her friends, neighbors, and relatives clapped and hooted. She kept her head on my chest, bringing her right hand up to slap my cheek teasingly to let me know who was boss. I had to hold her up. Emotion had drained the spirited lady.

Jen joined us. We pretty well had the porch filled. Jen held up her arms and said, "Friends, Aunt Velora may not remember Ben well, but she's right on the money with me. I was a beautiful child." Another roar erupted and raised glasses appeared. "My aunt is the most caring, unselfish human I have ever been a part of. She inspires me to this day. All of you are here as her friends, and what a tribute that is. I learned a lot from this cute little lady in her lovely gown. My brother was the exception. He tried, but he was a hard rock to mold."

I scrunched my face, giving her the most pathetic, mean glare I could muster. She raised her eyes. "My sister . . ." I started to say.

"Stupid and stubborn." She went on. "Can you imagine what he would be like without Aunt Velora's persistent help?" She paused. "Neither can I." Aunt Velora laughed and lifted her wet, reddened face. She whispered to Jen, "Velora would like all of you to enjoy the food." Jen continued, "She says she thinks she has laryngitis." An approval of noise began. Aunt Velora shook her hands in a move-on gesture, tears rolling down her reddened cheeks.

More folding chairs were brought to the yard, "Wulstups' Rentals" painted in white on the back of each one. They were laid out like a fence of Marines guarding the perimeter of the yard. Other partiers were grabbing long tables that lay against the neighbor's house and setting them up around the back yard. Still others slid chairs under the tables. There was no foreman, just helpful folks working together. I watched as my sister and I buttressed up our frail but vibrant aunt.

Within minutes, the lawn-side dining area was set up with bowls and trays of food. I'm not sure where it all came from. It wasn't burgers and dogs from the lunch barbeque. It was ham and turkey, rolls painted with butter, vegetables and fruits, honey-baked beans, and cloth tablecloths. I guessed the hamburgers were snacks. I'd seen a lot of people eating them.

I hadn't been hungry until the smells overwhelmed my senses. Jen and Aunt Velora seemed to be licking their lips, with eyes locked on to the front table. I escorted both of them down, my aunt still weeping like a disciplined child.

From behind us, a gaggle of ladies carried empty mayonnaise jars filled with white lilies and yellow daffodils. Each one was centered on the tables with thin fingers and prearranged care. Aunt Velora was giddy at the sight. My aunt's friends smiled with pleasure as she accepted this whole gift with a quivering smile and more tears. Beforehand, they had set out a special place for her with a high-backed chair from the house, real silverware, china, a cloth napkin, and a wine glass with her name engraved on it. The rest of us ate more like peasants—using paper plates, plastic ware, paper cups, and scratched folding chairs.

The food was good, though I hardly ate anything. The conversation was loud, somewhat slurred, and meaningless. My aunt was overjoyed. My sister and I sat proudly on each side, silent as we held in flashes of memory with sneaky grins while she took center stage.

The clouds were settling over us, giving rise to a veil of comfort and sunset anticipation. The leftovers disappeared, along with the tables. Chairs took up sentry duty again. People mingled. I leaned on the bar and watched, sipping a tart cheap wine that seemed to make my lips numb.

Jen's friend Andrea snapped pictures with her cell phone as if she were on her first trip to Paris. Her face beamed as she twirled, snapping away.

As the darkness descended, the trees Jen and Dad had haphazardly smothered in tiny Christmas bulbs turned the ambiance to one of romance and intimacy. I wasn't interested in receiving either of those. A band had set up and began the irritating sounds of tuning up and adjusting mikes. I winced a couple of times, as did some of the other lawn people. My aunt clapped and hooted as if totally blasted; I knew her drink was zero proof. A crowd fanned around her as she sat in her high-back chair. The time of her life glistened from every pore.

The band played sixties and seventies soft-rock and older country. They did a fair job for boys in their later fifties, who I'm pretty sure smoked something and crushed a lot of beer cans before the performance. The partiers were stomping their feet and bobbing their heads in approval. A form of dancing began that was taxing a lot of pacemakers.

My sister grabbed me by the hand and yanked me into the center of the lawn. She could dance, graceful and energetic. I more or less stomped out a nonexistent fire and moved my unsure arms back and forth to the side just enough off beat to appear clumsy and rhythm-less. I glanced around. Others were not too far off my version of dance. I sucked in a what-the-hell breath and kept on moving in spasms and quirks. Jen was a rock-and-roll ballerina, eyes closed, oblivious to her partner. I so admired her.

After a sequence of stork-walking I began to move to the music. Amy and I once took dance lessons, though she was more adept than I could ever hope to be. I remember the teacher saying, "Let the music move you, not the other way around." I relaxed and came out of my shell, twirling my sister around the grass dance hall. She gazed at me completely perplexed then smiled. In my ear she whispered, "Where do you have my brother and who are you?" I kicked off my shoes, and she laughed.

My eyes glanced over at Aunt Velora. The lady who seemed so meek before dinner had transformed back into the young social girl of the party. She exuded presence. She had so many amazing facets to her that I never knew. She definitely was not the same lady that I kissed on the forehead when I took off for college years ago. The lady back then was a little coy and quiet. She had been like air. No one noticed her. Nobody knew about her recipe room. No one watched her char meal after meal. Now she has hordes of friends and is busy with committees and projects. She wears stylish clothes, and she burned down the room of recipes.

Jen leaned closer to me. She pointed just beyond Aunt Velora. "Did you know the three men vying for our aunt's good graces donated most of the money and food for this affair? Affair being an operative word."

I strained to get a good look. The muscles in my neck tightened. I envisioned three horny half-dressed men with belt buckles hidden behind an outpouring of belly. I wiggled my head and licked the inside of my mouth to get rid of the nightmare. They were just three old guys dressed like three old guys. They all turned an attentive ear to whatever my aunt was saying, a little overboard, somewhat like they were listening to a Greek goddess. I noticed them before. My aunt had groupies. The thought made me grin.

"Aunt Velora isn't a tart to be bought by party gifts," I said. "She is a lady of grace and style." Jen began giggling.

"Actually, I talked to two of them," Jen said, "a Mr. Morris and a Cal Vandig. Both are well-off gentleman . . . and well fed. By the time they released me, or should I say I escaped, I knew they wanted female conversation and maybe a bridge night out. They're harmless."

"But, cute little Aunt Velora is a fine-looking septuagenarian. A great catch with a mortgage-less house."

"Ben, not everything is about money and glamour. She might could use a little lovin' herself."

My eyes narrowed. "Don't even go there." I was breathing in short gulps, my mind straying further than ever before. "There are certain parts of the human spirit I don't want to go to—especially with the woman who raised me and read stories to me and soothed me when I was sad."

"Good God, Ben, I'm not negotiating her out to prostitution. By 'lovin'," she paused and smacked my nose with an index finger, "I mean a walk in the park, dining out, conversation about politics, gifts of roses, four-person card games, and anything that breaks up the loneliness."

"Oh, good," I said. "I thought I was going to need years of therapy."

Chapter 10

After our dance, Jen grabbed me and hauled me into the house. Across the lawn, Klarisa waved at me with eyes that could burn plants black. I followed down the hallway, and Jen shoved me onto the empty couch. She dropped like dead weight beside me. My brain was shutting down; Jen's eyes drooped, without saying a word, both of us knew the other was exhausted. I had endured enough of people we didn't know, their many names swirling in my head but never landing.

We both glanced over at Albert. "He's the original party animal," Jen giggled. We sat with tired eyes, listening to Albert making soft disgusting noises from his trembling nose.

A fiftyish lady peered around the kitchen door. Jen and I nodded and mouthed hello as if we had laryngitis. She moved around, filling the doorway, hip to frame. Perspiration matted her once-curled hair.

"You two want a plate of something?"

"You have anything that doesn't resemble a ground-up cow?" I asked. Jen declined with a shake of her head.

"I've got potato salad, and I can slice up some cantaloupe."

"Potato salad sounds wonderful. By the way, I'm—"

"Velora shows me your pictures constantly. I'm Adele. I moved in two doors down the street about three years ago." Adele began rocking back and forth on the balls of her bare feet. We could feel her bouncy energy. "Your sweet aunt has me and two others over for coffee on her porch pretty much every day, even in winter. Course, we're so bundled up we probably resemble throwaways waiting for the Veterans Thrift truck. She's a hoot, that gal. We all love her."

Within moments, Adele served us up potato salad, a thin slice of cantaloupe, and a couple of radishes on two plates. I was completely hungry after mostly stirring my food in the back yard. We both thanked her. Jen shrugged her shoulders. Adele, our personal waitress, backed into the kitchen with a wave and a bump of the door frame.

It wasn't long before melon rinds and a plastic spoon were the only things left on our plates. Jen and I both laid back in contentment. Food has always been a great sedative for me. We closed our eyes, joining Albert for what would be forty minutes of noisy harmony.

Sirens blasted in my dream. I heard voices and moans coming from a distant place. The door banged open, and I sat up lazily, trying to focus with one eye. The eyelid on my left side seemed impossible to open. From one eye, I woke just enough to see two firemen racing for the kitchen and two others unfolding a stretcher in the front room. All hell was breaking loose. Adrenaline surged my system and put me on full alert. Fear unlocked my left eye, as I stared at bodies working frantically on something in the kitchen.

Aunt Velora. My heart raced.

It was Adele. She lay on the kitchen tile, moaning about chest pains and a hard cold floor. Two men I recognized from the backyard party began pushing their way to the front. "I'm a pediatrician, and Harold is an orthopedic surgeon," one of them said.

"I'm in touch with Saint Benedicts right now," said a fireman with a young face and a thin nose. "Heartbeat is high, but not unreasonable. Blood pressure one-fifty over eighty-seven. Pulse at seventy-two."

I found myself leaning in the doorway, not knowing how I got there. A dishwasher was cycling, people gazing down with open mouths, not saying a word. The pediatrician mentioned something about getting her on the gurney. I was pushed to the side and told to back up as the firemen slid a tray under her, moving her body from side to side. An IV had already been established. Sticky sponges hooked wires from her to a portable machine. All I could see was the screen's blue radiance shining toward the fireman in charge. Four men lifted Adele to the gurney. The gurney legs scissored up, and people were asked to move back.

There was a bit of a scuffle for authority between the two doctors and the paramedics. One paramedic finally relented and gave the doctor his stethoscope. The other doctor, Harold, listened to her chest with knowing indifference. He also tried the stethoscope on her bountiful belly. Harold handed it to the other doctor. He too listened to various parts. They both shook their heads in silent agreement. The paramedic grabbed the stethoscope back with a tiny bit too much force. The doctor scowled.

The doctor who had done most of the talking said, "We're fairly sure it's nothing more than intestinal gas, but you'd better take her in for blood work just to be safe." Adele smiled, holding the doctor's hand firmly to her bosom.

As they were taking her through to the front room, my aunt leaned over, scolding Adele, "I told you not to eat that last piece of pie." Adele smiled and nodded her head slowly in agreement.

Jen came through the front door and stood beside me. She leaned into me, whispering, "Adele seems bewildered."

"Yeah, sounds like she'll be okay, though."

"This is what it takes to wake you up."

We both glimpsed at Albert. His crumpled shirt and relaxed breathing made him part of the lounge chair.

"Maybe the paramedics should check my dear husband," she said.

"You think it would wake him?"

"Probably not," she responded.

My aunt was holding conference under the twinkling Christmas lights of a mulberry tree. Fifteen or so full chairs were faced attentively towards her. About twenty people in various stages of intoxication leaned against the back of the chairs, listening. For some reason it reminded me of a few of my college classrooms. At least, I had enjoyed the perception the students were listening. My aunt was all smiles and gestures. Her followers laughed and giggled.

Pride gathered in my chest then dissipated abruptly as I spotted my dear old dad under the mulberry tree just to the right of Velora. His royalty was sitting on the grass in front of the partial ring of chairs.

It was incongruent. Dad sat like a well-dressed bank manager as ladies in leisure tops and jeans and men in flannel shirts surrounded him. His cheeks and nose reddened from the sun; he gave me an acknowledging wave, almost a salute. I scanned the grass. No empty bottles. I nodded my head, pasting what I assume to be the most obnoxious, autonomic smile across my face. I was having a hard time doing even that much. I really needed to let him quit bothering me.

I strolled to the wine bar, asking for half a glass of something red with a donkey on the label. It tasted like colored vinegar. Whatever happened to the sweet, syrupy wines of my teens? I thanked the young bartender and set the glass back down, searched for peanuts or mints to quell the taste. I always assumed my father passed the fermented gene on to me, but I certainly couldn't drink that. I'm not sure my father could either.

I stood closer to my aunt's congregation. She was mesmerizing; all faces were waiting for her next sentence. She had a pause and timing to her stories.

She told about being a pom-pom girl in the fifties. I hadn't realized she was a cheerleader, though she fit the bubbly mold. She probably did bounces and flips all over the field. She said, "Back then, Keith was a quarterback for an opposing team." When Keith's team won the game nineteen to six, she said he grabbed one of her pom-poms and ran around the field. She chased him for twenty minutes. He would give it back to her only if she agreed to meet him at Charlie's drive-in the next night.

I was having a hard time seeing any of this. When I knew him, my uncle moved at the pace of a snail, and even that was rare. After three breakups with him and four other boyfriends spread over several years, she finally married Keith at the age of twenty-three. "I'm still waiting for him to run around the field again," she said.

I learned she won two blue ribbons and one gold-colored trophy for twirling the baton. We all watched as she pantomimed hand dexterity and an extravagant toss. All of our eyes went up to the clouds as she raised her arm. We saw it spinning in the air above her and dropping right into her fingers. She pretended to spin it over and around her back. She showed the serious demeanor of an athlete. Her dress heaved around her with grace and lithe billowing. As her fingers moved, she explained her names of each movement—the windmill, the propeller, and the helicopter. The crowd had grown; applause and yelps pushed everything else to the side.

I caught myself drawn in, and I snickered. Jen gave me an okay signal with her thumb and index pointing her head toward Aunt Velora. With a grand finale of two batons twirling, flying into space, and dramatically being caught again, Velora outstretched her arms and took a bow. She beamed.

When Aunt Velora sat down, the crowd dispersed like an exploding star. Aunt Velora grabbed her chest, taking in deep breaths. Her hair glistened around the seams of her face from the sweat of play-acting. She looked beautiful, happy, and just a touch frail.

Night fell without much notice. The spray of Christmas lights from trees to clothesline to trees illuminated the yard with a colorful glow. It gave my aunt's face a sparkle that hid the paleness of her battle.

I leaned down to her and whispered, "Can I get you a drink or something?"

With a deep breath and thoughts screaming through her eyes, she said, "Water, ice cold water—and not those silly plastic bottles. I understand they give you cancer." She gave me a lopsided smile and a wink. "I want real water in a glass, like a proper lady."

I rummaged through her well-worn wood cabinets, pushing aside aged A & W root beer mugs and K-Mart thin glassware. In the back I found two red glasses with deep-etched stars chiseled into the glass. I remembered those from childhood. She only brought them out on special occasions—Christmas and Thanksgiving, something with too much food on a candled tablecloth. There was a whole set of them at one time. I recalled how noble I felt drinking from them before pimples and crotch hair pushed me into the years of I-don't-care attitude.

Carefully checking out both of the glasses, my thoughts were lost in swirling memories. One had a tiny chip on the ring, so I set that one back in its historical residence. I washed the other with care and filled it up with ice. I let the tap water run until it was mountain-stream cold and filled up the glass.

Approaching from behind my aunt, I carefully tried to not spill the water. Moisture beaded on the outside. She was alone and "resting her eyes," as she would say. I sat on the grass by her and waited. Finally, I put her well-worn TV tray next to her on the grass. She woke up as if an electric shock had hit her. "What?" she said, sharply. It was a bit more scolding than she meant. "Sorry, I was just resting my eyes."

"A perfect glass for a true lady." I presented it with a bowed head and a courteous genuflect.

"Well, I'll be," she said. "I didn't know I still held on to any of these." She held it up in delight. Then she eyeballed me. "I hope you washed any dead flies out of it."

"Twice, just like I was taught. It's a lone survivor. The other remaining soldier is chipped." I stood up from my kneeling position. Old knee injuries made me listen for creaks and rubs.

Aunt Velora put a crocheted wrap around her shoulders and grinned as she gazed around. The night was cooling down, though the party was rising up again. She leaned toward me with her hand across her mouth, saying, "Here comes Tweedle Dee and Tweedle Dum and my cowboy."

"So, you like the cowboy?" I watched them jostle each other for first place.

"No," she said. "I adore all three. They are so enamored with me; I keep thinking they are going to drool at my feet."

"I think that sounds like a good thing in a sort of disturbing way." They were closing in, only fifteen feet away. Three grins were moving as fast as they could, which wasn't all that fast.

"Yes, it is. Three protective lovers bringing me things and taking me places I only dreamed about with Keith. He never even took me to a restaurant after the first year of marriage, other than the time the fridge broke down. These boys ask me out. I get at least three dates a week, each one treating me like a queen. All of them trying to outdo the other. It's like heaven." She stared off into the distance at nothing in particular. "Pure heaven."

"Velora." All three of them resounded like a barbershop quartet.

"Hello, boys." She sounded like a sixteen-year-old who had something to hide. "Boys, this is my nephew, Ben, the famous biologist from Florida." She winked at me in a proud parental way. "Ben, these three wonderful gentlemen are my boyfriends—Gus, Cal, and David. I am such a fickle, feisty, old woman, I can't pick one, so I pick them all." She pointed at each one as she introduced names.

I nodded. "You guys have a handful if you think you're going to sway this little woman."

"She's starting to fold," said Gus, pointing his finger into his chest, "leaning towards yours truly." He bowed as the other two moved in front of him with their elbows out.

"If she's doing any leaning," stated David, with his thumbs set hard behind a three-inch belt buckle with enough mounted turquoise to sink a boat, "it's on the road to the only 'real' man she knows. You two might as well back out now. Save what little dignity you have left." He tipped back his cowboy hat, leaving one hand nestled on the buckle. A proud glow and a smile filled his face.

Cal nudged him in the side with a doughy arm. David's face changed from egotistical to a grimace, but he quickly regained his testosterone level. Cal said, "She told me that I'm the funniest one, and you know how she loves to laugh."

"She's laughing, but not at your jokes." David elbowed him a little harder than could be considered playful, with the gleam of getting even. Cal made a guttural noise and coughed, spraying a fine mist of spittle.

"Boys, you need to behave," Aunt Velora scolded with a smirk, "or I won't let any of you passed the front porch." She used her finger to warn them.

The three lined up like diner salt shakers waiting to be refilled. Gus was attentive with his blue golf shirt tucked in, a roll hiding most of his belt. David stood Marine-erect. Cal kept his posture as adequate as his round shoulders allowed. All their eyes beamed at my aunt.

Velora smiled as she quietly asked, "My water is tasting like rusty pipes. Could one of you please get me a refill with lots of ice?" She winked at me. Her hand extended the glass. Cal, who was closest, grabbed it quickly. With an almost evil smile at the other two, he sailed away toward the bar. A short silence lingered.

David startled upright. "Velora, you really should have a new, clean glass." He disappeared with a grin. Cal followed, trying to get ahead of David. It was a race, complete with bumping shoulders.

Aunt Velora spoke to me in the most southern belle voice I'd ever heard. "Why, these boys just fuss over me something terrible." Both hands went to her heart as she took a deep breath.

"You are devious," I said.

"When you're my age, devious is better than sex . . . though I'm not sure I remember sex all that well." She clapped her hands, pleased with herself. "No, it hasn't been that long. I do remember sex. Maybe devious is . . . ."

"Aunt Velora, that's more info than I ever needed, thank you."

She pinched my cheek, shaking it slightly. A silence lingered as she sat down on her chair. She eyed the mumbling crowd, her head canted slightly. I took pleasure in the profile of a pleasantly weathered, happy woman, the lady who had done so much for me. The more I stared, the more my chest warmed.

Across the yard I spotted Dad. The warm feeling in my chest was sucked out. My head turned away, but not quickly enough.

Chapter 11

My father eyeballed me from twenty feet away. A stern, contemplative look glossed his face. He appeared relaxed, but ready to strike. He aimed a finger gun at me. I saluted.

He stood up, brushed off nothing from his pants, and straightened his jacket while walking toward me. I think I stopped breathing. He sat in the chair next to me. I glanced around for Jen. Alone was good; alone with my dad was always bad. My teeth ground together. Twice at the same party? I'm not sure I'm up for twice in the same year. I stared at the patches of grass blades and my scuffed shoes. *Did I need new ones, or did I have a second pair at the hotel?*

"Let's go fishing," Dad blurted out.

My ears perked up. My eyelids rose. "Now . . . ? I don't think the party is over yet." My back tightened. I crossed my arms, grabbing myself at the elbows.

I saw Andrea coming in our direction with a cell cam in hand. I shook my head at her; she raised her free hand and walked away, slightly dejected.

My sarcasm made him take a couple of short breaths. It was the first time I had ever seen him without a quick reply. In a kind and monotone voice, which I didn't recognize, he said, "Not now, sometime. How long are you here?" My eyebrows rose. We stared at each other for what seemed like a forever silence

Dad cleared his throat. The crusty sound made me think of stepping on crushed leaves.

"Dad, we have never done normal father/son things. We

wouldn't know how. Fishing? Really?" I paused. "Fishing? Do you even have a fishing pole? Are you serious? Are we going to play catch next?"

The wrinkles pulled around his eyes like creased wings. He started to say something, but bit his lip instead. His erect posture folded inside itself.

I had never seen him filled with dejection and worn the way he was at this moment. Had I gone too far? My spoken words finally brought the big man down, and I felt empty.

He sat down on the lawn and motioned for me to sit next to him. I joined him with my knees up and my arms wrapped around them. Uneasiness filled my whole body. Dad pulled at the grass with his fingers, seemingly without the strength to yank a single blade of grass from its roots.

The meanness he had taught me so well came out. I attacked him because of all the things he never gave me and all the horrors he had done. This battle had been staged for a long time. I never expected him to change, and I'm not sure I even wanted him to anymore. I felt superior for the first time. I actually enjoyed it when his shoulders drooped.

I couldn't help myself; once the meanness started, I couldn't slow it down. I kept naming all the terrible things involving him that had seeped through my lifetime. The party prattle faded out as my memories spilled forth, some distorted by time and circumstance, some dead-on accurate.

Finally, I slowed down enough to notice a face so full of sorrow and misery that my throat swelled up instantly. He was locked in a slump, his eyes sad and gazing at mine. I wasn't used to this situation. I felt sorry for my father instead of for myself. My mind raced back and forth. *Could this be an actual change? Was Dad sorry for the first time in his life? Was he baiting me?*

Silence emptied into the void between us. The air tasted stagnant and stale. The taste of vengeance still on my tongue, I tried to faintly suck in. Unknown emotions distorted my contempt as I stood on what I thought might be new ground. I wasn't completely sure. He had always been crafty. Would this be a charade he would break with his evil laugh?

I stood up and bent over, putting my hand on his shoulder

even though my mind screamed not to. I wasn't sure how to do this. It was like touching glowing coals. His head lowered, and he didn't speak. There was an air of satisfaction in that. Time slowed down. The Christmas lights reflected off the back of his neck.

My hand lifted off his shoulder, as if a hot iron had finally reached its temperature. He started to say something but bit his lip instead. Wrinkles pulled around his eyes like creviced wings.

"Sorry, Dad, but no, we cannot go fishing just like that." His face had pitiful, dejected wrinkles to it. He slumped down to something small and alone.

My mouth stayed shut as I battled between fight and flight. Flight won. I saw Jen a couple of groups away and darted to her, saying something to the sky about Jen signaling me.

Halfway there I started to turn back, but years of abuse pulled me across the weather-worn lawn. I'd never been a forgiving person. It had been left out of my genetic humanness. School bullies lined up in my subconscious, along with terrible teachers, girlfriends who had left me, and rude bosses. My dad led the whole pack with a bright red flag held high on a pole. Holding onto hate was comforting to me in some odd, distorted way.

Jen was yapping away. She didn't even notice I entered the group. Her smile and the excitement in her voice caused everyone to lean forward, just slightly.

A tall bean of a man came up to me from the side. He asked if I knew who he was.

I shrugged in a stupor, my eyes surveying his face. There was a distant familiarity to him. The jawbone dropped down. The chin was square with a deep dimple. He waited in anticipation.

"I owned the pharmacy on 20th and Meyer Street," he said, "Russell Montague."

I was still puzzled. A quick mountain breeze came up, lifting what was left of sparse hair on his abundant forehead. I tried a smile as though I fully knew him.

"Your dad had the office above my pharmacy for years," he said, somewhere between a question and a statement. He held something in a dish towel that he tapped gently against his leg.

I'd never been in my dad's actual office. I had an illusion of what his office would be like, all oak bookshelves filled with volumes of knowledge and a hardwood desk as big as an old Cadillac. And of course, a fully stocked bar, empties in a metal can behind his desk.

Whenever I endured the misfortune of going to his office, the rule of my father was for me to wait in the reception area on an unpadded chair. His revolving-door secretaries would ask me to wait there until he was done—that is, when a receptionist was actually behind the desk. They seemed to quit a lot. Most times, I sat myself down and did homework. I never knocked on that door, even though I had never been told not to. I wasn't sure I ever wanted him to come through the door. Many times the door didn't open, so I'd walk the twenty blocks home. I would catch a glimpse of his car driving slowly home the next day as my school bus rounded the corner. Nothing was ever said about his forgetting me—him to me or me to him. It's just the way it was. Luckily, I was sent to my aunt's by the second grade.

"I remember the office and the pharmacy, but I wasn't there a lot," I said.

"I've changed. I stare at myself in the mirror and ask, 'Who's that'?" He pulled at his cheeks, one hand still clutching the dish towel. "Anyway, I found something of your dad's still there a while back and kept it. He left that office years ago, and I've had fourteen renters since then, but all of 'em left this sitting on the top of one of the bookshelves."

Andrea came by and snapped our picture. She whirled away.

He handed me the towel. "Will you give this to your dad? Or maybe, you would want it?"

The towel was worn and faded, with dark marks around the rectangle inside. I unwrapped it as carefully as if it were a land mine, the whole time wondering why he was giving it to me. Inside was a five-by-nine framed picture. I spied Dad on a chair hardly twenty feet away and glanced back to the photo. A cheap wooden frame with part of the shellac curled stared up at me. I let out a gasp, though I'm not sure anyone heard it but me.

I stared. I remembered the day, but hadn't thought of it in a million years. My breath became shallow. That time was all happiness, root-beer floats, and a slowly picked out Cherry-A-Let candy bar held tight in my grip. We were out in front of the downtown Walgreen's. I could see part of a yard-long, red licorice rope Jen had tucked behind her with a mischievous grin. My eyes wouldn't blink as I stared. Jen and I were standing all decked out in front of Mom and Dad. Jen appeared to be about two years old and was grasping my thumb. Our parents smiled behind us. Dad was holding my shoulder, and his stance was different. He wore the face of someone who actually cared about his family, a slight show of front teeth and deep dimples I didn't recall him ever having.

I remembered the day, but not the picture. My throat tightened. I nonchalantly rubbed my eyes, then returned wet knuckles to the picture. My head bowed and I kept my feelings to myself. Mr. Montague remained silent. His feet shuffled in an uneasy way. I glanced over at the old, worn man on the chair and wondered if he had been looking at this in his office for a lot of tortured years. He was still an asshole, but maybe he carried a few reasons to be. My eyes fell back to the picture. They were two different men. The one in the picture was fantasy. And Mom— wow, she was pretty. I always envisioned her with dark eyes and an apron. It was a whole family I didn't recognize. It brought up feelings I wasn't sure I wanted.

I started to hand the picture and cloth back to Mr. Montague. A hoarse, quivering voice came out of my mouth. My head turned, discovering where it came from. "You should give it to my father." I pointed him out, even though I knew I didn't need to. Mr. Montague glanced his way several times. Dad's head was tilted back, his mouth slightly open.

"No . . . . No, you hand it to your father." His hands waved in protest. "Fact is, your dad and I haven't gotten along so well after I had to evict him on unpaid rent." He looked uneasy. "I'm not sure he even knew he hadn't kept up on the payments. The whole time was rough for him." He gazed down at the ground for a time. "Larry wouldn't accept a thing from me. I thought about giving it to Velora, but someone pointed you out, so there ya go."

"Thank you," I said reluctantly. "I'm sure he'll appreciate it," came out with even less conviction. I handed him the dish towel.

Both hands came up again. "That old filthy thing," his voice softened. "I'm sure it's your mom's."

TATTERED PORTRAIT

I held the rag outstretched in two hands. I gazed at it with a little more respect. Mr. Montague stood back with a smile. Air filled my lungs, and I began to notice the party again. Stretching my neck seemed to relieve my taut throat and dry mouth.

I peeked over at Dad, thinking, *I'd better treasure it; I'm not sure he wouldn't throw it in the garbage.* Then I started wondering why he left it behind. I glanced over at him. The life seemed to have been sucked from him. He showed little for his years—a worn and weathered house—one child who put up with him on a limited basis, another who spoke his name in harsh, abusive tones. . . a wife who disappeared long ago . . . and the ravages of alcohol and bitterness etched in his skin.

I darted off to find Jen, mouthing a "thank-you" to Mr. Montague. I seemed to have lost my voice, and my tongue tasted like parched earth. I knew I was abrupt. I peered over my shoulder. Mr. Montague stood with hunched shoulders seemingly lost, his mouth partially agape.

Jen acknowledged me with a wink. The glow of happiness filled her face and mannerisms. She kept on babbling. By the conversation that was going on, I assumed the two ladies were old friends of hers. They laughed and bobbed their heads with thorough enjoyment of Jen's wit and way with people.

Watching her, I felt socially inept. I wasn't exactly an anti-people person. I loved listening to others on a limited basis. My comfort fell on the sidelines, watching others tell stories. I was a fence-sitter if any kind of debate entered the conversation. Sometimes I'd venture through the gate, say a few scattered words, then bounce quickly back to the fence. I was always the inconsequential member of any group, even with my best friends.

There are only three people I have no problem interacting with—Jen, Aunt Velora, and Amy. Maybe Klarisa, but lately I'm telling myself we have nothing in common. I'd run and jump into a burning house for the other three. My shyness must be a genetic thing that I received and Jen didn't, like blue and green eyes. Luckily, neither of us received the heavy drinking gene or the pawn-your-kids-off gene (though, since I'm still without kids, we'll have to see how that turns out). I actually love to interact with kids and the feeble old, even if I do spend most of my time with octopuses. I have respect for all three. I probably don't have any gene barrier with children and octopuses. Or old farts, unless it's my dad.

I remember a quote from John D. Macdonald: "A friend is someone you can say any jackass thing to that enters your mind and with acquaintances you are forever aware of their slightly unreal image of you, and to keep them content, you edit yourself to fit." By that definition, I have only three friends, not counting my sea creatures.

Jen was too involved with her cute stories and fun quips to break away anytime soon. Her audience doubled, and all of them were giggling and touching hands intermittently. Very little had changed between Jen and her friends over the years. As many times as I waved the cloth-covered picture in her periphery, she ignored me. And she's my friend . . . and my sister.

I faded back into the party, grabbed a ginger ale from the bucket and looked at the growing crowd of well-wishers, and set the ginger ale can down on the bar, untouched. Aunt Velora was across the yard looking radiant. Her three boyfriends followed her like rock-and-roll groupies. I ordered a merlot from the skinny kid with too much Adam's apple sticking out. I needed something to hold on to. I saw in the bar kid's eyes a worry stamped deep within. He had those loose part movements that reminded me of junior high, the age of gangly. It seemed to take him a minute to decipher between wine and beer.

"Is that the red or amber one?" he asked. He pulled out two bottles and a boxed wine and began reading on the back of each.

"This one's close enough," I said, touching the cork of a nondescript brand of young merlot. It had a friendly label of two bears sitting on a hill. I asked the thin boy how old he was. He became self-conscious and covered a family of pimples on his chin

"Not old enough to drink." He raised a cherry cola from behind the counter and danced it in front of me then took a swallow of it. "Oh, sorry," he said, realizing he forgot to pour me my wine; he fumbled, dripping it across the counter. *All these underage kids serving adults liquor, make me wonder if some are their parents. At his age, I spent my time hiding the drinks.*

Thirty years ago, I was this kid—pimply, arms and legs too

long, having a hard time controlling my muscles. Now I'm just the adult version of the same thing, without the pimples and the thinness.

Sitting down on an empty group of chairs to the left of the young bartender, I sipped my wine. My lips tightened and my throat convulsed. I knew I wouldn't finish the plastic cup of merlot, even on a dare. I rarely drank more than a half glass of wine anyway. I barely touched the merlot to my tongue, but I pretended to sip for some time. It was more for something to do and to keep me from conversation, than due to any desire to drink. Boy, I wonder why? They say children usually follow their parents' over-indulgences. I must have missed the memo.

Chapter 12

At midnight, when I thought the party should be over and most of the folks should be back at Sierra Rancho Retirement Home in the comfort of their tilting beds, surrounded by pills, three more men I didn't know struggled onto the dance floor of grass. They tugged a child's swimming pool surround to the worn-out scab of grass. The tin pool was green with blue Smurfs dancing around the perimeter. There was no plastic liner. Talk was whispered around me about a cock fight. As a biologist and a civilized man, I wasn't too sure what I thought about this. The older men seemed incredibly excited as four metal cages were brought in. My stomach became queasy. Jen glanced at me, and I pointed to the surround and pulled a face.

She raised her eyes.

Two large birds were dumped from cages into the Smurf fence. As they began pecking the earth, I realized they were chickens. The chickens searched the ground for food as the old codgers yelled at them to attack. I smiled at Jen. She mouthed, "I know." After five minutes of watching chickens feed, one man decided to spice up the fight. He dumped the other two cages into the surround; two more chickens fluttered for a moment then went on a search for food, bobbing and pecking the earth. I had no idea my aunt's neighbors were aspiring rednecks.

I slipped over to my sister and whispered, "My bet's on the chickens. I think they are going to beat that grass to death." She laughed.

The serious anticipation of the fight began to wear off.

TATTERED PORTRAIT

People gathered around, betting on whether any of the chickens would lay an egg.

Everyone laughed at some big guy named Ralph who hatched the grand idea. "I thought it was a chicken fight I saw on TV. I'm from Cincinnati; I didn't know there was a difference between roosters and chickens." Ralph kept saying, "I can't believe I paid thirty bucks each for them to peck the ground."

Aunt Velora head quivered with obvious distaste. Ralph got the message, disappearing with his cohorts and the four skinny chickens.

The party ended about 2:30 a.m. Everyone helped put the yard back in order. Chairs were folded and piled up. Garbage cans were brought in from neighboring houses and filled. A team of octogenarians hosed the tables and chairs off, squirting each other from time to time like eight-year-olds. I looked at all the life still left in their old carcasses as they scrambled in the backyard. I shook my head and yawned. People slowly dispersed.

I went in the house to help clean up. The dishwasher was roaring, and the counter was spotless with patches of wet still drying in the air. The scent of cleaning liquids filled the room; any signs of a party had been sanitized. Jen, Velora, and a few friends were sipping coffee on a wet kitchen table. I poured half a cup and leaned against the counter. The ladies were all leaning in, seeming to all murmur at once. It seemed conspiratorial, so I kept my distance, catching only a few words here and there. I wandered into the front room, where several thirty-something-year-olds with heavy eyelids sprawled on couches and chairs.

The next thing I remember, Jen was shaking my shoulder and pulling my ear. I had fallen asleep on a chair in the front room. I wiped spittle from the corner of my mouth tried to figure out where I was. Jen said, "You're going to have one stiff neck if you sleep like that. Didn't you get enough sleep earlier?" I didn't answer but stared through eyelashes with hazy thoughts. "You want me to take you to your hotel or to my house? I have a small bed downstairs. There are people in the extra rooms here."

Squinting at the light and feeling the heaviness in my limbs, my mouth opened with a hesitant response. "What?"

She yanked my ear, saying, "Get up. I'm taking you home." I

followed the direction of my ear. I knew her persistence. I grabbed the towel-wrapped picture from the chair.

Waking up the next morning with my feet hanging over a blow-up mattress, I rubbed my face, trying to restore circulation. Sunlight spilled over the window sill. The walls were pink; a mirror and a sewing table gleamed back at me. Pulling the furry cover over my head, I hid for a few minutes, even though I knew falling back to sleep was not an option.

My eyes burned and my head throbbed. I tried to organize my thoughts. They came slowly. From just outside the door, I heard a whistling, banging sound and high-pitched voices. They belonged to children. Jen didn't have children. I slithered my head beneath the pillows. It didn't help. I peeked out from under the covers. It sounded like New Year's Eve.

From the doorway I heard, "Oh, great, you're up. Come up and get some coffee and breakfast."

Rising slightly, I gave an affirmative moan.

"It's already nine o'clock," Jen said.

I waved her off, squinting my eyes and collapsing back onto the bed.

An hour later, I was up and wandering through Jen's house, searching for coffee. The smell lingered from earlier, but the pot was in its cradle, clean. With half-shut eyes and the ambition of a sloth, I searched cupboards for a coffee can. I shut each cupboard hard enough to mean business, hoping Jen would come to my rescue, but the house was hollow and vacant. After several exasperated minutes, I spied the jar on the counter marked in two-inch letters, Coffee. After fumbling fingers, spilled coffee grounds, a wet shirt sleeve, and the timing of a watched pot, I sat down to a cup of freshly brewed coffee and proceeded to burn my tongue. "Shit!"

"That's a bad word." I turned my head toward the sound. Two children with big eyes and tight mouths stood rigid in the doorway.

"Who are you?" I said in a slow, threatening voice.

A girl about six glared at me. She won; I finally turned my eyes away. "I'm Audrey. Who are you?'

I pushed the ice button on the side-by-side and tossed one

quarter moon into the sink and another into my coffee. "I'm Ben, Jennifer's brother."

"Aunt Jenny?"

"Yeah. I guess so." *When did Jen become an aunt? I know I'm no uncle, and I'm pretty sure I'm no dad.* "Who's the little one there?" I pointed.

"That's Tornado."

"Tornado?"

"She's Tory, but mom calls her Tornado."

"I think I heard her this morning. Does she talk?"

"Course. All the time. She's just 'fraid."

They disappeared down the hall, laughing and screaming. Their voices muffled into the basement.

A cup and a half later, I heard a rise of adult voices outside the kitchen window. I figured everyone was outside. I was in no hurry. I slid my tongue, which still stung, across my teeth. I needed a toothbrush and a gargle. I found her bathroom and the toothpaste, and I brushed my teeth with my finger, which is kind of like combing your hair with a notebook. I smeared more toothpaste on my tongue then rinsed with a handful of water. Not respectable, but adequate.

With a clean face and a sore but peppermint-smelling mouth, I found the back door.

"Ahhh, the living dead," said Jen.

I rolled my eyes and stuck out my burnt tongue.

She was sitting at a round redwood table with Dad and Albert. She was excited, Albert appeared comatose, and Dad appeared worried. Jen motioned for me to sit next to her. I hesitated, then obeyed. Waking up to Dad in daylight hours was disconcerting. Then I remembered last night. After my blowup, we had enjoyed a couple of moments that were less battlefield and more dove and olive branch. Of course, they were short-lived, but moments just the same. I gave a hesitant half-smile and sat down.

"You want coffee?" Jen wore a denim skirt and a blouse so white her perfume had the backdrop of bleach. Dad wore a faded blue shirt under a sports jacket with elbow patches like those favored by college professors in the seventies. A distasteful grin was painted on his face, as he stared at me.

"Made some myself. Hope you don't mind. I cleaned the spills and put the cup in the dishwasher."

"Well, aren't you the perfect Mary Modern?" said Dad.

The spell of any truce was broken. I glared at him. "And you—"

"Boys, enough of that," interrupted Jen. "This is my house. My rules. You start again, and I'll slap both of you across the face with a rake." She pointed at some garden tools leaning against her shed. "Do I make myself clear?"

Her eyes stared with intensity. My body didn't have the ability to even move, but I nodded my head in the affirmative. I saw timidity in Dad's face as he also nodded. Jen had a power I never understood.

She rolled her fingers in a motion that gave us permission to talk. "When did you become an aunt?"

She giggled. "You met Audrey and Tory. They're Andrea's kids. You remember her from the party. She's at the doctor. She'll be here shortly." Jen eyed at her wrist as if checking the time. She was wearing no wrist watch. "They didn't wake you up, did they?" Everyone laughed but me.

"Great. Now, let's talk about our plans for the day. And other happy things."

Dad and I gave each other an uneasy look.

Jen's eyes went back and forth between me and Dad. Albert watched the grass. "You can speak now."

"Thank you," I said. "I was just waiting to be put in time out."

She smacked my arm.

"Are you going to do anything about that, Dad? Jen just hit me without any provocation."

"My shoulder's still sore from last night. I'm not getting into the middle of this," Dad answered, holding his arm and feigning a wince.

"You beat up on Dad, too? Maybe I do love you." I took in a deep breath.

"Ben, you're almost to fall off that fence. Watch yourself." Jen paused, "Albert, tell them I don't go around hitting people. I've never hit you, right? Tell them." She made a fist.

Albert remained disinterested then slowly turned his head facing the three of us. "I don't get hit. I listen to authority." He pointed at Jen with a nod of his head.

"Albert, I think you made a joke," Jen laughed, shaking her head.

"I did?" He cowered a little.

"I like it," said Jen.

A smile formed on Albert's face.

"It's settled. I'm a great sister, wife, and daughter. So enough with the accusations." She pounded on the table. "I have plans for our day. We are going over and picking up *my* sweet Aunt Velora," she said, emphasizing *my*, "and the five of us are going out to lunch. After that, we're going to a miniature golf course or bowling, I haven't decided. Then we'll decide what to do after that."

"*We* will decide, or *you* will decide?" I asked. The sun on my shoulders was hot, without the usual comforting warmth. The wind was stagnant, and the caffeine from the coffee hadn't kicked in.

"No one likes a smart ass. Today is my day for all of you, so I make most of the plans."

"Sounds great! I need to run back to my hotel for a couple of hours, and then I'll meet you."

Jen glared.

"Jen, I need to take a shower, brush my teeth with a real toothbrush, and change my clothes." I wasn't sure why I was perspiring.

She rubbed her chin and creased her forehead. "Okay. We'll all go to your hotel and wait for you. We'll pick up our party animal aunt on the way. I've talked to her this morning. It shouldn't take you that much time, and we will be there to hurry you along."

"I have phone calls to make and emails to send out."

"Well, I guess you'll have to be quick about it."

"You really think she's going to bend?" asked Dad.

I held up my hands and said sarcastically, "If it wouldn't be a problem for all of you, it's fine with me. Be aware it may take some time, I wouldn't want you to miss out on anything because of me."

Jen bit her lip. "No problemo. We have all day and night. If it takes a little longer, so be it."

"Where's my car?"

"Don't worry; we'll take the Explorer. You can pay for the gas."

The hotel was quiet as we marched to the elevator, Jen led the way. As I felt for my room card, Jen whipped it out and slid it quickly. As the light went green, she pushed her way in. Everyone followed. I strolled in last, as if I were intruding.

Jen rushed me into the bathroom right after she searched the closet for my "outfit," as she called it.

I stuck my head back outside the bathroom door. "Are you going to find me some boxers too, or can I pick those out?" She reached into my suitcase and tossed me a pair. I twirled them on my finger. She scooted me in with her hand. I started to get in the shower. After a minute, I got back out and locked the door. There's no way my sister was going to scrub me if I didn't shower quickly enough.

Out of the shower, clean, and dressed, I walked into the room to everyone laughing. I assumed it was about me, because the pitch rose then fell.

"We're just talking about that time you chased down an Alka Seltzer with a Budweiser at Karen's summer party. I can't believe you took that dare. You were foaming out your nose, and your eyes were as big as moons. Karen's brother drove you to the hospital. The whole staff in the ER couldn't quit giggling." Jen was on a roll at my expense, as usual.

"It wasn't funny then, and it isn't funny now. I thought I was going to die." I paused and folded my arms. "I thought we were going to go?"

"Sure Bubbles, let's go." She stood up and ushered everyone out, still laughing. Aunt Velora was erupting in little lady snorts down the hall. Dad patted me on the back.

It was 2:15 by the time we pulled into a Mexican restaurant called La Flor de La Montaña. It was decorated by an American architect who, obviously, never visited Mexico. The entrance was bright, with a college freshman in a bow tie and wrinkled shorts taking reservations. As I peered into the dining area, patterned glass sombreros on white walls threw a hundred watts down on each table. Tip-hungry waiters laughed loudly and shined plastic-surgeon smiles at everything. I put my finger in my mouth as if trying to gag. Jen hit my shoulder. I decided to behave and make the best of it.

Dad peered at the menu as if he had terrible indigestion. I snickered. Aunt Velora radiated a stoner smile. Arthur watched his shoes as he stood in the background. Jen seemed to be dancing with her shoulders to the music of Vincente Fernandez. He sang about his corazón filled with amore.

Starving, I held my fork and knife upright in anticipation. The anticipation turned to drinking Jen's and my glasses of water. I also downed all the chips in a bowl the size of a teacup with red salsa—two fingers from a shot glass poured delicately in the center. I felt like I was sitting down with a niece at a small table with two dolls, sipping empty cups and proclaiming, "How delicious." When the food finally came, everyone browsed each other's plate in slight disappointment at their own.

The portions were small and expensive, but at least the water pitcher seemed to settle my stomach. Jen beamed, waiting for my positive approval. I smiled and nodded my head with as much energy as I could master. She ordered everyone flan. Two bites and a scraping of the plate, and I was done. I slid the plate to the side. Jen's eyes met mine. I pushed out my belly and rubbed it gently. Jen giggled, taking a fake bite of my flan.

As we got up to leave, things started to move. Our forks and glasses danced across the white linen. Overhead ornaments swayed crazily from the ceiling. A rumble, then glass breaking. Something cracked like a whip behind us. There were glimmers of terror all around. People clung to their children in horror. I grabbed Aunt Velora's and Jen's hands in a vice-like grip and ran them to the archway, motioning to Dad and Albert with my head to follow. My teeth clamped tight enough to shatter them.

As we huddled in shock, something crashed in the kitchen. The tables began bouncing. People panicked, moving like sheep in a storm. A lady I didn't know held on to my waist, pushing Jen to the side. I pulled Jen back as the six of us huddled under the large archway. Though, I was not a religious man, I found a need for

God for a few moments. It passed, but not easily.

The movement finally subsided. Jen let go of my hand. Dust sparkled in the air as the lamps swayed in different directions. The lady behind me kept a firm grip on my waist while yelling to her husband, who cowered under a table. I glanced around. Most of the glassware was shattered on the tile floor. The waiters had disappeared. The walls appeared stable, but I was no engineer.

Everyone darted for the door, silent and wide-eyed, not waiting to see if it was going to happen again. The sound of stepped-on glass crackled in the air. We followed, stepping carefully over tortillas, frijoles, and splattered arroz. The bow-tied maître d' helped a scared, silver-haired lady move carefully across the floor. Bits of Mexican food stuck precariously to her face and her flowered blouse. Bow Tie kicked a path in front of her with his lime-green, florescent shoes. The waiters were still missing. I assumed they were all out back smoking.

Outside, the parking lot was a madhouse of honking cars and jerky movements, with everyone trying to gain a one-foot advantage. I noticed cracks in the asphalt that hadn't been there before. The nice spring day appeared out of place. I stared across the street at a leaning tree. Did the quake do that, or was it just reaching for the sunrise?

I suggested we walk to the park across the street. Everyone agreed. I watched the woman, who had attached herself to me in the archway, departed down the street with her husband in tow. I held a bile taste back as one girl held another who was throwing up by the gutter. People were exiting buildings up and down the street. Most wore the same disoriented facade—zombies without all the blood and missing body parts. Some stood in the middle of the street whispering. Others were texting or slowly walking with cell phones to their ears, their mouths moving wildly. A few went on as if they were doing nothing more than brushing a fly from their shoulder. Some went from shock to excitement.

Jen was a shock-to-excitement person. Dad was disoriented. Aunt Velora sat down on the grass as if readying for a picnic and motioned everyone to join her. Albert remained inconsequential. As they sat, I stood guard.

I realized I was kind of relieved that the earthquake

happened. It thwarted plans of miniature golf or throwing a heavy plastic ball down a wooden lane. I was more of a tennis dabbler and a bike rider, but I couldn't see the four of them doing either of those.

"Sit down," Aunt Velora said. By her tone, I knew she'd asked several times before. She patted the grass to her side. I smiled and sat as told. The others did too, all except Dad; he leaned on a tree looking uncomfortable and shaken. I couldn't recall many things that had ever taken him down. Of course, a lot of things pass by inebriation.

"That was incredible," Jen said. "I've never seen anything like that. The tables bounced. Everything tap-danced across the floor." Her eyes got big. "I was scared shitless. What a riot!"

"Me, too," said Aunt Velora. "That hasn't happened for thirty years, maybe longer. We should have taken pictures." Dad glanced her way as if he were sick.

I groaned. Dad coughed. Albert sat fidgeting uncomfortably.

Jen pointed a finger at each of us. "You three are no fun. That was amazing. My heart's still pumping a million miles an hour."

I said, "That was a hoot. Maybe next we can frolic in a tornado. Or perhaps get lost at sea during a tropical storm. Maybe in the meantime, just for fun, we could slam our heads in a fridge door."

"Every party has a pooper," she said, sticking out her tongue in my direction.

Jen and my aunt high-fived each other.

I twirled my finger around my ear.

"It's a sign," said my aunt. "Angels are speaking to me."

"Literally? Or are you thinking the angels caused the earthquake just for you?"

She held up a hand to silence me and gave me a glare that could sizzle flesh. A fire truck zoomed past the park with sirens blaring. *I may be needing the paramedics.*

"I think I received the gift of time. It was a sign. The angels have stifled my cancer. I can feel it." She held both hands to her chest and let out a forced breath. Dad bowed his head.

"I would probably get a second opinion," I said.

Jen and Dad silenced me with their glare. Dad mouthed

Quiet. Jen reached behind Aunt Velora and smacked my arm.

"Oh, he's okay," Aunt Velora said, referring to me. "He doesn't understand. He hasn't felt what I've felt." She stretched her arms out like a graceful bird and straightened her spine. Contentment fell over her face.

Even with Dad there, it felt good to be in her presence. The feeling left. A whiff of something ghastly snaked up my nose. I frowned at my right. Albert readjusted himself. My aunt was the only one who ignored it.

Aunt Velora kept her eyes on the sky. She was peaceful and thinking. Jen glanced at her and tried to emulate her. Dad stared at the two of them in silence with disdain, as if he were watching two crazy ducks. His hands folded in front of him, he concurred. *The drunk is putting down a happy cancer patient?* I turned toward Albert. He readjusted his back pockets again. I held in a giggle.

I decided to let the monks enjoy their tranquility, and I reverently stood up. I walked thirty feet over to a maple tree. The street was empty except for a few stragglers and an occasional car. I called Amy. I needed rational.

I thought about hanging up when it took Amy so long to answer.

"You have time for a psychological phone conference? I'll pay."

"Sure. Sandy's out to lunch. I barely finished McNeil's session, and I'm about to finish yesterday's sub. No appointments for two hours. I have an overwhelming urge to go check on new shoes at Macy's, but I think you trump Macy's."

"Wow! You sure? New shoes sound important."

"You're right. Maybe we should make it quick." She giggled with that little-girl voice she sometimes uses. "What's up?"

"We're sitting in the park after the earthquake."

"Who's we?"

"Aunt Velora; Jen; her husband, Albert; and my dear old dad."

"Well, you keep them off the swings."

"You didn't catch the part about the earthquake?"

"Yeah. Is that a euphemism for something?"

"No, we had an actual moving-chairs and stuff-falling

earthquake." My phone beeped. I peeked at the screen. It was Klarisa. I ignored it for the third time today, along with her text that stated "We're waiting" in caps with a picture of cleavage—I presumed hers.

"What? You okay? Your aunt okay? Is Jennifer all right?"

"We're fine. We were able to eat first. And now we're lounging in the park, digesting our small portions."

"Smart ass. Quit being a shit bird and tell me what happened."

"A shit bird?"

"Something my great uncle used to say. It's not a real swear word—Never mind! What happened?"

I explained the whole day from this morning until the present.

"You're okay, though?" she asked. "I thought I heard a siren."

"We're super. A little shaken up, but okay. Aunt Velora thought it was exciting. Jen cried for a minute, then her toughness took over. Then she thought it was a riot—her words, not mine. People are gathered all through the park, huddled in bunches exchanging earthquake stories with eyes wide open. The power's out here, and there's smoke coming from somewhere about a block over. People love a good disaster. You should see their faces." I paused. "It actually was scary for a time, but it's over now."

Amy sounded more panicked than we were. I changed the subject, told her about the picture of my family with loving smiles and waking up to child noises. She wanted to center on the picture and my feelings about it. I didn't. We decided to talk later that afternoon. Her voice ended in disappointed, curt sentences.

When I arrived back at the group, I noticed Aunt Velora's left eye was slightly purple and bulging. I leaned down to touch it. She ducked backwards.

"Don't touch. It hurts," she said.

"What's that from?"

"You elbowed me when you tried to save me from a moving table."

"I did?" I held my hands out in disbelief.

"You did more human damage than the earthquake. Check

out our wrists," said Jen. They were red and blotchy.

"Sorry for getting you to safety," I replied, my voice a little nasty.

Dad giggled. "Thanks for not saving my life."

After forty minutes of regrouping and exchanging what-if thoughts, I decided to go back into the restaurant and pay our bill. Bow Tie was sitting on a chair, his head bowed, shoulders slumped. He didn't seem to hear my crinkling entrance across the broken glass. He was alone, but I could hear banging sounds and arguing voices from the kitchen.

I stopped in front of him. His head lifted, his eyes dazed. Bow tie said nothing, but scratched the floor with his feet in a sliding motion. The power was out, and the lamps hung in stillness.

"Hey," he said.

I handed him a fifty and two twenties. He inspected it, puzzled at first, then waved me off. "This should cover our lunch. I assume the credit card machine isn't working?" He stared at me. I noticed a spot of blood on his hand and cuts on his knuckles. I tucked the money in his shirt pocket and walked out. *He'll probably just use it to buy a baggie, oh well.*

Chapter 13

We skipped miniature golf (thank God) and ended up at Aunt Velora's for coffee and a slice of some mystery berry pie. None of us were hungry, but if one comes to Velora's house, one must be prepared to be force-fed. The pie was good—flaky crust and way-too-sweet filling. I dumped mine in the garbage can halfway through when my aunt went for the coffee pot. Jen laughed as I rinsed my mouth at the sink. I could almost feel cavities developing and my heart racing. Jen enjoyed another slice.

Jen said, "Wow. Ben finished his pie before me."

I winced and mouthed "shut up" to her.

"Where's your plate, Ben? I'll get you another slice. You want á la mode this time?"

"Thank you, Aunt Velora, but I already cleaned my plate."

Jen giggled.

"Nonsense, I have a dishwasher. What's another plate?" She began sliding an enormous piece of pie onto a white plate laced with roses. She scooped on some burnt almond fudge ice cream.

Anxiety raced from my stomach to my throat. My idea of sweets was a few grapes or an orange. I looked down at the chocolate heap mounded high on the triangle of pie and forced a smile towards my aunt. She held out a fork for me to take. Jen poked me in the leg, smiling. Turning to Jen as I sat down, I mouthed an expletive I rarely used. Jen slid a glass bowl of cherry cordials my way. I sneered.

"Are you teasing your sister?" asked Aunt Velora.

"Oh no, I love my sister," I added with as much evil as I

could muster in my eyes, which wasn't much, "to death."

I thought about the picture. Where was it? I rubbed my temples trying to remember. I thought about my car, the backyard, and Jen's house. Nothing unfolded. My short-term memory was down there with paramecium and protozoa. I folded my arms and sat back in a kitchen chair.

"What're you thinking about, oh brilliant brother of mine?"

"I have something for you. Something I want to show you." I paused, still clutching my chest and gawking without focus. "I can't remember where I left it."

"Well, if it's new shoes, you'd better find it quickly. Is it a necklace? I'd love a necklace that matched my new shoes." I knew without glancing at her that she was staring at me.

I talked more to myself than Jen. "It's something even better. I think you will really love it."

"Better than new shoes?" She giggled.

"Much better."

"What is it?"

"I'm going to show you. Telling doesn't have the same impact. Besides, I need to remember where I put it. It will make your day—maybe your whole year."

"Benjamin, you can't tell a girl—who is your sister, mind you—that you have a surprise and that you don't know where it is, and just put it out there as some secret. What kind of brother are you?"

I jumped up and hurried to the backyard. At the cement porch overlooking the back of Aunt Velora's house, I saw the crumpled lawn, an empty redwood table, and the tiniest of litter scattered like stars on the lawn. Disappointment flowed through my veins. I turned around to walk back in and ran head-on into Jen.

She acted as if nothing happened as she rubbed her nose. "Is it back here?" Blood started to trickle from one nostril. I turned her around and headed her back to the kitchen.

"I need a cloth and cold water." Aunt Velora was already running the tap.

Jen started batting at my denim pockets. "Is it in one of these?"

I forced her into a chair, tilting her head back. She kept trying to lean forward, but her nose was dripping freely. She was relentless with her questions, and she refused to keep the rag over her nose. Red was flung everywhere.

"Sit still!" boomed the normally quiet voice of my aunt. Jen relented while glaring at me.

"You owe me shoes," she mumbled. Aunt Velora pointed a finger at her, and she cowered slightly.

***

Over at Jen's house, Albert answered the door. The TV was babbling. The house had that well-lived-in look, magazines strewn, half-filled glasses on the coffee table, and a bowl on the couch with un-popped corn kernels stuck in shiny, congealed butter. He wore yesterday's clothes and yesterday's face. He stood back as I explained, "I need to check something downstairs, where I stayed." As I walked past the kitchen, Albert sat back down on the couch.

"I need to check for something downstairs."

Albert nodded.

The blow-up mattress was still on the floor. I peered around as I folded the blanket and sheets. There wasn't a trace that I had ever been here. I felt in my pocket for Jen's car keys. I had snuck away while my aunt was binding Jen's nose with the wet towel. She was going to be mad when she found out I borrowed her car. Oh well, she shouldn't leave the keys on the counter.

The gas gauge said a quarter-tank as I drove through the underground parking of the hotel. My head flipped from side to side as I searched the gas-fumed garage for a space. It made me nauseous, so I slowed down and rolled the windows up. By the time I finished the search and pulled into a parking stall, I was lightheaded and dizzy. As the girl at the check-in desk made me another key card, my phone rang. It was Jen.

"Don't worry, but some jerk stole my car. Luckily the police are after the thug. He should be roughed up and in handcuffs as we speak."

"Hi, Jen. Your voice sounds so raspy when you're irritated."

"Where are you?" There was a pause, then she spat out, "Buster?"

"Buster?"

"I'm with Velora, or I'd use the language I'm feeling right now. Albert told me you stopped by my house."

Aunt Velora grabbed the phone. "Did you really steal Jen's car? I told her you would never do that. You must have had an important errand to run."

"No." I came across so innocent it fooled even me. "Jen let me borrow it. She left the keys on the counter for me. She must have forgotten. Does she have a temperature?"

I could hear Jen in the background. She must have been listening, because in the background her language around my aunt evolved.

"I'll see you shortly," I said quickly and hung up.

With a smile on my face, I searched the room. There was no trace of the picture. I was starting to worry. Rubbing my chin and hunting once more didn't help.

***

I pulled into Aunt Velora's driveway. Jen, Dad, and my aunt sat on yellow lawn chairs on the front lawn. Jen rose as I put the car into park. As she was coming toward me, my cell rang. I quickly answered it while opening the car door. It was Amy.

"Hey sweetie, your girlfriend is missing you. Is this a bad time?"

"Not at all. I'm just here with my family in the front yard." Jen came over and stood by me, grabbing the keys from my hand abruptly. I winced and glanced down at my palm for injuries. "I'm so glad you called." Jen asked if I was faking a phone call as she stepped on my foot.

"Who's that? She sounds irritated."

"It's Jen. She sends her love. She endured a bloody nose earlier and it put her in a sour mood, but I'm doing great. Tell me about your day."

Amy went on to tell me about two "wackos," as she called them, and a couples' conference that put her to sleep. She always gave me the highlights without names or gender. I laughed at her excitement as I watched Jen pulling faces at me. Dad and Aunt

Velora gave me privacy as they sat on the chairs and talked. Amy asked if we had had any more earthquakes. She said there was nothing on the news in Florida. I mentioned a slight movement about two hours after the main quake, but assured her nothing else happened.

I tried to walk away from Jen. She followed for a time then gave up and sat down on the lawn chairs. I stretched out the conversation as long as possible, my way of avoiding conflict. Amy finally had another client arrive, so I said good-bye. After her picture vanished from the screen, I continued to listen as if deep in conversation. Jen kept looking over her shoulder at me. She flipped me off. I stuck out my tongue and forced the cell into my front pocket.

"Do you know where my car is?" I said to no one in particular.

"Did you fill my gas tank?"

I remembered it was only at a quarter-tank when I first abducted it. It was probably on empty by now. Without peeking at Jen, I said, "Let's go fill it now. It's the least I could do. So, where did you say my car is?"

"Didn't, but maybe if I see the gauge on F and walk around for a while in my new shoes I might remember." She smirked. I shook my head.

"Jen, where is my car?" My tone was demanding.

"Guess we both have secrets?"

"It's a rental, and I need to return it."

"Oh, c'mon, crybaby, I'll take you to it, but I still want a full tank of gas."

"Done!"

We passed a Conoco station. I pointed at it. Her eyes narrowed. "I don't care about a few dollars of gas. I was making a point."

"Really?"

"Don't act so shocked. I've matured."

"Lot of changes in five years. I can't wait for the next five."

Jen stuck her tongue out and feigned a hit to my side. I jerked back, rubbing my arm as if she had made contact, and returned the gesture. We laughed.

We drove around for a while, talking about people at the party and the changes we'd experienced. We stopped and filled the gas tank, arguing about who was paying for it. I ended up paying, which was probably her plan all along. We pulled around the corner and up to Jake's plantation house. My rental car sat in front. We both giggled. It was where I left it.

I gave Jen a sideways glance. "You realize we drove around for forty-five minutes to arrive around the corner from Velora's?"

A sweet smile formed and her features softened. "Sue me! Sometimes I want to be with my brother, and he never visits. You're leaving tomorrow, and I just wanted to talk with you."

I gave her a brotherly hug, whispering, "I miss you, too."

Jen twisted my ear. "I didn't say I missed you. Did you hear me say I missed you?"

***

The Elantra had nothing in it except a blue water bottle and a Twix wrapper. Birds had splattered the blue hood and stained the windshield, but the inside of the car was fairly clean. I checked under the seat and in the glove box, bumping my head on the door frame. Listening to Jen's laugh in the background, I stood up; I wanted to rub my head but controlled the urge with pride. Searching the empty car three times, I still found nothing.

"You really have lost the secret present you claim to have. I hope it's not another one of those academic ocean magazines you publish crap in. Tell me now and let me fall asleep early."

"No, I think it may even keep you awake at night. And that crap you mentioned? You have a whole scrapbook of it—I saw it on the end table."

"Yeah, I need more time to throw things away."

I nodded and raised my car keys in the air. "I'll see you at Aunt Velora's."

From behind me I heard, "Ben, I thought you may be the owner of that affordable little blue car. If you have time, come on in and have some coffee. I was given a bag of Flor De Altura beans, and I'm dying to try them out." Jake stood between the pillars, wearing khaki shorts and a faded orange shirt buttoned to the top. Hand motions signaled us in.

"I'm intrigued. How about you, Jen?"

"You boys have fun. I've got to return some plastic containers to friends, and I'd better check on Albert."

Following Jake to the doorway, I glanced around at a gleaming hardwood floor and lawyer's bookshelves filled with eclectic carved figures, hats, bowls, and feathered things from around the world.

"I didn't realize you'd traveled so much. This is great," I said.

"The only traveling I do, except for Puerto Vallarta once a year with Rick, is on the Internet. With a credit card you can buy anything." He motioned at the bookcases as if conducting a symphony. "Rick thinks I'm indulgent. I think of myself as more of a renaissance man."

He led me to the kitchen. I sat down. Within moments, I heard the grinder churning and smelled the flavor of ground beans. When the grinder stopped, the house stood still and silent. I really didn't want any more coffee. We chatted about my sister as he filled the coffee maker with water. If he was straight, he said, he would have married my sister, without a doubt. He told me my dad had taken one addiction and traded it for another, but at least the current one was less frightening. He also mentioned that Aunt Velora is a goddess

As the coffee finished and the room filled with my favorite aroma, the most ungodly sound came from his back room, like the room was coming apart. My breath stilled as the sound came again and something fell.

"Excuse me," is all Jake said.

"What the hell is that?"

"Simon and Garfunkel must have woken up. They're hungry. It must have been the coffee smell. Give me a minute. I need to check on them." His calm drove me crazy.

I held tightly to the chair as Jake grabbed something from the fridge and scooted off down the hall. The screaming continued, followed by a pounding on the walls. Did he have panthers in the bedroom? I knew it was something feral; I had heard the noise before. I thought about leaving, but decided there had to be a logical explanation. Quiet ensued as I heard Jake talking softly down the hall. I leaned back in my chair in an effort to see better, just as the door down the hall closed and chattering started up.

Suddenly, the door ripped open, and the biggest spider monkey I'd ever seen came barreling toward me, mouth open, teeth bared. Its mouth was wet, and I could make out a hissing noise. He ran up over the table, clipping the edge of my chair back and sending my coffee cup splattering to the floor, before flinging himself to the counter. Then, he was on top of the cabinets, chattering.

Jake walked into the kitchen with another spider monkey clinging to his neck; eating an orange. The placid monkey had reddish-blonde hair—the demented monkey had a reddish-brown mane. He sat staring at me with crazy, wild eyes and an open mouth that displayed white spikes.

"You met Garfunkel; he gets a case of enthusiasm when strangers visit." Jake rubbed the head of the monkey that nestled in his neck. "This is Simon. She is the calmer of the two, but don't get her riled. She can be a b-i-t-c-h."

My mouth sat agape. "Are you crazy? These are your house pets? Are you crazy?"

"Shhhhhh," he whispered. "These are my and Rick's children. They don't know they are monkeys. You have to be considerate of their vitality."

"Trust me, they know they're monkeys."

"That's what Rick says. He doesn't understand them like I do." The monkey on the cabinet began throwing feces toward the window behind me and chattering with his arms flinging out. His hair stood erect. Yellow splattered the cabinet and floor, barely missing me.

"No, no, Garfunkel," Jake said in a harmonious soft voice. The monkey bore his teeth and hissed, his hands waving wildly. Jake stroked the other one, "Look how good Simon is being." The monkey on the cabinet screeched.

Backing out of the kitchen, I waved good-bye. Jake didn't notice. He was too busy baby-talking to Simon and Garfunkel. As I opened my car door, I could still hear Garfunkel screaming as if tortured by demons.

I went back to the hotel to call Amy and rest. Amy didn't answer, so I left a message about earthquakes, screeching monkeys, and a picture of a happy family I didn't recognize.

An hour passed as I watched the TV without sound. I was as inactive as a person can get. The couch formed a question mark from my body. A ringing musical tone hit my ears; it was many seconds before I figured out my cell was singing.

Jen was on the line. "Where are you?"

"Here."

"Your voice sounds weird. Are you okay? Your car's gone from Jake's."

"Yeah, I left. I'm here now."

"And that would be—?"

"Oh, the hotel. I stopped to get something and call Amy." I rubbed my eyes, then clicked the TV off. I needed sleep. "I'll be over in a minute."

"Dad's been waiting here for you. We've eaten enough chocolate chip cookies and drunk enough coffee to power a downtown city block. Should we come to the hotel?"

I glanced around and shook my head, almost setting the phone down on the table.

"I'm waiting?"

"I'll be there in fifteen minutes, I need to brush my teeth and wash my face." I heard a loud growl and a click. I knew it would take me an hour or so because I wanted a shower and a change of clothes, but if I said that, the whole family would arrive at the hotel.

***

"What's on the agenda now?" I asked, not really wanting to know. My mind faded to the picture. I wondered if we had any other good times as I was growing up. Nothing came to mind.

"How about I order Chinese?" said Jen.

My aunt spread both hands out in a fanning motion. "I have leftovers from the party that have stretched the limits of my fridge. You're not leaving me with all that food to rot. I'll pull some out if you're hungry." Her voice was old and chiding, her eyes tiny and tired.

Jen and I jumped up. "We'll throw something together, Aunt Velora. You sit down and rest," Jen said.

"What have I done for the last three hours?" Aunt Velora retorted.

"You and Dad come sit in the kitchen and guide us to what you want. We'll serve you," I agreed.

Aunt Velora didn't listen. She went first to the fridge, pushing us aside and pulling out bowls and trays of meats and salads and fruit of many colors. I gazed at Dad; he was being way too congenial and quiet. This whole sober personality was throwing me off. His eyes wandered, and there was hidden thought going on in the background, but his mouth lay pasted on his face like a paper drawing—no dimension, no anima. He caught me staring and almost smiled. Instead, his lips fell flat, and he dropped his eyes to a point on the table. Maybe it was remorse. I believed it was more of a hidden agenda

"I received this picture . . . ."

Everyone glanced up at me. My eyes flickered to each one of them as the words hung suspended in the kitchen along with the aroma of the unwrapped trays of food. I bit my tongue lightly and began humming an unknown song. I was trying to think, but the gears were slipping.

I've got to find that picture. They have to see what we could have been.

Dad spoke. "You nuts?" The silence was broken. "Are you trying to remember lyrics? And what's this about receiving a picture? I'm positive that's not the words to the song. You're acting a little crazy."

"Thanks, Dad. I assume you would know first-hand about crazy?"

"You two knock it off," Jen said. "Ben, you did have a weird look on your face. And then mumbling and humming?"

I glared at her.

"You two leave Ben alone." My aunt always stood up for me. I grinned and nodded at her.

"Okay!" said Dad, "But if he pulls out a tambourine and starts up with a ballad, I'm eating on the porch until Amy can get here with his daily dose."

Jen laughed. I snarled. Aunt Velora crossed her arms, letting everyone know that was enough.

A solemn quiet fell over the table. Even the silverware clinking against the plates was muffled. After dinner, we moved to the front room for coffee. Throats were cleared. I heard the fridge compressor kick on. We all cuddled our cups as if holding tiny warm babies. We all waited for Aunt Velora to let us know if we could talk again.

Aunt Velora broke the spell. "Anyone want a soda?" she opened the fridge and held out a couple of cans. Everyone shook their heads. "I've got to go out back for a minute. I'll be right back," she said.

"Where's Albert?" I asked.

"Home doing whatever Albert does when I'm not around. Probably sleeping, though I left him a list of to-do's."

The three of us talked about the party. We were all glad to have visited with Andrea and Jake again. Dad kept telling stories about Willey. I had no idea who that was. Jen acted puzzled too. She kept trying to change the subject. I broke away and went looking for Aunt Velora. I had heard the back door open a few minutes earlier.

She was on the back porch step, sitting with her back to me. As I opened the door, she spun around, holding something to her side. As she spoke, smoke came out of her mouth.

"Aunt Velora, are you smoking?"

She giggled. "It's not what you think. It's medicinal." The distinct odor of marijuana floated around the back porch.

I stopped and tried to mull that over in my mind. I thought I smelled it the other day, but shook it off as something else. Standing there, I considered retreating as though nothing happened.

"My doctor recommended it."

"Who?"

"Doctor Rattenborough. He's famous on the Internet. He's the doctor to several celebrities. Helped cure Demi Moore. She's cancer-free."

"She had cancer? I asked.

"Of course. Why else would he put her face and others on his website?"

"And," I adjusted my thoughts as I spoke, "when did you see him?"

"Silly, he's not at a hospital; he's an online doctor. I signed up for his website membership, and he gives me personal advice about what to eat, drink, sleep, exercise, and all sorts of things. His vitamins keep me healthier than I should be. Marijuana shrinks the tumor. He has studies and results from all over the world. He's not a quack like that oncologist, Doctor Bratten."

"Don't tell me you've quit seeing your oncologist?"

She blew air out like I was being ridiculous. "Doctor Rattenborough say's we should all see our own doctors, but when we need the big guns we check in with him. He runs the PCI and knows all about new treatments even before they're through their trials." Her voice was excited as she talked.

"What's the PCI? How do you know if he's a real doctor? You realize it's the Internet—he could be an elementary school student."

"PCI is the Psychological Cancer Institute. I'm sure you've heard of it. Of course he's a real doctor! You think I'd go to just anyone?" Aunt Velora turned her head in disbelief. "He's listed as a doctor, but he prefers the title 'cancer psychologist.' He treats cancer from the mind out."

I could tell she was getting a little irritated as she noticed my responsive gestures. I took a breath and told myself that at her age, she could do whatever she wanted.

"Beth Ann Bandolyn showed me his website. Her breast cancer was almost gone."

"Almost gone?"

"Well, she died first. She wouldn't stop using those sleeping pills."

"She was on the pot remedy too?"

"Beth Ann was the one who introduced Prudy to me. Prudy's such a dear; she helps with my dosage. I couldn't have done it without her. Most states have made medicinal marijuana legal. Utah is asleep when it comes to helping us ladies with cancer. What do they want us to do—drive to Colorado or California? At least I'm not paying taxes on it. The taxes alone would probably wipe out this old lady's bank account."

Snickering and nodding in agreement, I held out my hand to help her into the house. Even if it was only psychosomatic, if it helped her, I was all for it.

"Where ya'all been?" asked Dad.

Jen crinkled her nose and took a sniff. "Appears you've found out about the bridge club remedy," she giggled.

Dad tilted his head with a frown. "My sister thinks she's Snoop Dog or something. Disgusting, the whole damn group of them."

Jen and I gave Aunt Velora a hug, and the three of us shot out giggles as we tried to keep our lips tight.

Chapter 14

Jen's car hurled us down the lined asphalt towards the airport. Trees whipped by, and Jen's hair pulled toward her open window. She'd insisted I drop off the car at Hertz the night before so she could drive me to the airport. We left way early, and I wondered about the ride as I clung to the door handle, trying to catch a breath of air inside her open-window wind tunnel.

I had driven by my supposedly reformed dad's house prior to returning my rental. The car glided by slowly without stopping. I wanted to stop and didn't want to stop at the same time. One trip of handcuffed humiliation in front of the man was enough for one home visit—maybe even for my whole life.

Aunt Velora had given me a lot of forehead and cheek kisses. She cried and hugged me. We finally said good-bye with few words and thickened throats. I secretly hoped the next time we were together it wouldn't be to put her in the ground. The dry air had been mysteriously damp on my neck and forehead. Jen had shoved me into the car, and we were off. The last I saw of Aunt Velora's face were tears and reddened cheeks as she waved frantically.

When I had seen my dad the day before with Jen, he and I had thrown barbs at each other. I called him a "drunk," even though my voice didn't have the conviction it once held. He called me an "ungrateful son" and a "biologist." The first one, I had heard a million times before. I wasn't quite sure how to react to the second. I didn't have a rebuttal. Perhaps that's why he had said it. He said it like Parisians say *American.* Our conversation had stalled. A slight grin had formed as I thought, this is the first time he's acknowledged my occupation. After that, the anger had mellowed. I had breathed easier.

There had been no hugs or tears when I left him standing on his yellow, patchy lawn. That would have been too hard for either one of us. We nodded at each other and parted as if on cue. His listless wave was the last gesture before we headed down the road. I should have waved back. I had just nodded.

***

I watched Jen as she mumbled the words of a song on the radio with the lips of a ventriloquist. She was happy and content in this city of despair and darkness. Her head bobbed to the music.

I loved my sister more than anything in the world. She always brought me up out of deep waters. Her glow was genuine. She should have been an inspiration for dealing with family, but I felt content in my bitterness. Jen had floated above all that for years. I often wondered why. I always wondered how.

Her car shimmied as we rounded corners and barreled away from the street lights. It was one of those indistinctive vehicles that gets lost in traffic like stampeding cattle. I tried guessing at the make or model—it was a boxy Ford. An Explorer, I think. I glanced around at use and wear. The seats were stained. The console was cracked and faded. She smiled at me as if oblivious to anything bad in her life. It was almost irritating.

"Should we stop at the mall?" she asked. "We have time."

I regarded her as if she were crazy.

"You should pick up a gift for Amy."

A puzzle filled my brain. "Why?"

"Because you've been away, and she's your significant other," Jen paused, "and she's a girl."

She hit me in the shoulder as she turned into a parking lot filled with more cars than parking spaces. We went up and down aisles for a minute. Between craning her neck and searching for an open space, she fluttered her head towards me, mumbling something that sounded like stupid dumb men. I assumed she was referring to me, so I kept my mouth shut and then I didn't.

Jef Huntsman

"I could get her something at the airport," I mentioned meekly.

"And she would know, it was from the airport."

I wasn't sure what that meant, but I knew better than to cross my sister. Besides, my arm was sore from a week of sister smacks, and I was starting to flinch whenever her eyes narrowed and her lips sucked in.

"You need to get away from your beloved octopuses and ocean-what-nots once in a while." She found a car pulling out and zoomed in with a shudder. Her smile faded to determination.

"Does Albert know these things?" I asked.

"Of course he doesn't," she said rather loudly. "He's more of a relationship invalid than you. I buy myself presents, wrap them with glorious bows and ribbons, and pick out my own card. I hand it to Albert; he signs the card, slips it under the ribbon and gives it to me later that day. I feign gratitude. It's a system that has worked well all our lives. If I left it up to him, I'd probably receive an iron or a vacuum for my birthday. I still have those damn striped, fluffy, knee-high socks nailed to our bedroom wall. He is not allowed to buy presents, but he is not you. You are," she hesitated, "trainable."

"Thanks," I said. "Sounds like in a few years I'll be able to use the potty by myself."

"All in time," she answered.

***

I listened to voices for a time. There were distant sounds . . . someone very familiar . . . another I didn't recognize. I strained to hear the conversation, trying to pull myself out of the blackness. Sentences were muttered in soft tones. I felt the rhythm of each person's voice, picking out a word or two every so often. It was soothing. I fell back to sleep without the strength to keep listening. This semiconscious fade-in-and-out happened over and over like a cycle. Was I dreaming?

On my final attempt to pull myself out of a stew of vowels and unrelated letters, the distinct sound of Aunt Velora's voice pulled me in. My head was suddenly filled with coherent

126

conversation from the three wonderful women in my life.

"His nose is cold." Then muttering and "a heated blanket."

The second voice was my sister's. I concentrated harder, willing myself to wake up. I tried to say hello, but my mouth didn't seem to work, and a pain shot across my jaw. Then I heard Amy's non-client voice, soft and worried.

"Did his lips just move?"

I could feel her close to me. I counted to three and forced my eyes open. It was only a squint, but I saw a blurry Amy, then I felt her hand hold mine. Her other hand brushed my forehead. Glimpsing through eyelashes and under heavy lids, I watched the ceiling tiles sway and a faint outline of someone at the door. My neck wouldn't turn. Something was restraining it. I turned back towards Amy. I could sense her more than see her.

"Can you hear me?" she asked.

I blinked. It appeared to be the only thing I could do. No, I found something else. I squeezed her hand lightly.

"You're going to be okay. You are in Saint Joseph's Hospital. You were shot."

I didn't recognize the voice. I tried to eyeball the other side. After a few moments, a lady with a stethoscope around her neck and a name tag pinned to hospital scrubs came into view. Amy leaned back. I blinked and raised my finger.

"I am your nurse, Shonda. You are on a lot of pain meds, so waking up will be difficult. Your neck is in a brace to keep your spine straight. You won't be able to talk for a while, but we'll work that out. Get some more rest. That's best for recuperation. I'll let your doctor know you're awake, and he'll visit you as soon as he can."

The nurse glanced up, then back at me again. She had a deep, reassuring voice. Why couldn't I talk? What was that all about? I think I went to the mall with my sister. Amy squeezed my hand again, and I forgot about the nurse. Amy's eyes were caring. She leaned in close to me and kissed my forehead. Warmth spread through my chest, and I tried to move, but pain flew up my jaw and above my ear. I mentally told myself to relax, but I didn't listen. Unknowingly, my elbow pressed hard on the nurse button. A long time fell between deliberate breaths. The nurse touched the monitor and moved the call box from under me.

Another nurse took one look at me then her watch and came back shortly with help delivered through my IV. Pain meds began drifting me between pain and stupor. My bed was elevated slightly. A lightheaded blur filled the room. I was out for a long time.

Much later, a loud noise broke the spell. Shapes began to appear—some smiling, some with worry. Four loving ladies came into full view.

"Hello." My voice was raspy and sounded like "o-low." I struggled to stay awake. Damn, that hurt. I wanted to scream but forced myself to relax. They all laughed as if I had uttered an incredible punch line.

They all started talking at once so I closed my eyes. I could make out voices, but the clatter was disconcerting and foggy. A loud voice said, "Quiet, he's trying to say something." I tried to talk. My lips were dry and my neck hurt with every movement. A noise came out like slaughtered mutterings from a chicken coop. I swallowed bile back. Forever passed before I realized the sound came from me.

I opened my eyes and touched the bandages around my throat. Amy held my shoulder carefully, her face contorted with concern. Jen and Aunt Velora wore the same mask. From behind them, Klarisa's head popped to the side with a smile.

Klarisa said, "Good morning, handsome." The other three glowered at her. Amy's eyebrows lifted as she took a noticeable breath. Amy grabbed my hand, looking at me with a slight aura of ownership. Klarisa pushed her way through, across from Amy and began combing my hair back with one hand and lightly tickling my chest with the other. Even dazed, I could feel her sensuality. She was dressed in a tight blue blouse with enough buttons undone to spy her belly button. Her hair had a windblown style as if she just left the beauty salon. Her nails were the blue of her blouse with white roses painted on each one.

The air thickened as I glanced around. Amy had obviously met Klarisa and seemed unsure about her. I winced as muscles in my neck pulled. No one uttered a sound. I felt a bit like a zoo animal peering through bars.

"We need to let Ben rest," Aunt Velora said. She grabbed

Klarisa and Jen by the hand and led them out. Both were reluctant and grabbed the door frame as my aunt yanked them through.

Amy squeezed my hand with a gentle touch. My tight chest released as I exhaled deeply.

"You need to get better," she said. "Donald and Goofy miss you." She giggled. For a brief second I missed my lab, but the feeling faded with my strength and concentration. "I miss you."

I tried a smile. Even that hurt.

"Mind if I stay here while you rest?"

I twirled my finger around the side of my head and pointed at her with the index on my other hand.

"You think I'm crazy?"

I tried shaking my head. The brace held it in place, but she understood.

"No?" She paused, "Oh, what about my patients?"

I pointed both fingers at her.

"They'll be fine. I have Doctor Langosta and Mary taking care of them. Also, I've been talking to several on the phone. Phone psychology, I call it. I have also been doing the ridiculous and texting with a few. They seem to prefer it. I'm starting to wonder why I pay rent at all."

***

I was awake—well, sort of—by the next day, writing notes to my three women. Amy told me it was my fourth day in the hospital.

I ignored Klarisa. Probably better for my health and my relationship.

Three smiles filled the room as I uttered grunts and groans to keep the sympathy from fading. I tried to give some back, but wasn't sure a smile formed at all. To talk hurt my whole body, so I was speaking sparingly, waiting between agonies to begin again. I assumed my aunt had banned Klarisa from the hospital—either that, or she had become disenchanted with the sick boy. To keep my pride up, I decided she had been banned.

Noticing Jen's discolored eye socket, I pointed at my eye and then hers. At first she appeared puzzled, then nodded.

"When you threw yourself on top of me at the mall, your mad elbow gave me a black eye. It matches the one you gave our sweet aunt at the restaurant," she snickered. "Our lawyer will be bringing up the abuse charges later. Until then, heal up, big brother." I noticed a tear flowing down her cheek from her good eye. She turned, wiping it away as if adding makeup.

My cheeks flushed as I watched my sister try to hide her caring. It trickled through me the way the desert invigorates and blossoms after a spring rain.

My doctor—whom I had never met—and a nurse I slightly recalled came into the room. He had a knowledgeable, caring face with hair like unkempt fur on his head. We were about the same age.

My three girls left me alone with him as the nurse silently scooted them out with subtle gestures. Aunt Velora's face held worry, Jen gave a slight wave, and Amy blew me a kiss. I started to assume this was the part where they tell me how many days I had left—to get my things in order and so forth.

"Well, Ben," the doctor said, "this is the first time I've seen you awake. I'm Dr. Tormini. I'm the surgeon who worked on you the other day. How are you feeling?"

I rolled my eyes. I knew the question was rhetorical.

"Can you roll over on your left side?" he asked.

I complied, knowing that whatever pain meds were oozing through my veins would do nothing as I moved. I tightened my face as the roll began. A fiendish sound filled the room. I initially thought it was someone else.

Dr. Tormini loosened the neck brace. I tried to squeeze Amy's hand in anticipation, but her hand wasn't there. Once I moved and settled, the Percocet kept the agony down, but the thought of turning back over made me wince. The doctor reached over and analyzed the back of my neck, prodding as if releasing the demons. That part hurt. My face creased, and I held the bedrail with enough force to bend it. The nurse gave me two extra pain pills. I bit one in half, swallowed it with a full glass of water, and tossed the other pill and a half on my food tray after the nurse left. I would rather have pain than be a lightheaded zombie lying placidly against the white sheets.

I think I'm better, I thought with my jaws clamped shut. I formed an okay hand gesture, waving it slightly.

Dr. Termini patted my arm. "I see your dad every Sunday at church. He's quite a character." His nurse smiled appropriately at the end of the bed, her arms crossed.

Whatever he did, I'll try and compensate you. I unconsciously raised my eyes, giving away my thoughts.

The doctor sat up straighter with a puzzled look across his face. "Oh, no, he didn't do anything. He's not the scoundrel he once was. I knew him only by reputation before." He paused as if having to think about it. "He's a good man. Of course, you know that already."

A good man, I thought. *Oh yeah, he's a saint.*

"Lawrence has been in the hall since you've been here. I'm not sure why he doesn't visit. He has taken this very hard."

After a pause, Dr. Tormini said, "You seem surprised. I'm sorry; I thought—"

Dad's outside? I tried to move my head. Pain ripped across my cheek and into my shoulder. I smiled, thinking, *Dad's probably out checking carts for rubbing alcohol.* I glanced at the doctor. I could tell he thought my reaction was for something else. I was ashamed at my attempt at humor.

He smiled. "Moving on to things at hand, you should be able to move your jaw and speak without much pain in a few days. The muscles were torn up pretty badly. There's still some swelling and internal and external stitches. The wound will take time to heal." He rubbed his chin. I noticed acne scars below deep-set eyes. "Your prognosis is expected to be favorable."

The sun reflected off the lamp above my bed. A shot of light hit my eyes as he moved to the side. I squinted and my cheeks puffed. Stabbing pain slid down my spine.

"Do you remember what happened?" he asked.

I raised my eyes.

"You were shot through the leg, and one slug lodged in the back of your neck. The bullet clipped the femur after passing through the muscles at the back of your leg. It missed the femoral artery by a few centimeters. You were lucky. The second bullet punctured through the jaw here." Dr. Tormini pointed to just below his cheek. "It shattered your molar, which apparently slowed the velocity down slightly. It finally lodged in the muscle on the back of your neck. I made an incision and excised it from back here." He gently touched the bandage behind my neck.

His touch wasn't gentle enough. I squirmed and held my breath. He didn't seem to notice.

"You had extensive tissue damage and a shattered molar, as I said before. My team and Dr. White, the oral surgeon, worked about eight hours on you. In time you should be fine. You were carrying a barrel full of luck; the bullet missed anything that could have been fatal. Any questions?"

I pointed to my throat and raised my eyes. I could talk but it hurt like hell.

The nurse stepped forward and reached into her pocket for a pen and turned over tomorrow's menu. Her hand made a gesture of writing as she handed both to me.

I wrote down one word in all caps: "VOICE?" I tapped the word several times.

The doctor smiled. "You can talk now, though it will put a lot of strain on your healing tissue. Just give it a few days. There is a lot of internal swelling. Okay?" After a nod of my head, the doctor patted my shoulder and walked out. The nurse followed.

He sounded reassuring, but it didn't untie the knot in my stomach. I kept wanting to massage my neck, but the brace stopped that. I tried mentally to speak, then thought better of it. My throat felt like a pineapple was lodged in it.

I could hear the doctor's voice in the hall, letting my family know how I was doing. I tried to smile. Damn, that hurt.

Jen, Amy, Aunt Velora, and the nurse came back in. The nurse checked my IV and typed something in the computer. She asked if I needed anything. My three girls held my gaze with expectant eyes. I said no, and the three moved in. My pillow was fluffed, my full water topped, my bed cart rearranged, my sheets and thin blue blanket tucked softly to my neck, and chairs brought to each side of my bed. The ladies sat down. Mission accomplished.

I pulled the covers back down and waved my hand in front of my neck. Feeling obliged, I drank from the glass of water, but no more than a few drops. It was perfunctory at best.

Aunt Velora said, "My brother's outside."

I acknowledged it with an okay sign. All three eyes gazed at me with the question: "Want to see him?" I turned my head into the pillow and closed my eyes, feigning sleep. I heard noises of frustration. After what seemed like an hour, I fell asleep. One way to avoidance.

Several days later, I was talking meekly. I had asked for five minutes alone with my father. Nothing was said. He sat and watched the monitor. I raised the bed up and down.

Jen told me we were both bullheaded and cut from the same tree. I pointed at her. She said she knew now that she was adopted and said something about bloodlines and stupidity. I held my throat and tried to look pathetic. She made a fist, and I slid to the other side of the bed, holding my shoulder.

Chapter 15

The rain pooled in low pockets of uneven asphalt. Tires squealed as cars tried to find parking places closer to the hospital. Two glass office buildings across the way glanced back with distortion from the downpour. I favored one crutch, leaning into the cool of the hospital room window. Exhaling slowly, my lungs missing the outside air, I tried to remember an old song about rain. I could hum the tune and knew when they sang the word "rain," but the title and the rest of the lyrics escaped me.

"I knew I'd seen that butt somewhere. My brother, the singing streaker."

My torso turned quickly. Teeth ground together from the pain that exploded within my spine as my body moved. I waited a few seconds for my breathing to slow, then tried to pull the gown around to cover my chilled rear end. Pain shot through my shoulder, and all I could think about was where my boxers where. Dizziness filled my head. I sat on the edge of the bed.

Somehow I had knocked over the plastic water pitcher and felt it dripping down my good leg. I didn't care. I was still glancing around with faded vision for my underwear. A million miles away, I could hear Jen laughing. She was trying unsuccessfully to stifle it. The head of the bed was elevated at a forty-five-degree angle. I lay back slowly with short breaths and pulled the wet covers up to my chest. Pain radiated from everywhere. The tendons and muscles of my face were pulled tight enough to make me look like a plastic surgeon's mistake. I moaned deep and loud, barely noticing that Jen was gently rubbing my shoulder.

Jen pushed the nurse's button. I twisted my neck no. At least I think I did. Jen ignored me anyway.

"Just relax. Your sister's here. Who the hell let you out of bed?"

I love my sister, but man, I was getting tired of her and all the other Florence Nightingales. The phone calls and a visit every few years worked nicely. The shooting had put me in mother-hen hell. If Jen wasn't making me blow my nose, my aunt was pouring water into a full cup, Amy was stroking my forehead for what seemed like hours, or Klarisa was sneaking in late at night to offer sex therapy. I declined.

The nurse and Jen made my bed while I feigned sleep, pretending the pain had magically disappeared each time they rolled me over to one side, then the other.

"I know you're not asleep." Jen said. "You need family, and I'm going to be here whether you like it or not. By the way, Macho, you need to tie your gown strings when expecting visitors." She was holding my head by my temples and talking inches away from my face.

I giggled. Another bolt shot down my spine. I winced, waiting until my fists unclenched.

"See, you love having me here." She turned to the nurse who walked in. I watched Jen through squinted eyes. "Hi Calvin. When was his last pain pill? He seems to be hurting."

Calvin gazed at the computer, punching keys as rapidly as an executive secretary. He glanced over at Jen. His lips were tight and he stood frozen, as if thinking.

"Well?" asked Jen.

"He hasn't had anything since late last night and only one eight hours before that. The computer says he doesn't want them."

Thanks, tattle-tale. Without even looking at her, I knew my sister was crossing her arms. Calvin walked out without saying another word.

"You're in pain, aren't you? Heavy pain? Are you trying to be some manly asshole?"

I spoke without opening my eyes, but turned my face in her direction. "No. I plain . . . don't . . . like . . . pain meds. They make my brain swim. I can't think right and they give me headaches. A little pain is much better than the remedy."

Without turning, I knew her face would be red by now. She hated anyone disobeying. Always had. Every instinct told her to slug my arm, but she resisted. I'm sure that made her even angrier. She sat down by my side, accidentally bumping my bad leg on the way. I held my breath and silently went through a string of expletives in my mind.

"You lay there in pain. You won't change your wet gown. Your rump is flying in the wind. There are probably a hundred other things I haven't noticed. We're just trying to make you more comfortable."

"Who's this helpful 'we' you're talking about?" I laughed. It's hard to be mad at someone who cares. "Jen, I can't find my boxers and pain is relative."

"Pain is relative?" She bobbed her head between her shoulders. "No, pain is pain, Mr. Philosopher." She opened the door of a cabinet, reached in, ripped open a package of boxers Amy had bought me, and threw one at me. It was camouflage khaki. I caught it on my forehead.

I smiled up at her. "Thanks for caring." I meant it, even though one couldn't tell from my sarcastic voice. We stared at each other for longer than was comfortable. "This is what too much TV and a small room will do to you. I'm irritable, pathetic, and rolling back and forth between wanting help and needing no one."

There was a knock on the door, and it opened. Aunt Velora and Amy walked in. Jen got up to greet them properly with hugs and smiles.

After an hour and a half of the three of them talking about me as if I wasn't there, I fell asleep. My gown was still damp, my new boxers under my chin, and I didn't care.

I was awakened for vitals and another person asking me how I was doing. The nurse untangled me from the IV that had tied the neck brace to my ear. My dad sat in a rocking chair watching with boredom, his idea of concern. He cleared his throat three times before he told me the girls were down getting a bite to eat. His face and posture made him shy and inconsequential. His black suit and paisley blue tie showed the ruffles of too many days worn.

I thought back to childhood with Dad's starched collars,

tailored suits, and alcohol-glazed eyes. He was more relaxed and timorous now than he had ever been after Makers Mark on the rocks. Jen watched his evolution over time. My infrequent visits made these changes seem abrupt and pointed. He was now a stranger with a resemblance to someone I had known. I kept checking for the red in his eyes and the flush of his cheeks, but it wasn't there. I still couldn't lose the anxiety that boiled whenever he was near.

"Anything I can get you?" asked Dad.

My childhood would be nice. "No, I'm fine."

He reached in his coat pocket and took out a cell phone. He fumbled it in his hands, gazing into the screen. I assumed he'd never answered a phone call on it.

We were both uncomfortable. I rearranged the sheets several times and adjusted the patient tray. He kept pushing buttons on his cell, as if writing a dissertation. I coughed; it slightly hurt my throat and sent a spasm down my chest and through my ribcage. The sound echoed around the room. Then we listened to the air conditioner.

The girls came back, laughing and grabbing each other's hands like school girls. Dad and I both sat up straighter.

"What happened?" I asked.

They all stared at me and burst into laughter. I waited, curious. Dad grinned and got up from his chair, motioning for one of the ladies to sit down. They ignored both of us, laughing into their hands, their whole bodies quivering.

The laughter turned to sporadic giggles. Amy turned to me. "Your aunt and your sister stole wheelchairs and . . ." My sister began snorting, and Aunt Velora made choking sounds as tears filled her eyes. With a grin, Amy held her hand out, motioning everyone to sit down. "These two had races down the hallway, wheeling around, barely missing patients and people with food trays. They kept hooting as they stormed the hallways. I had to run to catch up. On the third hallway, this little ten-year-old with an IV joined the two terrors in his wheelchair for a pass back the way they had come. A race ensued. He would have won if that tall nurse with a beauty mark the size of a Volkswagen hadn't stepped in front of them."

"We were scolded," said Jen. "Can you imagine a twenty-five-year-old with big glasses scolding your sweet little aunt? Good God, she was wearing a pink top with Smurfs on it."

"I was embarrassed," said Aunt Velora, "until Jen and Amy just laughed at her. You should have seen her face. That nurse stood there between the two wheelchairs with her arms crossed tight enough to crack a coconut. She mumbled something about security. We ran for the elevator."

Amy put her arms around Jen and Velora. "I am having so much fun with your family. I can't believe you never told me about this wildness. Your childhood must have been hilarious." Amy peered at Dad, then me, and quieted down.

Dad held the arms of his chair, veins bulging on the backs of his hands, and stared at the floor. I raised my eyebrows.

***

The next day, I was released from the hospital. I kidded Jen about being thrown out because of yesterday's antics. She flipped me off. Amy laughed.

As we pulled into my Dad's driveway, behind his Eldorado with the crumpled license plate and rust-spotted bumper, a knot tightened in my stomach. Irritation and panic formed as the color drained from my face. I wanted to rip the console out from between me and Jen. Amy patted my shoulder from the back seat.

At first I couldn't think, then anger solidified. "I hope we're just here to pick up something?"

"I thought it would be nice for you and Dad to spend some time together. He has two extra bedrooms. It's only for a couple of days while you heal well enough to fly back to Florida."

"Are you effin' kidding me? I assumed we were going to Aunt Velora's or your house. What are you trying to do?"

"Maybe it won't be so bad," came Amy's small voice from the backseat. "I'm staying with you."

"This is like boarding the Titanic with previous knowledge of the iceberg. No, this isn't happening." I cringed as a biting pain shot through my spine. I took in slow, deliberate breaths as I realized I shouldn't yell. As the pain ebbed, I slowly turned and checked behind me, waiting for the car to back out.

"I'm sorry, but you're being a six-year-old. You can stay with me if you need to." Jen used that tone in her voice as if staying with her was the stupidest, most cowardly idea ever. She ground her feet into the car mat "I thought it might be a good idea. You always wanted a father. Now's the time to man up. He wants to make peace."

"Two-person group therapy. Sounds terrific, only neither of us talk to each other. As you recall, I didn't want to leave the house when I was six years old. I had no idea how much better life could be. Then, after spending a week at Aunt Velora's, I never wanted to come back."

Amy leaned forward. "It is a good idea. You need to try this. People change."

"Bullshit!"

Amy rubbed my shoulder. I flinched, but said nothing. Uneasy quiet filled the car as they waited for me to agree. My silence irritated my sister as she tried to bite through her bottom lip. I found some pleasure in that.

Jen broke the stillness. "Are you waiting for me to . . . pay you? Or what? She bit her upper lip, holding back a grin.

"Perhaps . . . how much?"

She made a fist and mumbled. I craned my neck as far as I could—about three-quarters of an inch—and willed the car to reverse. A hand grabbed my shoulder. I froze, waiting for sympathy.

Instead, Amy came at me with psycho-babble that centered on words like adolescent behavior. I wanted to be back in Florida, checking salinity and graphing beak movements of Donald and Goofy. The car just kept idling. Jen blew out a steam of air. She turned the key off, dropped it in her purse emphatically, and spied down her nose with a "so-there" look.

I noticed the window shades open slightly and the unmistakable eyes of my dad burrowed in me. His face was carved by cheap gin and regretful aging; he appeared as distraught as I felt. I turned my eyes away, just as the drapes fell into place.

"Ben, it's only a night or two. You are a grown man." Amy pointed at the door. "What could possibly happen?" Her voice was low and conspiratorial.

"I'm not afraid of him. I just plain don't like him. I don't want to be around him. I don't want to be in that house." I sucked air hard through my nostrils. "You never had a drunk for a father, one that cared so little for you. I was only wanted when he ordered me to give him a ride to the liquor store. He was all profanity and bad breath. He would call my aunt's house yelling at me to get home to drive him."

"Jen seemed to make it through."

"Jen's a forgiving saint. She'd forgive the devil if he came to her house."

"Now just a minute, Brother." Spit hit me in the face when she said *Brother*. Her whole body contorted and her neck reddened. "I spent years picking up bottles for him while he passed out or threw up in my car. All the therapy in the universe couldn't erase all the abuse and crap he put me through. I HAVEN'T FORGIVEN HIM. I don't know if I even care about him enough for that."

"Jen, I'm—"

"I just quit hating. It wasn't worth my time. It made me miserable and gave me stomach aches. I stopped myself from thinking that way. I went for a long time not answering my phone." Her finger poked me repeatedly in the chest; I was pretty sure she was trying to shove it out through my back. "Now he's nothing more than an old man who has found a God to believe in. Sometimes I give him a ride to church. I feel better. He has turned into the dad I didn't have, and my damn car seats don't smell. Don't come across like you're the only one who was affected."

Jen was crimson, breathing hard, and sometime during her tirade she had squeezed my fingers so tight they were numb and white. Amy sat stunned. Jen finally let go of my fingers.

I waited carefully for the steam to settle. "I'm so sorry. We never talked about it before." My heart was pumping so hard that I placed my hand against my chest to quiet it down. It didn't seem to help.

"No, we never talked about it, and I don't want to ever discuss it again."

We were all silent, peering around at nothing in particular, but especially not at each other. I thought about checking my cell, even though it hadn't squeaked out the silly notes of my ringtone. I was afraid to move. The drapes opened again. I saw his eyes, dark and deep. They backed away, leaving the heavy fabric to glide for a second, then drop into place.

After trying to force saliva into my dry throat, I finally spoke, my voice cracking as if I were going through puberty again "He'd better have clean sheets on the bed." Laughter filled the inside of Jen's car.

"It's about time. I was afraid I would have to drag you to the front door, kicking and screaming, with all the neighbors watching." Jen paused, "Besides, how dirty could unused sheets get in thirty-plus years?"

The car door was heavy as it opened. Jen popped the trunk to grab my things and Amy's. I heard a car honk behind me. It was Klarisa in a purple convertible. My breathing ceased. I tried not to glance at Amy. My ears perked up when Amy welcomed Klarisa over like an old college chum. I couldn't have been more uncomfortable. Pain seemed to rattle down my back as all of my muscles tensed involuntarily.

Jen sent girl-hate signals wavering through the thick air. Molecules exploded as Jen held her hands on her hips and sent Klarisa a piercing glare that could shrink daisies, but didn't affect K-pop.

Chapter 16

Klarisa was carrying a fancy wrapped package, striped in rainbow colors. The giant bow bounced with her as she pranced up to me.

"This is for you." I reached out as she thrust it towards me. She pulled it back. "I'll carry it in for you." Her face scrunched. "Oh, you just look horrid."

She turned directly to Amy. "Hi, girlfriend. You okay after those two giant Margaritas? I told you Rafael's would hit the spot."

My eyes scanned from one to the other. "What?"

"I sat in the lobby for an hour while the room kept spinning, nurses and people heading this way and that," Amy said.

Jen scowled and her face puffed like she was going to pop.

"I didn't know you two got together." I said. Jen's mouth widened, her cheeks turning an irritated shade of red.

Klarisa planted a kiss on my cheek. I could feel the red lipstick streak as she parted slowly. I assume my flushed face hid the smear. "Of course," she said. "You were sleeping when I stopped by, so we two girls did lunch at Rafael's. Amy's a blast." She held the present with one arm and hugged Amy with the other. Amy nodded happily with a newly formed trust that made my stomach knot.

"This girl's naughty." Amy joked pointing to Klarisa.

Oh shit. I shook my head at Jen over Amy's shoulder. Jen set down one hospital bag and tightened her grip around the other. She wanted to swing the grey plastic bag at Klarisa. I could feel it.

Klarisa had an arrogant grin as her eyes landed on Jen. Amy

was oblivious to the fact that Jen was behind her.

Amy went on, "You know, I seldom drink, and I never have anything like Tequila, especially at lunch. This girl is persuasive." Amy put her arm around Klarisa. Jen steamed in the background.

"We gulped down two Margaritas and didn't pay for either of them. Klarisa used these two gentlemen-quarterly types to buy us drinks and pay for our lunch, though I don't remember eating much. We didn't stop laughing. She kept the boys at bay. Wouldn't let them join us at our table. They kept toasting us from their corner table. This girl gets more in an hour, batting her eyes, than most girls do their whole life."

Klarisa held up a hand for a high-five from Amy. A puzzled face held for three or so awkward seconds before Amy understood. She started to raise her arm, then pulled away quickly, not sure about locker-room comradeship. Klarisa appeared unfazed.

Silence ensued as eyes darted back and forth.

Jen's face turned demonic, though she faked a crinkled-nose grin when Amy turned around, mentioning that Jen should have been with them.

Jen and Klarisa having lunch? Yeah, that'd happen. "Why don't we go inside?"

Klarisa grabbed Amy by the arm and started for the door.

"Klarisa, Amy . . . why don't you help Jen with the bags?" I couldn't believe Jen was keeping her mouth shut.

They both turned. Amy took a step towards the trunk.

"Jen's a strong girl. She appears to have them covered," Klarisa said and grabbed Amy, pulling her forward. "We need to help get things ready for our favorite patient."

My dad opened the door. He had been peeking through a three-inch gap in the curtains, waiting for us with one hand ready on the knob.

Amy hesitantly followed Klarisa, but looked back at me, questioning what was happening.

"Mr. Parch, can you help your daughter with the bags?" asked Klarisa in her demanding yet flirty voice. I caught my dad checking the curve of her soft, bare shoulders.

Dad obliged. Jen mumbled what sounded like words from a locker room. He leaned in, saying something to Jen. She mumbled to him in a terse voice, he raised his hands in surrender, then picked up one of the bags and closed the trunk.

My eyes swept the house as I entered. It had been years— probably twenty or more had passed—since I was last inside. The rooms appeared smaller and exhausted. The house was tidy; everything in its place; but it smelled of musty, hidden dust and decades of worn age. The shelves and furniture were that of a man's place with a hint of womanly care buried deep on the shelves in aged nick-knacks and faded paint colors. For a moment I could see that young boy running through the house with a ball and his favorite Tonka truck, his mom scooting him outside with a broom at his heels.

Jen bumped me with the suitcase. "You're blocking the entrance." No post-hospital sympathy there.

I glanced back at her and moved out of the way. She stared at me with an almost evil smirk on her face. She put the suitcases down as if they were filled with concrete and exhaled loudly. Her irritated features changed completely. She began to giggle lightly. "Dad," she said, "Ben's in here remembering good times. You'd better grab your camera."

"I am not. This house has an odd feeling to it, like it's possessed. I'm just not sure I should venture any further."

"Admit it! You have some good memories here. I saw that look."

"I didn't have any look. You misread indigestion."

Dad peeked around Jen. "Is that true? You're having good memories?" Each word came out deliberately and expectantly. He stood a little straighter. A gaze I had never seen before came from eyes like those of a child at Christmas, instead of bloodshot and disappointed eyes.

"He is," Jen stated with her hands on her hips, "but he'll never admit it."

Walking away, I slowly made the trek up the stairs. Amy helped me from the front and Klarisa pushed my buns from the back.

A quick reversal sent Jen back to aggravation. With a spear in her voice she said, "Klarisa, thanks for your help, but we can manage from here on out."

TATTERED PORTRAIT

Klarisa squeezed my butt, pushing me further up the stairs.

My old room hadn't changed much: a single bed; unframed Disney characters dotting the walls; a tiny, empty desk; a kid's wooden folding chair slid under the desk; and one shelf with a 1960's model Corvair leaning haphazardly and missing one wheel. Amy opened the closet. It was stacked with boxes labeled by school and year. *That was odd.*

With all of us in the tiny room, I was claustrophobic. Amy opened the only window with a hard nudge to break the binding of age. The air felt good, the sunshine delightful. A thunderstorm of animosity rolled back and forth between Jen and Klarisa, darkening the room.

"This will be cozy. Right, Amy?" My voice sounded hollow and weak. The feud broke momentarily, as the two glanced at me. It didn't last. Jen took short, even breaths through clenched teeth. Klarisa smiled as if winning at a poker table.

"Considering your injuries, I'll probably sleep on the couch." Amy said hesitantly.

"You two could have some fun on that bed," said Klarisa. She winked at me a bit too obviously.

"Okay!" Jen broke in. "We need to let Ben get settled. I made a casserole earlier. I'll bring it by later tonight and the family—" she evil-eyed Klarisa, "can have a nice dinner together." She paused. "Alone."

My room was antiseptic clean. It smelled of spray cleaners and Clorox. Even the window sill was dustless. Amy leaned in, whispering, "I think your Dad has affectionately endured wife-wannabees as they helped him this week."

Dad laughed behind us. "I have a few prospects. No hurry though."

"You just want free maid service and a home-cooked meal now and then," Jen said. "Trust me; he won't be out buying rings any time soon. Dad strings them along, and they're too lonely to care."

"You make me sound like I'm using them."

"Duh, yeah."

"It's a give-and-take relationship. I give back as much as I receive."

With twinkling eyes, Klarisa asked, "Really! How much do they give, Mr. Parch?"

"Whatever." Jen twirled a finger above her head, raising eyebrows in my direction. "Anyway, you should be feeling right at home here. It even smells the same as your hospital room." Her nose crinkled.

I pulled the top blanket back as I sat on the bed and patted the sheets, saying, "Amy, this might solve all my childhood fantasies." My eyes raised a couple of times.

"I don't do that kind of child therapy, especially when the single bed has little green robots all over it. Yikes. I'm sleeping on the couch until you're better."

Everyone laughed.

Jen turned towards me. "Yeah, like you're ready for that."

I scooted everyone out with the backward flip of my fingers. They backed out, one at a time. The room still felt insignificant, but clean. Everyone clattered down the stairs except Amy, who stood in the doorway with eyes on me, thoughtful and radiating care.

"Anything you need, let me know," yelled Dad from the bottom of the stairs. His voice bounced off the stairwell walls. It sounded lifeless with a fringe of sincerity. I raised my eyes. Amy shook her finger at me. Her lips tightened.

I lay back on the bed and pretended to snore.

"Your sister's right. Sometimes it seems as if you never left puberty," said Amy.

I snored in horrid bleating sounds with great sucking noises in between until Amy stormed down the stairs after the others. After she left, I grabbed my throat with both hands, trying to subdue the pain I caused by being stupid. I wanted to scream, but the absurd pride of manhood left me chewing the pillow instead.

After the pain eased, I rolled carefully out of bed and opened the closet. A touch of anxiety filled my chest as I bent over between my three hanging shirts and peeked through the top of one of the boxes that were stacked neatly on the worn varnish of the floorboards. Surprised and pleased, I found my aunt had organized boxes of my homework. Artwork, math tests, and weekly spelling words were next to pictures of animals, a crayon-drawn color wheel, cut-out bears, and penguins. All my old school papers were neatly stacked, from elementary to early college papers.

I turned wrong and too quickly as I searched closer. My jaw sent a sharp spike from the bullet wound to a spot above my ear. I grabbed the bandage and held my position solid until the pain eased. My breathing returned to normal, though I concentrated on each breath.

Dad must have picked these up from Aunt Velora.

I remembered all those cardboard boxes having been in her garage. I kept telling her to recycle the damn paper or burn it before someone actually saw how pathetic I was. She ignored me. My stuff filled the top shelf of the garage, and Jen had the one under. I had kidded my aunt that if the tax man ever saw all that paper up there, they would definitely audit her.

I chuckled to myself as I thought about the shuffling of my homework from desk to desk at the IRS building as they searched for concealed money.

Why did my dad have these? Had he been through my papers? An uneasy satisfaction filled my chest.

Twenty minutes later I was downstairs, faking a smile in perfect control with an immobile neck. Rest was out of the question. Everyone appeared to be in the kitchen, laughing and passing around trays of cookies. The fragrance of fresh-brewed coffee and cinnamon stopped me in the hall. I listened to happy banter for a minute or two. Turning, I strolled into my father's "drunk room." Some might call it a den or an office, but all I remembered was water-marked tables and hidden bottles.

The desk was still there, but it was polished; and a stack of papers was neatly set an inch from the corner. As I approached, I noticed the shine. Several thick layers of polish had been applied. The lines of the dark oak came out as I'd never seen them before. A copper cup of pens and pencils waited expectantly. A maroon office chair was tucked partially under the desk. There was an end table with a lamp and a short stack of *Field and Stream* magazines fanned perfectly. My dad, the fisherman?

The bookcases that followed along the exterior walls of the room were tidy and dusted. Sun came through a vinegar-polished window. I tried to recall if I had ever noticed that window before as I scrunched my nose from the caustic odor. I remembered olive green drapes of some fabric that I always believed could stop a bullet. They never allowed light through, not even late-sunset afternoons on the west side of the house. He had replaced the drapes with thin macramé window coverings that were tightly pulled back against freshly painted trim. Lots of changes.

As I turned to walk out, something shiny caught my eye. The closer I got to the corner of the room, the more reflective lights twinkled like stars. "What the hell?" I muttered.

I bent down to make sure. Yep, it was broken glass, a pile of it, all dusty and cobwebbed. Partial labels of Stolichnaya Vodka, Johnny Walker Red, and Bacardi Rum were crumpled in the heap. Stains of syrupy liquids were aged so long that a hammer and chisel would be needed to clean them off. As I glanced up, I noticed dents and chunks taken out of the bookcase directly above. Bottle pieces lay on untouched shelves in the corner.

"You found my memorial."

Startled, I knew the voice well; it had always given me shudders. I didn't turn around. My chest seemed to collapse, and my face flushed. I felt like a sneak. I felt the usual fear creep over me.

"That's what happens when you finally give up a lifestyle. Some people nail cigarettes to a wall. I threw bottles at a bookcase. I'll be damned if anyone cleans or picks up or dusts that corner. I look at it every day as a reminder. It's the final burial ground of Lawrence D. Parch."

I turned. "A little dramatic, don't you think, Dad?" My eyes bored at him like he was nuts. I had somehow lost my fear.

"It captures a lot of the wildness and pain I endured before I stopped craving those bottles." He pointed to the corner. "I lay on the floor shaking and screaming for days, curling up in my own vomit, until my blessed sister found me and called an ambulance. I lived in a Florida rehab center for five months. I was your neighbor, and you didn't even know it."

"Where?"

"Jacksonville. At something called The Florida Palm Facility. It looked like beach condos and smelled like human waste, covered slightly with disinfectant." His whole body shuddered. "When I go, if I end up in hell, it will be The Florida Palm Facility. It was run by Neanderthals with online PHDs.

"The moment I came back home; I threw all the hidden bottles at the corner. The thought of ever going back there helped me quit—that, and discovering God. Your sweet aunt had already found most of them, emptied them, filled each halfway with water, and put them back in their hiding places. I swear I never even knew. She later told me it was just a precaution. I couldn't have a better sister, except the fact she forcibly shipped me off to the Florida boot camp of drunks. I can't understand how you can live there. Of course, the only time I spent out of the facility was with the Adavan Nazis."

Jen stuck her head in. "There you are. Checking out the glass shard shrine? Come eat; food's here."

Embarrassment defined my father's face. He had a hard time pulling his sight from the corner, and glanced back a few times as he walked out.

I felt like a Peeping Tom watching him.

We had a frozen casserole that Jen reheated, made of broccoli and noodles and cheese and hamburger. I was so hungry I slammed it down in seconds. Lunch went down my sore throat like barbed wire, but with six glasses of water and tiny moans, I successfully got it to my appreciative stomach. Afterward, I snuck upstairs; lay down on soft pillows in my old, barely used bed; and fell into a deep sleep.

I woke up to a note taped to my old desk:

> *I've gone with Jen and Velora.*
> *Be back later tonight.*
> *Go talk to your dad.*
> *Love, Amy*

I reread it and then glanced at the clock. I could hear someone downstairs putting away dishes, clinking glassware, and shutting cabinets. I turned toward the clock again. Still 3:05. The feeling of water storming over the sides of my boat and waves as high as a corporate insurance building washed over me. I pulled the sheets tight to my sides, crumpling them in my fists.

What did Amy mean by tonight? Surely no later than four o'clock. Why am I thinking four? I've never cared about stuff like that. I could feel the anxiety growing. *Damn, why do I care if Dad's the only one here?*

I could hear whistling downstairs. I sat up, trying to listen more closely.

Crap, it's Dad's voice. What's he doing whistling? It's unnerving.

I wanted to go downstairs and get a cup of coffee, but the blaring happiness wouldn't stop. Maybe he was trying to wake me up with clattering dishes and that incessant whistling. I have to recuperate and get back to my home in Florida. This is too much for one visit. Dad's a sober, happy Mormon who whistles like those damn dwarfs in Snow White. He is messing with me. I glanced back at the end table. The stupid clock hadn't moved— probably wasn't even plugged in.

Dad stopped whistling. The silence soothed me. I could hear him answer the door. I hoped the girls had arrived. I dangled my feet off the edge of the bed and started to get up. I stretched, and a sharp shot of pain slipped up my leg.

Klarisa bubbled into the room, stopped briefly to eye me over, and came barreling her womanhood directly at me.

"Still in your boxers. At least you were expecting me."

I jumped back into the bed, clunking my skull on the headboard and craning my neck so hard I saw shooting stars through closed eyelids. My breath almost returned to normal, then I felt her hand on my thigh. I brushed her hand away, searching for the bed covers. My face blushed, more from anger than anything else.

"Bennie, I have seen you in boxers before. Don't be so shy." A pout spread across her red lips. "Don't be embarrassed. I'll pick you up new ones." She pointed at my groin. "Did you buy those from the Amish?"

"Amy will be here any time now."

"I don't have a problem with Amy. She's my new BFF. Now your sister, on the other hand, scares the hell out of me. I cruised by and saw her car was gone, so I figured it was a good time to check on you." She patted me on the tummy.

150

TATTERED PORTRAIT

I kicked the sheets up toward me with my good toe and grabbed a corner, yanking them over my chest. It wasn't much of a barrier, but it made me feel better.

"Amy is with Jen. They'll be here shortly." As my words came out, Klarisa glanced at the note.

"It says tonight. That means six or seven." She stared at the clock, absently figuring things in her head. "It's barely past three."

"I don't think that clock's been plugged in for years."

"Well let's just figure we have three hours. What do you want to do?" She winked.

"I need coffee. You mind scooting off the bed for a minute so I can get up?"

Klarisa stood up smiling. It's hard to stay irritated at someone whose red lips and girly smells melted you into adolescent goo. Historical significance—that's all it was. We had a history. Sure, she looked fantastic, curved in all the right places with eyes you could swim through, but really, it was just past history. I started to get up with the sheet wrapped around me like a toga. She let out a sing-song laugh.

"I've never seen this modest side of you before. I like it. Coy is kind of attractive and stimulating."

I pulled on some denim pants so fast I danced one-legged in a circle with one foot in, the other out. My head pounded as biting pain shot down my back. My brain was spinning, so I sat down on the end of the bed and waited. Klarisa came over and began rubbing my back; as she stretched over my shoulders, her breasts rubbed softly against my cheeks.

"Hello!" came Amy's voice.

"What the hell?" said Jen.

I pushed Klarisa back, and her hands slid quickly up my spine. My face flushed. "I got dizzy."

"I'll bet you did," said Amy.

"Was that before or after Klarisa began nursing you?" Jen spat.

"We were just . . ." said Klarisa, her fists into her hips, elbows out.

She seemed to be holding back a grin. This wasn't going well. I took a breath, realizing I hadn't inhaled for what might have been minutes.

"You should leave," echoed both girls.

"But, Amy . . . ."

"Go!" Amy's voice was decisive and loud.

Dad poked his head in. "Anyone want coffee? I just made a new pot, and dear Miss Abbott just dropped off homemade cinnamon rolls." His smile faded, replaced by caution. He ran over his own feet trying to back out. His spine jabbed into the doorknob, and he let out a pained yelp.

Klarisa brushed by his side as she glanced back over her shoulder, giving me an innocent roll of eyes. We all listened to her heals clacking down the stairs. The front door slammed. Silence ensued.

I began rubbing my temples with the balls of my thumbs. The quiet was more painful than my throbbing bullet wounds. I tried to think, but I could pull up nothing more than a blank screen. Someone finally cleared her throat, and I glanced up.

Amy turned to Jen and Dad, saying, "Give us a minute." They left the room without a word, though I knew Jen was bursting with things to say. Instead, her top teeth clamped tightly on her bottom lip.

Amy turned around and closed the door. "That . . . ." She chewed absently on a nail for a few seconds. "What the hell was that?"

My throat constricted more than it already had been. I felt as if I had swallowed sand, as I stared at the shelf on the wall. In my mind I hadn't done anything except maybe enjoy Klarisa's attention too much. Yeah, that was bad.

"Klarisa came by as I was getting up to go downstairs for coffee. I moved too quickly and became dizzy with back pain. I sat back down, and Klarisa came over and began massaging my back. That's all." I paused as the air thickened. "I'm really not sure why she was massaging me." I watched Amy's intense eyes, they didn't even blink. Her deep tan face was pulled tight by the cords in her neck.

"It looked a lot like she was rubbing her breasts into your face." Amy crossed her arms tightly against her belly. Her posture was stern, almost condescending.

152

TATTERED PORTRAIT

I didn't say anything.

Amy came closer, lifting my head up by my ears. "Well?"

"I know, I know. She can be a bit overzealous." I thought Amy was going to pull my ears off. I wasn't about to complain.

"Overzealous? She was giving you a lap dance."

My ears were starting to ache, but I was afraid to pull away. Amy's grip was strong. Finally, she removed her fingers from my ears and slapped the top of my head.

"You were holding her waist."

"I was?"

Her eyes rolled.

"If I was, I didn't even know it. Really, my back is in so much pain." *Did that sound as stupid as I thought it did?* I cupped my ears in case she came at me again.

"Yeah, whatever. I'm sorry your back was hurting, but Klarisa is not a pain pill, and whatever was going on was definitely inappropriate." Her fists tightened by her side. "I just want to pop your head off." She made a horrific moaning sound.

"I'm sorry. I'm not even sure what all happened. I didn't invite her into the house or into my room. Ask Dad."

Why does Klarisa have to be so . . . Klarisa? She has always been a bomb waiting to go off. And I sit there and hold the damn bomb with the fuse lit and hope for confetti. My mind has never worked right since junior high. I could barely control my sentences when talking to her. One time, she walked over from her table to mine in the cafeteria. She looked like an angel. She asked me to hold my hand out, and she emptied her milk into my palm, then walked away while the girls at her table laughed as they mimicked the whole scene. I didn't wash my hand for the rest of the day. I smelled like sour milk by the time I arrived home from school. What a dweeb I'd been.

"You're deflecting the guilt towards your dad?" She shook her head, then a softer aspect relaxed her body. Amy's professional persona took over. She sat down by me, though hesitant.

I felt the top of my head getting slapped again. I didn't even move.

Grinning like a child caught in the don't-touch cupboard, I said, "I wasn't sure which angle to take. Seriously, I love you . . . I

153

want only you. Klarisa is an aggressive presence, and I admit she pulls me into her little games. I am a stupid male that likes the attention, even though I know I shouldn't. I'm sorry, I'm sorry, I'm sorry." My hands formed a teepee as I banged them against my chin lightly.

"Stupid male is right. You are all pathetic. I swear most of you carry your brain in an appendage. I have to deal with this crap in sessions. I don't need it in my real life." She gave a devilish laugh. "Why do I care about you so much? Actually, right now I want to kick you where it hurts and fly back to Florida by myself."

We stared at each other for several minutes without a word. Her eyes stuck on mine, but hers focused deep, towards the back of my skull. I started several times to say something. She put her index finger to her lips and glared. It felt like the hair on the back of my head was singed and dropping off in patches.

Amy stood up, motioning me to do the same. She wrapped her arms around my neck as I stood up. We held each other for several minutes. Pain shot down my spine and radiated out to my shoulders, but I said nothing. She whispered in my ear, "I have a lunch date with Klarisa tomorrow. I think I'll pass." As she released her embrace, she slapped my head again.

I knew this wasn't over. She needed time to organize the facts psychologically, then she'll sit down and talk to me like I was a client. We'd been through similar face-offs before, but nothing this bad. I had never before seen more wrinkles and redness in her face. This one was costly. I knew she wouldn't demand that I never see Klarisa again. That wasn't her style. Of course, I'd better never be alone with her again, or those slaps would come with a hatchet.

I finally drank my coffee. Jen and Dad fidgeted at the table. They wanted to ask us questions, but knew better. Jen crinkled her nose at me. It wasn't affectionate, but I smiled. Amy held my hand under the table, slowly and absently twisting her neck, and tightened the grip on my fingers ever so often as thoughts crossed her mind.

At least it was a really good cup of coffee.

Chapter 17

I woke up relaxed and wound around Amy. The sheets twisted like a giant rope off to one side. I kissed Amy's head and squirreled around, trying to get upright. Her sleep purr reminded me of Florida and a bed that was wider than a kitchen counter. As I got up to empty my bladder, her arms and legs stretched to the outer edges of the mattress.

The cold water felt invigorating on my face, so I kept splashing more on. I brushed my teeth, then went soundlessly back to the room of childhood nightmares and sat on the wooden desk chair. The silly smile on my face was one of contentment and absurdity.

Through the open window, the smell of the neighbor's bacon seemed to relax me a notch more. I watched Amy's chest rise and drop with each breath. She could sleep better than anyone I knew. Her lithe, full body rarely changed position. She always lay on her right side with the pillow crumpled into a ball and her legs offset enough to look like she was running. I was surprised she slept all night cuddled up with me. That was something she used sparingly. Cuddling was only after sex, and lasted only twenty minutes at the most—then she'd bunch up her pillow to a perfect sphere and take her jogging pose, which lasted until morning. It worked for me.

I watched her another five minutes, then followed the pleasant smell of breakfast and the morning kitchen sounds. I could hear the sizzle of something frying as I stepped lightly down the stairs. My neck was stiff, and I was limping with renewed pain. Post-coital affliction, I assumed, and grinned with each step.

The aroma of bread dough hit my nostrils as I stepped into the kitchen. Dad was frying scones. A plate piled high sat next to him. It was the first time I'd ever seen him in front of a stove.

"Dad, I love the apron."

He scowled as he set the plate of fried bread on the table.

Jen and Albert were sitting around the well-used coffee table. To some, the table would be an antique. To me it was plain junk, scratched until the surface had more dull spots than shine. The scones were a pleasant centerpiece.

"Where's Amy?" asked Jen.

I pointed my index finger upstairs.

"Are you going to tell us what happened after Klarisa was kicked out?" She bunched up her nose, and her mouth tightened as if she'd swallowed a lemon when she said "Klarisa."

"No."

"I'm your sister."

"And?"

"Look, Ben," she squinted, "I need to know why Amy would forgive you so quickly. She saw what I saw. You were like the king of a whorehouse."

"Is there any more sugar?" I began fumbling through cupboards. Albert watched his feet stay put.

"Top left," said Dad as he yanked the apron off and sat down.

"Ahhh."

"Forget the damn sugar. Tell us about last night."

I watched Albert reach over and grab a scone. He lathered enough butter on it to clog his arteries for a month. Jen absently pushed the honey towards him.

"You know I can't drink coffee without sugar. Is there any Tylenol down here? I don't want to run back upstairs. My neck won't quit throbbing, and my ankle kills me with each step."

Jen stood up suddenly, startling Albert. "Benjamin Parch . . . ."

"What's up with the yelling?" I heard Amy say from the doorway. She stretched her arms high while everyone stared at her. She wore a Tampa University sweatshirt and my baggy running shorts. "I smell coffee and scones. Wow, I may just stay another week."

156

She turned to Jen. "Why are you yelling at Ben? What did I miss?"

She was wonderful—messy hair, smudged makeup—and I gazed, realizing how much I cared about her. I sighed and wondered what that was all about.

"Ben's just hard of hearing. I was trying to tell him where the Tylenol is."

"Yeah, my sister's excitable in the morning. Isn't that right, Albert?"

Albert peeked up at Jen, then his eyes found his shoes again.

"I'll grab it from upstairs," said Jen.

The kitchen was quiet as we all sipped coffee while Dad made more scones and bacon. The room actually smelled like a home. Aunt Velora slipped in just as the next heap of fried dough hit the table. She pulled up a chair, and Amy poured her some coffee. I caught a whiff of a flowery plant smell as Aunt Velora leaned over and kissed my cheek. The daze in her facial movements made me laugh out loud. She was stoned.

I planned a full schedule—reading my assistant, Simon's paper on jet propulsion of para larval octopuses in planktonic movement, checking stats from my Florida lab, visiting Dr. Anders this afternoon for an evaluation, and hopefully getting some alone time with Amy. I listened as Jen recited her ideas for my day. I scrunched up my face and the grip on my fork bent the tines. Amy mouthed, "Don't worry."

"Ben has a lot to catch up on with his associates back in Florida, and he needs rest. Perhaps we'd better play it by ear for today," said Amy.

Jen sunk like she had lost all her air as she folded down towards the table. Albert actually seemed happy. Jen glanced back and forth between me and Amy and waited for me to say something—preferably something to do with everyone following her "suggestions," as she would call them. I sealed my mouth. Her face stayed sour.

After an unbearable thirty seconds of silence, Aunt Velora said, "We need to let Ben heal. I'm sure he's stressed by not being able to return to work."

Jen smiled. "Yeah, watching eight-legged sea creatures must

be quite demanding. Now that's responsibility."

"Eight-armed," I said.

"Whatever, but later on we're having a barbeque at my place." She waited a couple of beats with a scrunched forehead. "And don't give me THAT look."

***

That evening, I was staring at the ceiling in a quiet room with the door closed. Elation swelled my chest, and a feel-good smile spread that couldn't be wiped off my face. I let the silence roll over me for a few minutes then picked up my cell and called the lab. Anthony answered. It seemed the night crew was getting squirted by Goofy, my temperamental octopus, as they checked on her throughout the late evening. She didn't like the flashlight being shined on her when she slept. Everything else was good, except the last shipment of crustaceans had been delayed. Anthony worked it out with another lab that filled in with two hundred cuttlefish. I hung up wishing I was back home in real sunshine and humidity. *Damn, I miss thick air.*

Bunching up the pillows, my mind thought about initiating another study. Goofy's squirting after being awakened made me think of it. Scientists have always questioned if octopuses sleep with alternating halves of their brain, as do birds and whales. If she was waking that easily, perhaps she's only half asleep. Maybe I could use subdued light that turned on and off a couple of times a night, or maybe I could experiment with sound. I fell asleep somewhere between setting up an experiment and writing for a grant, as ideas flowed lazily through my mind.

The next morning, I woke up to the scent of hot coffee and whispering between Dad and Amy, who had come to my bedroom, I guess to check on me again. I feigned sleep and listened for a while, which was hard, because the coffee seduced me into slightly opening one eye. I watched Amy's throat bob as the liquid slid down under her narrow, curved chin. She almost caught me as she glanced over, laughing about something unintelligible Dad had said. It was kind of upsetting to watch her having such a good time with the man who had embarrassed and humiliated Jen and me as far back as I could remember.

Amy and Dad were quite at ease with each other—another conspiracy. His voice seemed almost pleasant. In my mind, I growled like a rabid dog. They kept laughing as I heard my name mentioned more than once. This had to end.

Sitting up quickly, I asked for a cup of coffee. Actually, it was more of a demand—and I could tell from their reaction that my voice was rough and sharp.

Rolling her brown eyes and crinkling her forehead, Amy said, "Good morning to you too, Mr. Petulance."

"Sorry—I'll get up, and you can have coffee downstairs."

Dad walked out without saying anything.

"You okay?" asked Amy. "This morning and last night you have taken rudeness to a new level. What's up?"

"This room, I guess. And slow healing."

"You mean this house and your dad?"

"Well, that too."

"Let's get you some coffee. My plane leaves at three, so you'd better get up if you want to see me. Work on the attitude, okay? I'm so tired of you and your dad's subtle nothings left unsaid. When you get back, we're going to have to get you into some regular therapy; I personally know someone with a degree and everything." She winked and gripped my shoulder.

"Does that mean sex?"

Amy shook her head. "Hardly, but it may not be entirely out of the question."

"For that, I might learn to smile at the table and ask Dad to pass the pepper."

"There's an expression people try sometimes, and they put feeling into it: 'How are you doing today?' You should try it on your father."

"I thought we were doing well with the head nods and planned avoidance."

"Do this for me and actually mean it. Larry is a good man."

"Larry? I liked it better when he was Mr. Parch."

She pinched me hard on my upper arm. My teeth gritted, and I rolled my elbow to check the damage.

"Okay, okay, I'll try."

Chapter 18

After Amy left, the house was quiet. I sat watching a cup of coffee with its steam rising warmly to my face. My body was more liquid than anything with structure, and I felt brain dead and floating. A loud noise sparked me out of my self-induced coma. Looking up, I noticed Dad sitting across from me. He pulled his chair across the linoleum, scooting his belly closer to the table. We both cleared our throats at the same time. I waited for him to speak. He was waiting for me. Out of my peripheral vision, I watched him stare at a spot on the white wall, as I rubbed the tabletop with my index finger. A minute, then another went by. I almost felt relief when the fridge compressor turned on.

Dad cleared his throat again, this time so hard I checked to see if he had hurled.

"How about we go get a bite to eat at Sid's?" he said. "I have a few things to talk about, and this empty, silent house is giving me the creeps."

"Wow, Sid's is still there? He was probably seventy when I was a teen. I assume someone else cooks the grits and fries in the grease?"

"His daughter runs it now. His wife gave birth to only girls, so when his fourth daughter came, he named her Sidney. She's twenty-two, every bit as moody as he was, and almost as tall."

"Have the same greasy burgers and hand-cut fries?"

"Of course; they still haven't heard of cholesterol. She did add a Cobb salad to the menu a year ago. I doubt anyone's ever ordered it."

TATTERED PORTRAIT

"I'm in. Let me change and clean up a bit, and we'll go." I almost sounded excited. It was unsettling. I stood up from the chair quickly. The soreness in my leg and back stopped my breathing for a count or two. I went slower. Luckily, Dad hadn't noticed.

"With those old booths, I'm not sure cleaning up would save you."

We both laughed. I headed up the stairs with a bounce in my step; I wasn't sure why. When I entered the room, depression hit me. *What am I doing? What does Dad want to talk about? I need Jen here. I want to see Amy's tilted smile.*

***

As we pulled up to Sid's, I read the signs in the windows. They were all in two-tone markers on see-through paper. The sun had yellowed the edges. Two eggs, ham and hash browns, $5.99; BLT and fries, $7.99; stack of pancakes with scrambled eggs and sausage, $7.99; roast beef, potatoes and gravy after four p.m., $12.99. A new roof had recently been done; I could smell the tar as we got out of the car. It was the only improvement I could see on the worn façade. There was always a comfortable feeling at Sid's. Gladness filled my chest as we walked in, and I listened to that same volume of conversation from years ago, loud and forceful.

Then the thought hit, *this may be the first time I've ever been out to lunch with just Dad.* I began hyperventilating.

A stand-up sign on a black pole greeted us: "What are you waiting for? Seat yourself." The message was the same as when I was a teen, only back then it was hand-printed on a blackboard behind the register. I chuckled as we searched the high-backed booths. Some time ago the room had been expanded into the old Gail's Beauty Parlor that resided next door. We found a booth just before the stained-trim opening into the newer-looking expansion. The table and seats were still wet from the two-second sanitizing. I sat down anyway. Dad wiped his side with a paper napkin.

We both inspected the place in admiration. A large sign above the opening next to us read, "We don't count calories, just tips." Sid was always big on sayings. Sid Jr. seemed to be carrying on the tradition.

A waitress with raccoon eyes headed our way with determination and two cups of coffee on a tray. The cups were set down in front of us without our ever ordering them. I glanced at Dad, puzzled. He nodded his head and smiled. "Menu?" she asked. "Oh damn, Vina missed a spot." She bent down and stared at the tabletop. Her black crucifix hit the edge of the table. She stood up and rubbed at the spot with her stained apron. Smiling, she reached into a pocket on the wall and plopped down menus in front of us, then turned to walk away.

"Could I get a water?" I asked timorously.

She turned back to us, her pupils constricting above the scowl on her face. She stood as if ready to say something. Her lips slightly opened, then she turned to the kitchen and walked away.

"I take it water isn't on the menu?"

Dad hid a smirk under his hand, mumbling, "There are rules here I'll never understand."

She came back with my water and stood silently, waiting with pad and pen in hand. I ordered a Sid Burger. Dad asked for the soup of the day, which was minestrone.

After a few more minutes of father-son talk, which amounted to a few words dangling between long periods of soundless avoidant gazing, the waitress brought our lunch. I smiled. The smile wasn't returned.

We listened to the two of us chew and plates clack as tables were cleared. Dad finished the last slurp of soup. I dabbed my mouth with the napkin enough times I worried about a rash. As I glanced at my father—not straight on, but covertly—I thought about the picture. That happiness had morphed so much; I wasn't sure we even had blood ties anymore. *Could genetics dissolve with age and distance?*

"So, without discussing the weather, I believe you wanted to talk to me?"

We both glanced at the waitress eyeballing our table. She had already asked us twice about dessert. We declined both times. Dad's eyes met mine and stayed there. I swallowed, hoping he would look away first.

"Your mother is living 30 minutes from here in Bountiful." He waited to see if this affected me. His eyes kept blinking as if an eyelash had fallen in.

I thought over all my illusions about my mom. They swam in and out of focus. I knew so little about her except for the few pictures of her and my distorted imagination. I tried to form a picture of her from the family portrait. I needed to see it again. *Where was it?*

"She has two children, your half-brother and half-sister. She also has a husband with a pension from the military, and I understand he now teaches school at a private college downtown, one of those business schools that advertises on billboards and TV commercials."

I noticed my mouth was open. It took a while to figure out how to shut it. Wiping slobber from the corner of my mouth, I tried to speak. No words seemed to form. I shook my head, stared at my father, and shook my head again.

Dad nodded. "Yeah, I assumed she was in Iceland, or maybe Texas, something like that."

I thought about the picture again. Now, she would be with different children and a different husband. I hadn't thought about her for so long—at least not until I saw that smile and those loving eyes in the picture. It didn't make any sense to me. She truly loved us at one time. But she had left.

"How do you know?" I asked.

"We've talked. Actually, we've spoken several times in the last three years. I don't hold anything against her anymore. I was a drunk with a mean mouth. She had good reason to leave." He stared out the window. "And good reason to stay away."

"You've talked?"

"Well, she found out I've been sober—her and that neighbor with short skirts, too much rump, and a head the size of a prize pumpkin." Dad bit his lower lip and dropped his eyebrows. "What's her name?"

"Mrs. Beanful?"

"That's it, Joyce Beanful. Anyway, Joyce and Anna have been sending letters to each other for years. They were coffee buddies every morning before she left me. I'm not surprised they stayed friendly. I see Joyce at church on Sundays since her husband died. She never let on a bit, but she told your mom I

changed my ways. It was kinda nice talking to your mom, instead
of about her. I've been told I have a lot of anger." Dad stared at the
table and used his napkin to wipe up a small glob of spilled soup.
He drew a long breath. "She seems happy. Even now, she has the
same beautiful lips and rosy cheeks," he paused, "only brighter."

I didn't say anything. My mouth kept opening, and I tried to
consciously shut it several times. *Mom and Mrs. Beanful? Wow! I
think I talked to her at Aunt Velora's party. She actually still
knows Mom?*

"Anna, she—I mean your mother—asked a lot of questions
about you and your sister. Everything I told her seemed to cause
her to swell with pride."

"Does Jen know?"

"Not yet. I'll talk to her tonight."

My mind bounced from elated to irritated. My heart was
trying to pump itself out of my chest. My palms were so wet I
could drink from them. "Why didn't she call me? Why didn't she
come?"

"Her option."

I never thought of Dad as someone who would listen to
anyone. My mom hadn't seen me in 30 years. And I was holding
this against Dad. My mind already had a thousand basketfuls of
stuff I held against him. I felt bad adding more. It wasn't logical.
My thoughts were drowned in emotions, as the dam broke and the
spate carried me to new and unwanted places. My palm wiped
tears from my eyes as nonchalantly as possible. I inhaled strong
breaths through my mouth, letting the air out through pursed lips as
if blowing up a balloon.

"Does—she want—to see us?" As soon as the words came
out, I wasn't sure I wanted to know.

Dad raised his palms and cocked his head to the side.

Putting my elbows on the table, I rubbed my temples.
Nothing was said for a full minute or two. I was actually glad we
were in a public place. I wanted to scream at myself, at Dad, at a
mom who abandoned us, at Sid's, at my sister, and even the stupid
spoon I kept stirring in my cold coffee.

"Does Aunt Velora know?

"Your mom's more afraid of her than anyone. She especially

didn't want her to know she was anywhere near striking distance."

I took in a breath that flowed like fire into my lungs. My cheeks heated. "She has kids?"

"Yeah, one 19, a boy, and a 23-year-old girl. From the picture she showed me, they both look a bit like you did at that age—homely and introverted." He laughed; I didn't.

"No, the girl's all smiles and beauty—smart, too. Anna said she was valedictorian at Viewmont High and now vacillates between pre-med and geology at the university. Her name's Autumn or Summer, one of those season names so popular a few years back. The boy is named Adam, like the first man. He works with a landscaper right now, and Anna's hoping he'll go to college next quarter. She says he won state at tennis in high school. Anyway, that's about as much as I know."

I took a sip of my cold coffee, then regretted it. I held it up for the waitress. She still didn't like me, but she obliged after I poured the remainder into a water glass. She grabbed the water glass as if I were a vagrant passed out on her porch. "I'm not making any friends here." I reached for the check. Dad slapped my hand and grabbed it, ripping off a corner.

After drinking four cups of coffee, receiving life-alternating news, and spending time alone with Dad, I was exhausted, but I wanted to talk to Jen. "Can we stop at Jen's? I want her to know about this immediately."

Dad said nothing. He just headed towards Jen's house.

Chapter 19

Sitting in Jen's kitchen, Dad started into the whereabouts of Mom. My sister turned crimson and seemed to be holding her breath. I added my thoughts in a few places. Jen said nothing, her forearms tight as her fists kept pushing into the kitchen table.

When we finished and silence ensued, Jen said, "You want some pie?"

We kept staring at our placemats, as if for wisdom.

She got up, grabbed a fresh cherry pie from under a clean dishtowel, and cut two pieces. She put the pieces of pie on plates and placed them in front of Dad and me. I was stumped. She gave us both a look, so like obedient children we began eating. Nothing was uttered. The only sounds were forks clinking and a few uttered sounds of appreciation.

We left after eating the pie, saying our good-byes, I gave Jen a hug. Her arms stayed at her sides.

On the drive to Dad's, he said, "She needs to process."

"Yeah, that was almost spooky."

***

I woke up to someone patting my arm with substantial force and repeating my name. My eyelids felt glued together. Next, my forehead was getting tapped. I glanced through thickened eyelashes and sleep sand at a dark, blurred object. A light turned on by the bed. I squinted and began swatting the air in front of me. My cheeks pulled up tight to my eyes, wishing her away.

"Ben . . . Ben . . . ," escalated in repetitive rhythm. I hoped it was a dream. I rolled over. She pinched my nose shut and caused me to gasp for air. My own bitter morning breath broke the barrier, and I opened my eyes. Jen stared down. She scooted me to the far side of the bed with rapid backhand motions. As I moved, I cursed at my wounds. They didn't want to wake up either. I pressed my cell phone to life, grinding my teeth as I noticed the time through weighted eyelids.

"Jen, it's two in the morning. What the hell are you doing here?"

She appeared hurt momentarily, then laughed and clapped her hands, as if I said the funniest thing ever.

"We have a BROTHER AND SISTER!"

I inched myself up, remained silent. My mouth felt pasty and dry.

"Yeah, I guess we do," I said with irritation.

"We need to go see them."

"Two in the morning's a bit early for a family reunion." I cocked my head. "Actually, it's not a reunion if we haven't ever met them. Is it?"

"WE HAVE A BROTHER AND SISTER!"

"You mentioned that. And be quiet. Dad's sleeping, which is what we should be doing. Why are you up so early?"

"Don't you think this is exciting?"

"That our missing mother lives so close by and has another family?" My tone was sarcastic.

"I don't give a shit about Mom," Jen said. "She left us. She walked out, leaving a drunk to take care of us. I want to meet my brother and sister."

"Stop. They have only Mom's blood, unless Dad didn't tell us everything." I laughed. Jen ignored me.

"We're going to visit them all the time. At least once we meet them. Who wouldn't want a big brother and sister? This is incredible."

"Dad was right. You had to process."

"What?"

"Never mind. I suggest we get some sleep and then plan a day in the future to go introduce ourselves."

"We can't sleep after this kind of news. We need to plan it now. You think they're up by five or six?"

"Jen, nobody's up by five or six. You're going to freak them out. You need to calm down."

"I want to take my sister shopping for dresses." Her eyes bulged so far I cupped my hands in case I had to catch one of the little suckers. "I wonder if they've seen the zoo? It's a cool zoo. All those giraffes walking around . . . and the penguins—you remember the penguins?"

"Slow down, Sis. They ARE fully grown. They're probably more interested in Starbucks and Rihanna concerts than two 'old' people claiming to be relatives. Can you imagine a couple of goofy strangers hugging them and calling them our brother and sister? It's insane."

"I am neither goofy nor insane." She pointed her finger against me and pressed deep into my rib cage.

I let out an odd sound, like a deflating balloon.

"You're probably right, but maybe they know about us and are as excited as I am about a meeting." She paused. I could see the gears grinding behind intense eyes. "Okay! Let's make a plan."

I turned my cell on and held it out to her. "It's now 2:30 in the morning."

"Great. We'll have all the time we need to figure this out by morning. How do you think we should approach them?"

"Jen," I said a little too loudly. "Let's sleep on it. I know you're wired to the hilt, but I need rest—preferably eight hours of it. Remember the mall, gunshots, my rehabilitation, you caring for your favorite brother? People don't do things at two in the morning unless it's illegal and sirens are going off."

"What about nurses, and those people behind counters selling beer and potato chips at all-night markets, and cops? We used to do all-nighters in high school up at Murphy's Lake. Get a little adventure in your life."

"Being shot by a crazed gunman was all the adventure my body can handle for this year." I stuffed my face into the pillow. I pulled a muscle on healing tissue, and became very still with a tight grimace on my face.

Jen laughed, until I raised my head up, searching for a

Lortab. "You don't look so well."

I chugged the pill down with stale, warm Seven-Up.

"Okay, I'll be back at eight. You get some rest. You really look horrid."

***

I smelled coffee just before I heard Jen whisper in my ear, "I'm back."

Jen made Dad, Albert and me breakfast. Actually, she poured milk over our cereal and sliced up a couple of oranges. Dad tried to talk Jen out of running over unannounced to our mother's house, but she shook her head and gave him a string of no's. I was feeling surprisingly better, so I ignored the Tylenol bottle Jen pounded down in front of my bowl. She kept whistling. Dad and I exchanged weary glances. I groaned inside as I glanced at the wall clock, which read 7:35.

The front door opened, and Aunt Velora came into the kitchen. "How's the patient?"

"I'm feeling incredible."

Aunt Velora raised her eyes at Jen.

"So he says. He went through a hard night. He was irritable and in pain. He probably needs more rest, but this morning he seems great."

"You need verification from my sister?"

"No, it's just nice to get a second opinion." She winked at Jen.

I chewed on an orange slice. Jen told Aunt Velora all about our mother and our new brother and sister. Aunt Velora always bit her bottom lip at any mention of our mother, and this time was no different. A couple of expletives squeezed out between her clenched teeth. Jen kept smiling and talking with the excitement of a kid blowing out candles on a birthday cake.

My aunt wanted to go with us to Mom's house. Dad forbade it, his arms crossed hard across his belly. Jen said a strict "No." I grinned a tiny bit at the thought of Aunt Velora and Mom fighting in the front yard. I didn't want my mom hurt, really, just knocked around a little—maybe a touch of blood, nothing major. My money

169

was obviously on Aunt Velora, even with her cancer.

I wasn't quite ready for forgiveness yet. Uneasiness spread through me, my thoughts about Mom's disappearance twisted my stomach. I tried to dismiss them, but it didn't work; they were already out there on a platter of bestowed guilt.

It was decided that Jen and I would go to the door, while Dad kept Aunt Velora company in the back seat. I hadn't noticed Albert until we were leaving. He mumbled something into Jen's shoulder about dropping him off at their house. She told him to stay at Dad's. Dropping to the couch, he seemed to lose all bone structure.

Dad said, "Remote's on the recliner."

Albert grinned as if this was the highlight of his day.

***

Each of us held our breath as Jen's car slowed and we scanned street signs. Pulling into the neighborhood, I instinctively knew which house was my mother's; of course, the white house numbers on the mailbox helped. An older Subaru sat in the driveway. It was sun-faded blue with a crunched rear fender. A man and a tall boy were hunched under the open hood. The sun reflected off the rear window, blinding us for a few seconds. Passing the house, we wound through some unknown streets so we could make another pass. The man was explaining something to the boy, using his hands and fingers as if demonstrating the workings of a combustion engine. The boy was nodding with a full head of long hair—curly, not straight like mine.

Is that them?

At my insistence, we parked across the street. Relief passed over our faces as Jen pulled to the curb with a jolt. She paid more attention to the two men than to driving. We bore up a stakeout as the four of us watched the father and son work on the Subaru. All of us looked like zoo chimps as we peered through the glass. I leaned hard on the armrest. I could feel Jen's breath against my neck. I wondered if my mom would peek out the drapes or something. My eyes kept searching the house. The door remained shut. The curtains didn't move.

After ten minutes of mechanic awe, I said, "Should we go

talk to them?"

We all argued about it in whispers for a while as if anyone could hear us with the windows up. Suddenly, the father noticed us and seemed to ask his son something. The son leaned around the hood and gave us a puzzled glance. They both disappeared behind the Subaru. We fought over leaving or staying, keeping our voices low. Tension escalated as a minute passed, then another.

A neighbor to the east who was hosing off his driveway gave us a suspicious glare. He glanced between us and his house with uncertainty.

The father and son both peered from around the edge of the raised hood again, and all of us scrunched down into the seats. I felt the annoyance of their gaze.

Dad kept mumbling, "Let's get out of here."

Aunt Velora said, "Just act natural." She clapped her hands, "Just act natural."

"This is ridiculous," I finally said. I wasn't about to get interrogated by the police again for loitering. My right hand pushed down hard on the door latch, and I slid my sore leg carefully to the asphalt. I grabbed the cane Jen bought me. I wasn't sure I actually needed it, but it might help with sympathy when they saw someone walk from the felonious car with a cane.

Jen grabbed me, pulling by my shirttail. A voice sounding like that of a little, scared child whined, "Are you sure?" Her eyes widened, her mouth shaped in an O. It was the Jen from years ago—an unsure young girl wanting her brother's hand and reassuring voice. I hadn't seen her like that in forever.

"C'mon, it'll be fine." My voice had an unstable edge to it.

We both stood outside her SUV, gaining strength from each other. I noticed the neighbor run into his house. The water was still running down the driveway. Holding hands, we walked towards the Subaru as two foreheads and four eyes watched us from the hood.

"How are you?" I asked.

Jen nudged me in the ribs, as if I'd just uttered the stupidest thing ever. I opened my palms, giving her a you-try-doing-better look. The father came around the car, followed by his son. They appeared to be the younger and older versions of each other—same wavy dark hair, jutting noses, bony chins, and angled stance.

I pasted on a grin that almost tore open my cheeks as I walked toward them. They smiled back, but their lips betrayed a touch of worry. The father's chest swelled and his shoulders tucked back as if he were headed for a confrontation.

"I'm Ben, and this is my sister, Jennifer."

"And the two in the car?" The father had an announcer's voice with a rhythm to it, very strong and low.

"That's my aunt and father in the back seat, fidgeting like disciplined children," I chuckled.

He relaxed his shoulders and laughed. "You always make them stay in the car?"

"No, just this time."

My sister, the one who usually took control of everything and everyone, remained silent but kept quietly clearing her throat. It was borderline annoying, though I felt sorry for her. She was so excited driving over. Her balloon deflated as soon as we left the safety of the car, though. I wondered what would have happened at 2:30 in the morning.

The father wiped his palms on worn corduroy pants and held his hand out. Suspicion turned to a harmless appraisal. "I'm Parley Anderton, and this is my boy, Adam."

Adam nodded his head. His bangs fell down over one eye.

They both smelled of grease, gas, and some kind of potent cleaner.

We shook hands. Good grip, firm and military. Then he shook Jen's hand. She bowed her head, glancing back at Adam. Adam kept his position behind the fender and nodded again.

A faint smell of cut grass and automotive grease flowed through my nose as silence settled. Parley and Adam waited for me to talk. We listened to birds chatter in a half-dead tree.

"We're trying to locate Anna, and we didn't know her married name, I assume it would be Anderton?"

This seemed to shake him a bit. "Anna's my wife's name. Why would you want her?" Suspicion with a hint of curiosity crossed his face.

Adam leaned forward.

My neck tightened and I kicked at the cement driveway for a

few seconds. "She was our mom—or she is our mom, I guess."

Both father's and son's jaws opened like broken hinges. Their stature seemed to diminish. I watched Parley glance back at Adam. The silence was so heavy that I struggled to get air to my lungs. Jen giggled. I turned and gave her a shake of my head. I could tell she was hurt. She wasn't sure what to do.

"You're here from Italy?" asked Parley.

Puzzled, I turned back to Jen. She returned my gaze.

"Italy?" I asked.

"Anna told me she had children in Italy. I don't recall the names, but they could have been Ben and Jen. Actually, Jennifer sounds familiar." His head nodded excitedly. "Your father died, I thought?" He pointed to the car. "So, who's that?"

"That's my dad."

The four of us stared at each other. I watched tears form around the edges of Adam's eyes. He shut the car hood and scrambled into the house. His dad twisted his body and watched his son's movements. He turned back around and after a moment said, "He's had a rough time this last couple of weeks. We all have. How'd you find out?"

"Mom talked to our dad. He just barely told us," I said.

"Told you?" Parley's eyes opened wide.

"Yeah, about her living here and having a husband and two kids."

"Where is she?" Jen's voice bubbled out like an excited teen.

Parley rubbed his forehead in tiny circles with his fingertips; the front edge of his tongue swiped back and forth along his upper lip.

We waited.

"I'm so sorry." A pause. "She passed away a week ago Tuesday." His eyes stared at us, dark and gloomy.

A catch hung in my throat.

"What the . . ." came Jen's voice, seeming so distant and soft that it merely hung in the air.

"It was sudden. She had a brain tumor." His eyes closed for a moment. When they opened, a sad, wet gloss reflected the light as he blinked. His cheeks flushed. "We didn't know. She kept it from us until two days before, when her face went numb on one side, and she collapsed. The ambulance arrived just before she lost consciousness the second time. Adam and Summer were here for dinner. We were about to walk out the door when she dropped to the carpet. It was chaos. We all stood in shock."

Parley's face and hands trembled, as if he was reliving it all over again. Tears began flowing.

I felt like an intruder, listening to the account of my own mom's death. I glanced back at Dad and Aunt Velora. My head swayed mechanically. They returned expectant and puzzled contemplation. I held up a finger, letting them know to give us a minute. My aunt's face became petulant as she sat imprisoned inside the car. Turning back to Parley, I couldn't think of anything to say, even if my throat would have let me.

"We didn't know what to do," he repeated, staring off into some unknown distance.

Jen stood sobbing at my side. I put my arm around her, and she nuzzled in. I braced myself. Jen gazed up at me with a look I hadn't seen since our mom left all those years ago. I patted her on the back.

Parley's chest expanded, and he straightened up, his cheeks now red and shiny. "I still don't understand why she thought she had to spare us. Anna knew about the tumor for months and didn't tell us until she lay helpless on the floor." His hands tented, and he bounced them against his lips. The sound of air rustled between his fingers for a time. "Adam took it the hardest. It seemed to have knocked him down deep. All he does is watch TV or sleep. He barely eats. Today's the first time I've gotten him outside."

He stopped. "I'm sorry. It must be hard for you too. I'm just babbling with no thought of the two of you. I can't believe you two didn't even know. It was such a lovely funeral." He stared off into the distance as tears carefully streaked his face.

"You came to see her. C'mon in the house and have some ice tea. I'm sorry. Sorry, I keep saying I'm sorry. Things have been tough."

I peered back at Jen's car. "Give me a minute to talk to my aunt and Dad." *How can you hate your parents so badly, yet feel so sorry for them and miss them at the same time?*

"Invite them in too. I think I have some homemade donut

rounds the neighbor made."

I left Jen and walked back to the car. Dad absorbed the news hard in his own way. He couldn't speak. He sat there staring at me as if I were a mugger.

After several minutes, he said, "Let me sit here a bit longer."

My aunt put her arm around him and shooed me away with the back of her hand.

Jen and Parley had waited for me on the driveway without acknowledging their own existence or each other's.

I broke through the barrier with a loud, "Okay."

The house was pleasant and neat, showing signs of living, with quiet sunlight reflecting the brightness of the hardwood floor. I noticed an old wooden stereo, more ornamental than usable. It held three pictures. Two sat guard on the ends with photos of family, one younger, one more recent. In the center was an outdoor photo of my mom, smiling and healthy. I started to pick it up, but noticed Parley reaching forward as if I had desecrated a shrine. I withdrew my hands, leaning forward slightly to get a closer view.

"Sorry, I'm too possessive of anything of Anna's. Go ahead and pick it up. It's my favorite. Adam snapped it this last spring. See the flowering trees and buds about to burst? It's our back yard. Anna and I had just returned from a cruise along the Baja in Mexico." Parley closed his eyes tightly then rubbed them.

Jen leaned closer, holding my elbow. "She's beautiful."

My eyes fastened on the picture. Mom had aged, but it hadn't been a rough age. The furrows around her eyes made her seem more real. She smiled more brightly than I'd ever remembered. I kept trying to swallow to get rid of the dryness in my throat. I was actually missing this damn woman who had left us two kids so long ago. I thought of the happy picture of times forgotten and had to pull something out of my eye.

***

After the second donut hole and slow sipping of terrible ice tea, I felt completely worn. Parley had told us about Mom and him, their courtship (as he called it), the birth of their two children, what Mom liked and disliked, how she could light up a room, and their adventures. He was reminiscing about wonderful memories of someone unfamiliar, a stranger, who had given me birth. It was completely incongruent with any perception my mind nursed. Adam never did come down from his room, though I'm not sure I would have known what to say to him anyway.

An hour or so had passed by the time I stood up to give my final condolences and say good-bye.

Jen blurted out a hurried sentence with pleading eyes, her neck stretched to the limit. She had been holding it in, perhaps the whole time. "I want to see my half-brother and half-sister. Can we?"

Parley glanced at the fridge and peeked around the corner at a calendar. "Summer will be home this Friday, if you want to stop by." He looked to the cupboards for an answer. "Probably after three o'clock. Would that work?"

I started to say I'd check and let them know, just as Jen said, "Perfect! But, how about we have you folks over to dinner?"

Parley nodded.

On the drive back, Dad was silent. Jen kept asking me questions about Adam and Summer as if I was holding out on hidden details. My mouth grinned, though no words escaped. She nodded her head as if her mind resolved answers she knew nothing about. My aunt slept purring against the window. We were all in our own worlds.

Chapter 20

My friend Jake stopped by that evening. Happy to have a reason to go out the front door, I hugged Jake and whispered, "Get me out of here."

I had snuck out a few hours before, but the mother patrol—Jen, Aunt Velora, and even Dad—followed. Albert had been happy to miss out, though I'm fairly sure I saw him blink in my direction.

I loved that they cared, but claustrophobia was swelling inside with everyone trying to set routines for me and shadowing my every move. My entourage ignored my pleading to walk by myself, though they stayed a couple of steps behind as a concession.

After passing two driveways, the air became stale, my anxiety peaked, and my step lost any bounce it started off with. Turning abruptly, I walked right through the three of them. My hope was they would keep on going. Aunt Velora asked me if I needed a coat as I headed back to the house. Curses formed on my lips.

I began jogging—actually it was more of a fast walk, and each step made me scrunch my eyes. Their tempo increased to keep pace with mine. I cursed again. Aunt Velora told me to watch my mouth. Jen agreed. Dad called me pretentious after re-opening the door I slammed in their faces.

Now, talking happily, Jake and I walked down the block. Jake grabbed my arm. "Why do you keep glancing back?"

"Oh, nothing." I peeked over my shoulder again.

We turned on the next street. The air was fresh and smelled

like evergreen. My ankle hurt like hell with each step. I noticed Jake wince every time I did. I didn't need the sympathy.

"You sure you're okay?" A look of worry washed over Jake's normal carefree expression.

"I'm just stiff." Pride managed to shine through the piercing ache.

He pointed to the park across the street. His face conveyed sympathy. "How about we take a sit on one of the benches over there?"

"If you want." I was breathing through clenched teeth and flared nostrils.

"If I want?" He laughed in that deep-base chuckle I remembered from years ago. "Don't pull that manly man stuff with me. I am the strong, emotional type . . . with acute sensitivity." He held his fists in the air and flexed his arms. The muscles bulged in places I'm not sure they should. "You're in pain, lots of pain. You are trying so hard not to limp, but each step stretches your face so tight you look like an x-ray."

"If you're tired, I could sit."

He laughed, and with his large hand on my back led me over to a wooden, slatted bench.

It felt like I'd been led to heaven as I sat. Pain shot through some places, relief through others. I closed my eyes as the skin on my face relaxed.

Jake waited.

It took a few minutes—maybe five or more—before my leg only slightly throbbed. "How many miles did we do?"

Jake raised his eyes. "We're about twelve houses away and we crossed a street. So what's that?"

"That would be about 80 miles in rural Nebraska."

His head cocked to the side. "Ben, see those mountains? We're not in Nebraska."

"Damn!"

We sat and talked about his construction jobs, old friends, Klarisa, my work with octopods, Amy, and his live-in boyfriend, Rick—whose real name is Calvin, but he thought it sounded too gay, so he changed it to Rick. When they fight, Jake calls Rick, "Calvin." A breeze picked up and scattered someone's school papers and a candy wrapper at our feet, then whooshed them away to the playground. We watched them as if it mattered. There was an unknown pride that came with visiting an old friend.

Jake pulled a cell phone out of his front pocket. "Should I call Jennifer to come and pick us up?"

"No," I said, with enough force Jake's eyes widened and he cupped the phone tightly against his chest. "Let's just head back slowly. I really do need the exercise, and there is no way I want to see my sister's I-told-you-so face. She's been giving me crap about my rehab."

After the second rest stop, I was about to find a tree branch to bite between my teeth. Jake's eyes dropped, concerned as a mother over her first child. I kept telling him I was all right, but my words came out more in a grumble than diction. The fourth stop was Dad's porch. I sat down and massaged my ankle, which only aggravated it. Jake waited in silence.

When do these damn wounds heal? I am so sick of pills and agony.

The front door flew open.

"Jen?"

"I saw you through the window. What happened? You were gone a long time."

Why was I feeling irritation at my sister?

Aunt Velora was a step behind, saying my name over and over.

"I'm fine. I just stepped off a curb wrong."

"Is that right, Jake?" Jen asked.

Jake folded his muscular arms and glanced at my pleading eyes. "He should be all right. He could probably use a couple of Ibuprofen, if you've got any."

Jen helped me up against my protests. "Your face is as white as a ghost. Where's your Florida tan, Mr. I'm Okay?"

Dad, Jake, Jen, and Aunt Velora all huddled around me as they hustled me into the house and up the stairs. I'm not sure my feet were even on the ground. I held my complaints behind sealed lips. Pain radiated down both my legs and up through my chest. I wasn't sure if it was from the walk or from being carried by family and friends through the house to my tiny bed. Later, I kidded Jen and Jake about huddling so close we were a ten-legged bug crawling up those stairs.

They laid me down on my childhood bed, that was hard enough to iron clothes on, and it felt amazing. My caregivers released their grip on me, tucked me in, and forced two striped pills down my throat. I closed my eyes, but I could feel all four of them standing with impatient eyes and hand signals to each other all around the bed.

"Dismissed," I whispered with eyes still shut, exasperated.

I heard feet shuffle, a few whispers, and the door shut.

My eyes opened back up. I watched the room for a while, feeling clenched muscles relax and my heartbeat slow.

I'm never going to walk that far again.

Chapter 21

We finally made my aunt promise to grit her teeth whenever she felt like ranting about Mom. The night before, she rattled on and on, no expletive left unsaid. Her voice boomed and echoed off the walls as Dad, Jen, Albert, and I listened to every vile thought with our heads bowed.

At one point that night, Jen and I retreated to the old recipe room. We had seldom heard anything about Mom, especially from Aunt Velora.

I went into the bathroom, dialed Amy's number, and let her hear a chunk of Aunt Velora's raving over my cell phone. She said it was incredible group therapy. I mentioned something about the rest of us being no more than large stones with ears and frightened minds.

"Stay that way," Amy said. "She obviously has years of built-up anger about your mom. She will be mentally healthier once it all comes out."

"This is what you listen to day after day? They couldn't pay me enough money. You should see her eyes. And she keeps dabbing at spittle with a Kleenex to the corner of her mouth."

"Velora has held this in a lot of years, for your sake and Jen's. She resents your mother for leaving, probably more than you or your Dad ever did. Let her get it out."

"What about her cancer? This can't be good for that?"

"The two aren't related, but getting rid of mental baggage sometimes helps with physical well-being."

"Have you fallen in? What're you doing? . . . You okay?"

came my aunt's voice through the bathroom door.

"I'd better get back in there," I told Amy. "She's knocking on the bathroom door. Love ya. Thanks for the advice."

"Let me know how it goes. And—trust me—it's incredibly helpful that you're there with cute little Velora right now. Bye love."

***

The doorbell rang. Even with last night's craziness and apprehension, somehow we let Velora slip past us. She greeted our visitors with a radiant smile. I could hear it in her voice. She'd been whistling all morning.

The clock on the wall read three-thirty; it was an hour slow. They were right on time.

Parley stood in the middle flanked by his children—our newfound brother and sister. Velora was congenial; she took their jackets off almost before they crossed the threshold. We all crossed our fingers, hoping she had said everything she needed to say about our mom the night before. I was ready to interject if any off-beat opinion came out.

Jen looked like a bubble about to pop. I was my bumbling congenial self, going for the standard hello and handshake. Adam's hands were sweaty, Autumn's were cold. They both wore smiles that tilted to the left, just like Mom's.

The conversation began with a narrowing on innocuous subjects like the house, the neighborhood, and the faint sound of a dog barking in someone's back yard.

Finally, Dad asked Parley, "Was Anna still an enchanting dancer?"

"The best. She could guide me as she floated around Madison's Dance Hall; she made it seem as if I was leading. We received compliments, as if I had anything to do with it."

"Yeah, she loved to dance." Dad gazed far off as the memory settled. A melancholy half smile crinkled his nose slightly.

"I moved like Frankenstein with hard, heavy steps when we first met. She used to laugh at me in that tender way only she could. I remember Anna made me spend weeknights in the kitchen training me to glide, as if I ever knew what that meant." Parley's eyes drifted.

Adam and I watched the two of them and giggled every so often. I didn't even know Mom danced, let alone that she liked to.

Jen and Autumn settled in a corner with Aunt Velora. All three mouths were moving at the same time. They appeared to be getting along well.

Dad held his chin. "She taught dance as a teen at the Terrace Ballroom." He nodded his head, agreeing with himself. "Yeah, that girl could move like water. She was a dance major at the junior college until we married, and then she accepted a secretarial job for the county while I finished law school."

I noticed then that Parley and Dad were talking about the same things, but were totally ignoring each other. It was obvious in both of their voices how much love they felt for the same woman. My chest felt warm.

Parley let out a low whistle. "She was an angel in dance shoes."

I broke the hypnosis. "Parley, I didn't know my mom well. I was only five when she left. What did she like to do?"

Adam sat forward on the chair with his arms folded across his chest. His father turned to look at him. "Adam, what were your mom's passions?"

Adam's face folded around his eyes. His voice was thick. "She was just a mom, I guess." He cleared his throat. "Came to my games, helped me with schoolwork, made dinner." He chuckled, "Lots of meatloaf . . ."

"Yeah, we ate meatloaf more times than I care to admit." Parley laughed.

"Like Dad said, she loved to dance. Made me learn to twirl my date before my first prom, but I still wasn't very good at it. I dumped Lila Pilgrim into a whole row of folding chairs. I'm pretty sure she didn't know how to twirl. Surprised the hell out of her." He paused with a grin. "Never got a second date."

The three of us laughed. I imagine we were fairly loud, because the girls glared over at us like we were convicts breaking into their tea party.

We all got along famously. We talked. We giggled. After a

couple of hours, the buzzer on the stove sounded. Aunt Velora shooed us into the kitchen to sit down to a Della's Restaurant reheat of lasagna, garlic bread, and Caesar salad. Adam mentioned something about how wonderful it was that it wasn't meatloaf, and Autumn chided him for disrespecting his mom. A little bit of time together and we were an American family, completely disjointed and friendly.

As the evening wore on, we were all melancholy, drained like a tide that keeps coming back to take a bit more sand with it each time. We could keep giving and taking, but the moon's pull was weak and the sand was heavier. The door was finally closed on the Andertons for the night with a flood of expectations and promises.

I slept soundly at Aunt Velora's on a hide-a-bed, caressing a ridge down the middle that wouldn't affect me until morning. I was asleep when Jen and Dad snuck out, and Aunt Velora went upstairs to bed.

Jen came back around midnight and woke me up. This was getting to be an annoying habit, but she seemed to need to talk so badly. I still had my pants and one sock on; she asked me to throw on a shirt and shoes and take a walk with her. She tossed my other sock to me.

Sleep slowly evaporated as I eased out the front door, dressed and hazy. Jen grabbed me by my arm and we walked around to the back yard, where she deposited me on the picnic table bench.

I waited for her to say something. She just sat next to me and stared somewhere past my right ear. I glanced back and saw nothing but a half-moon, so I waited. Several minutes passed.

"Do you remember anything about Mom?"

The question startled me. I thought she wanted to talk more about our brother and sister.

Jen's eyes were tearing up. "When I looked at her picture at the Anderton's, she seemed like a vague dream, as if we never even knew her—like she was always someone else's mother."

Her eyes never left whatever she focused on in the yard. Jen held the top of my hand, pressing it into the redwood board below. Her fingers were soft and strong.

I waited for her to say more.

184

TATTERED PORTRAIT

"Was she a good Mom to us?"

I sipped slow breaths and pinched my eyes shut in thought. Time slowed. A breeze came up, both comforting and haunting, pushing me to tell her something nice about Mom. My mind was blank for the longest time.

"Well, I hear she made a lot of meatloaf."

Jen flew out of her trance and began laughing, knocking her knuckles into my skull. I held up my hands in protest. After a few seconds of crazy, we held each other, our arms wrapped tightly around one another's necks. We both began crying. That turned into light convulsions of sobs and wet cheeks. The spasmodic crying finally eased, but it lasted forever. I'm really not sure how long we held each other, crying for a mother that we never really knew.

I put my arm around Jen, and she laid her head down on my shoulder. I told her about Mom having foot races with me in the back yard, and how she would tickle Jen's belly as she lay giggling in her diaper, and about the other good times I was able to pull from my memory of those too few years.

The moon was down and the sun was taking its time rising, leaving the night black as we walked through Aunt Velora's front door. We glanced at the clock and giggled. It was three-thirty in the morning, and we felt like we'd gotten away with something that was truly ours.

Chapter 22

After Dad picked me up, and I was fully primed with coffee, compliments of my aunt and a hazelnut latte from Starbucks, we drove back to the house. The journey upstairs was rough; my aunt's hide-a-bed and my gunshot wounds had conspired to make me miserable. I found myself wishing I'd slept on my old hard bed at Dad's. I'm fairly sure I groaned with each step.

I looked through my suitcase again. It had almost killed me to lift the mostly empty luggage onto my bed before I left with Jen the night before. Now, simply unlocking the latch was torture. I paced my movements and eyed the Ibuprofen on the desk. The meds won out, and I popped three into my mouth, swishing them down with the last of my cold latte.

Searching the luggage was futile. I had tried three times before, but I was hoping my results would change. Where was that family picture?

Dad stuck his head in the door while I was mumbling to myself.

"You okay?"

"Just searching for something."

"Need help? Or is this that mystery package you keep talking about?"

"Something like that. I'm done anyway. I want to wait until the Ibuprofen kicks in."

"Pain's back?"

"With a terrible vengeance. Aunt Velora's fold-out bed was the culprit. It was like sleeping in the sink, only less comfortable."

He turned his head as if he was envisioning it and couldn't get the thought out of his mind. "Oh, did you hear about your old girlfriend?"

"Who?"

"Klarisa." Dad waited a few seconds. A grin puffed up his cheeks. She was arrested yesterday for having sex with a minor. A 17 year-old who was teaching her tennis. My source tells me they never made it to the tennis court in six lessons."

"Your source?" *What has Klarisa gotten herself into now?*

"Well, Jennifer."

"Jen must be completely giddy." I was feeling a little sad for Klarisa, though I knew it was just her nature."

"Yeah, she's pretty happy."

This almost felt like a regular conversation. We'd been having a few of those lately. It was kind of comfortable. Maybe this is what real fathers and sons do. I knew I was still learning, and God knows Dad's still a toddler at family relations. What a pair we were.

He left, and I slid the suitcase over the edge of the bed and let it flop on the floor. Easing myself onto the flat of my back, I lay down and watched a couple of popped nails on the ceiling for relief. It didn't help.

Sometime after I memorized the patterns on the wall, the pills finally eased things enough so I could rest fitfully for a couple of hours.

My eyes opened. The ceiling was still there. I started to bounce up. That was stupid. My whole body throbbed for a time then settled into a piercing soreness. I thought about the saying, no pain, no gain and contemplated how ridiculous that was. Common sense dictated that I should be getting better. My brain knew it, but my body wasn't following.

I called Amy.

She answered with her usual sing-song voice. It sounded so happy I actually wanted to hate her, but I knew that wouldn't do any good.

"How're you feeling?" she asked.

"Well, mentally I'm in anguish, but physically I'm only miserable. How about you?"

"Is this a call I need to set the clock on? This is sounding professional."

"I just need to bitch to someone."

"First of all, men don't bitch, women do. Men complain."

"Is that true?"

"It's a law."

"Okay."

"So, what's the problem—or the problems?"

I couldn't seem to let it out fast enough. I told her about the hide-a-bed, my struggles with Dad being a dad, the hot chocolate that burned my lip three days ago, my sister slugging me, the two nails popping out of the ceiling, how my back pain was the most terrible thing on the planet, and about having been in this town way too long, and Klarisa. I'm not really sure how many minutes or hours I rattled on. Amy listened silently with small noises in all the right places.

I was sweating, but my back agony felt scaled down from a twenty-seven on a scale of ten to a solid three. We were silent as my breath settled from all the unloading.

"Feel better?" she asked.

"Yeah, I think I do." My head nodded slowly as I thought about it.

"Good, because I've got to rush to my next appointment. I'll call you later tonight. And by the way, the way you do it, it is bitching." She giggled. "I want to know more about your old girlfriend and the jock."

"What do you mean your NEXT appointment?"

"You figure it out."

"But—"

"Bye. I really have to go. Love ya! I think."

An hour later I made it downstairs, ate some Raisin Bran, and swallowed two more Ibuprofen. Dad pointed to the Lortab on the counter. I shook my head.

Jen and Aunt Velora stopped by halfway through my cereal. Jen was still high on brother-and-sister fever and the news about Klarisa. She kept the Klarisa thing to herself. I was relieved. It appeared she had memorized everything that had been said the day before; we listened to her reiterate even the hand gestures that were made. (Autumn pushed her hair back with two fingers, just like I do!) Even Aunt Velora caught the excitement.

After about 45 minutes that seemed to last the better part of a day, I put my hands over my ears and told her a little too loudly, "We were there."

Her mouth bunched all up.

"You're spoiling your sister's effervescence. Knock it off," said Aunt Velora.

I was irritable and knew deep down I resented these children who had actually had a mom. I became petulant. "You're always taking her side. You always have," I boomed and began to walk away.

As my aunt called my name, I turned toward her. Her eyes pierced mine clear back past the irises, through grey matter, and seemed to be focused on the back of my skull. She could always do that—look so deeply into me that it physically hurt. It wasn't an evil stare. It was one filled with knowledge and love, but one that always made my gut hurt and my hands fidget.

"Maybe," she said, "I take her side more because she's right more often than you are."

My aunt stood up, began laughing, and came over to wrap her arms around me.

My childish agitation floated away. I hugged her and laughed.

"Don't let him off the hook that easily," Jen said. "Isn't there a corner somewhere he could sit in?"

Aunt Velora released me, and I sat back down at the kitchen table. I glanced at the clock.

"Okay, tell me more about what Adam and Autumn said. Maybe we could act it out in the front room? I'll be Autumn. Dad, you be Adam. Jen, you tell us what to say, and Aunt Velora, would you mind ordering some lunch? This may take a long time."

Jen glared at me. "You're an ass."

"No really, I'm all in."

There was silence, but smirks all around.

"Are you sure there isn't an earlier flight to Florida? Tomorrow seems so distant." Jen punched me in the arm.

Chapter 23

It's crazy. I was excited to get home, but actually kind of glad I'd been shot and forced to stay so I could reconnect with the only family I knew. Aunt Velora with her frail little body squeezed the stuffing out of me. Dad shook my hand so long and hard, I felt like a car jack. Then he patted me on the shoulder, while Jen kissed my cheek and whispered, "You're gonna miss me, and you'd better visit more often, or I'll come to Florida and never leave."

Albert winked as Jen and Aunt Velora came back for a family hug. I turned away and feigned scratching my head while, I swiped at a tear with my index finger.

Back in Tampa, I flowed back into my routine. I said hello to my specimens as I walked between tanks. Goofy delivered her baby while I was gone, then followed her species' pattern of dying shortly afterwards. I missed her, but quickly fell for her daughter, Isla. She eyed me and stroked the glass with one tentacle every morning at eight as I was getting coffee from the pot just across from her tank.

I filled my days with charts and computer input from the undergrad staff. I wrote up grant packages to be sent out for future funding, always saying a short prayer after finishing (my attempt at religion). I rechecked the salinity and pH in the tanks every afternoon, always telling my assistants it was no reference to their abilities, just my OCD. They raised their eyes whenever I used the saying, "Measure twice, cut once." Anabelle, who was my smartest biology student, told me a number of times in her most assured voice, "I'm a college grad, not a carpenter."

TATTERED PORTRAIT

My relationship with Amy became much more than it ever was before. I paid rent for a place that was little more than a well-furnished closet. I stopped by there for a change of clothes, to feed cuttlefish to my moray eel in his 80-gallon aquarium, and to glance at my coffee table, which developed into a resting place for dust and dead flies. The air conditioner was set at 85 degrees, my mail was forwarded to my office, and everything had to be discarded from the fridge—it was nothing more than cold shelves and a humming noise. Several lights burned out, and I didn't care.

For months, I lived at Amy's. We shared the cooking and the cleanup and spit every morning in the same basin after brushing our teeth from the same tube of Aim. I read in the same comfortable chair every day. She read from the north side of her lime-green couch each day. Amy, of course, had better light. She took out the trash; I vacuumed. She put the dishes in the dishwasher; I put them away. We had sex 2.5 times per week. We both enjoyed conversation with one another and were both fine with sharing silence.

We worked on the event of being a happily married couple, and we didn't even know it. At least that's what Jen told me.

Amy and I talked about marriage several times. It seemed to be something we were both looking at some time in the distant future, like dentures and hip replacements. I didn't think we were in any hurry to get there, but sometimes I would catch a glance from Amy that made me wonder.

My sister bought Amy a subscription to Bride magazine. Jen was subtle. There was a small stack of them in the corner. I'd never seen Amy even look at them. I was pretty sure she had, but it was completely covert. Once, I noticed one was missing, I asked Amy about it. She stared at me like I was crazy, but the next day it was back in the stack.

***

I started to think about marrying Amy. Maybe it was because Jen kept sending me emails about how she looked forward to having a sister-in-law and asking what percent chance I thought she had of becoming a bridesmaid in Florida. Or perhaps it was that watchful, dreamy look Amy got when she saw a giggling young couple or a smiling, grey-haired couple holding hands as they watched birds bounce from branch to branch.

I'd been calling her my fiancé for three and a half years, and she used the term about as freely.

I finally decided to formally ask her to marry me. I wasn't considering buying a ring yet. I was much too skittish for that. Amy would have to pick out the ring. My job would be to pay for it. I wanted to do this romantically, even though heart-rending passion was not my strong suit. I checked on the Internet for the best way to proceed.

My computer spilled forth so much utter crap it made me dizzy. I wasn't about to skydive to her work and propose, or make some Italian noodle dish with a ring in it, or hire a fifteen-piece band to play her favorite music—which was something between Taylor Swift and Madonna. Skywriting was too old-school, and texting was too new and impersonal. We were adults; I was in my forties, and she was peeking at forty next year. What would an adult do? And what if she said "not yet"—or worse, the big "NO?" I decided it would be best to wait a couple of days.

Two days later, she asked me while we were driving to a bookstore, and I said "yes." It was so spur-of-the-moment that I lost control of my car for a few seconds and almost hit a lady with two Welsh corgis; her hair extension fell loose to one side. I waved sorry, and Amy laughed as loud as I'd ever heard her laugh.

We decided on April Fools' Day, two months away. I was elated and relieved. She appeared to be the same. We ate cherry pie and ice cream for dinner, began giggling like teenagers, then ended up on the floor entangled together in the most memorable, passionate night ever.

I woke up at four that morning on a cold kitchen floor with Amy tucked against me, between chair legs with a hot pad sugar-glued to her cheek. Her head rested on a cereal box—Lucky Charms. I carefully got up, then slid on something shiny on the floor. I went to the bedroom to get Amy a blanket and pillow, noticing in the mirror that my face and neck scar were streaked with red lipstick, or was it cherry filling? I smiled, disgusted and pleased with myself.

TATTERED PORTRAIT

Moving the chair, pushing the table back a foot, and carefully replacing the cereal box with a pillow, I snuggled up to Amy and pulled the blanket over both of us.

Chapter 24

On March 30th we boarded a plane for Salt Lake City. The wedding was two days away, and my ears were still sore from Jen's elation over the phone when we agreed to get married in Aunt Velora's back yard. Jen agreed she would keep it small, but thoughts of a marching band and relatives that were two and three times removed gave me a migraine. Amy was up for anything. "Let-er-rip," she proclaimed, as I explained my worries about Jen and Aunt Velora organizing our cozy, intimate wedding.

Amy's parents were already there. Seems they adore my sister and my lovely aunt and were thrilled to meet my father. My first thought—eloping to Montego Bay, Jamaica—was looking better and better. All my girls told me how silly that was, even Amy's mom.

It wasn't so bad.

We were married by Dad's Mormon bishop. Amy was enchanting in her white gown with tiny lime-green bows circling her waist and scattered perfectly in her hair. I wore a tux I'd bought for a formal biology affair in New York that I'd never actually attended.

My aunt's lawn was filled with chairs and guests I hardly knew. There were so many floral arrangements around the front, courtesy of my sister, that it appeared more like a funeral for a foreign dignitary than a wedding. Jake was my best man. Jen was the maid of honor, which thrilled her, she seemed to float above the lawn with a gracious, glowing smile. Amy's approach to the whole affair was much more low-key—a mirror image of mine.

TATTERED PORTRAIT

We both thought marriage lines were stagnant and boring, so we opted to float among the guests, despite Jen's disapproval. Jen had been voted down when Aunt Velora reminded her, "It's their wedding, not yours."

She had sulked for a few minutes, but it didn't last.

I quietly counted the chairs, figuring the guest count to be about 140 or so. I leaned over to Amy and said, "I know about twenty of these people."

She replied, "You beat me—I know about 12."

Parley and his two children came, and it was nice to talk to them again. Jen had given us weekly tabs on them. She was seeing Autumn every Wednesday for lunch, and sometimes Adam came along.

Two soft hands covered my eyes. I knew by the way Amy squeezed my hand and straightened her posture that it was Klarisa behind me.

I turned. Jail apparently hadn't helped her; seems she was headed into a cycle of recidivism. The young boy with her was at most 21, but he looked about 17.

I backed up as she lunged forward. It didn't help. Amy's hand tightened and twisted my hand out of joint as Klarisa gave me an open-mouth kiss. I couldn't pull out of it, especially with her arms wrapped around my neck, constricting what little movement I could manage with my damaged neck muscles.

Suddenly something happened, and Klarisa backed up, gasping for air. Amy smiled and wiggled her knuckles.

"It's been a long time, Klarisa," said Amy. "I didn't realize you had a son."

Amy reached out and grabbed the boy's hand. He was trying to hold onto Klarisa and seemed confused, but smiled gamely as he shook Amy's hand.

Klarisa regained herself, forming the light-up-the-room fake smile that she had perfected at a young age.

"This is Andrew. He is teaching me tennis and agreed to come with me since Raymond is at a dental conference in Georgia."

Andrew nodded. His curly blonde hair bounced freely across his forehead. He seemed pleased with himself.

"I thought you and Raymond were considering divorcing?" I asked.

"Oh, the silly man changed his mind. He just couldn't get along without me."

Amy and I shared a glance. Amy wished her well at her tennis game and we hurried off.

"You think good ol' Raymond changed his mind because he wants to be with her or because he couldn't afford the cost of her leaving?"

I smiled at Amy. "Definitely a monetary thing."

Dad was happier than I'd ever seen him sober. He asked me, with a nudge of an elbow, if I needed the sex talk, then laughed so hard at his own joke that all heads turned to check if he was all right. He danced so gracefully with my new bride that I teared up, thinking about Mom.

Wiping my eyes nonchalantly and grabbing Aunt Velora, I strolled out to the center of the lawn to dance. My aunt helped lead enough that I almost appeared to be graceful. At first she kept her distance, trying to out-step my size ten black shoes. When she realized I was trainable, she moved in a bit closer. I couldn't match my dad, or most of the people who were out dancing, but I enjoyed myself.

After my aunt's prepping, Jen cut in. I took most of the shine off her new heels and turned her head-on into someone's elbow. As I led her over to a chair, her face reddened. I apologized.

She kept rubbing her feet. I ran over to the bar and grabbed her a glass of wine. When I got back to Jen, she half-jokingly told me, "It'd better be Tequila in this plastic wine glass."

I nodded my head yes and walked away.

Aunt Velora caught up with me a few minutes later. She leaned in close. "Don't worry, she can't dance much better than you."

***

That night, we played chess on a soft bed and finished a bottle and a half of champagne, before we totally passed out. Waking at four in the morning, we made love again and finished off the other half bottle. I was enjoying this married life, even though it appeared to be little different from the one we lived before

We had taken our honeymoon the week before we were married. I know that's backward, but the trip to Jamaica was planned and booked nine months earlier. Montego Bay was beautiful. Amy made me limit my snorkeling, or I probably wouldn't have eaten lunch or dinner or gazed into her happy, carefree eyes. We walked our hotel's private beach and battled for bargains in the marketplace. We truly learned baskets full of wonderful things about each other in those six pre-wedding days.

We believed we knew each other so well, but the thought of actual marriage drawing near prompted us to snip off all those dangling strings we hadn't realized were a part of us. With a lot of the frayed seams gone, the anxiety of the following week dissipated. Insignificant spats ceased, and our eyes gazed just a little deeper.

***

Dad spoke with me after the wedding. He was worried about Velora. Her treatments seemed to make her feel worse. She was lacking energy, but pretending to be a young school girl. Dad called it a "façade." If that was true, she fooled me.

Amy and I spent a few hours with Aunt Velora at her house before our plane's departure. She fussed over us. She tried to make us sandwiches. She gathered apples into a bag for us to take on the trip. I told her I'd put them in my carry-on, which pasted a satisfied grin on her face.

Though her stance was more bowed, Aunt Velora's movements were quick as always, but unsure. She seemed so frail, though the fireball inside never dimmed. Somewhere during our conversation, she told us she was feeling like life was draining from her. It was the first time I'd ever heard my sweet aunt mention her mortality. I turned my head as a tear found its way down my cheek. Amy knew and drew Aunt Velora's attention to something else.

As we began to leave, she slipped me a twenty, folding my

fingers around it. She tilted her eyes and winked up at me, as she had so many times before, and said the same sweet words— "Just in case." with a nod of her head.

***

Amy and I didn't know then, that we would be back for a funeral in just a few short months.

Chapter 25

The smell of decay and flowers carried through the door, opened gratuitously by a heavyset man with a black suit, wrinkled shirt, and scuffed brown shoes that pressed deep into thin carpet. He escorted us down a hall to a room with heavy, mustard-colored curtains hiding one wall. The quietness was disturbing. My mind sailed through days of near and far in a haphazard order of flashes. Even the name, Manson's Funeral Home, sounded dark and laced with ivy. The abundance of flowers only made the scene more distasteful. Someone offered me a cup of water. It was clear but tasted miasmic, as I forced a swallow down my tight throat.

The heavyset man introduced himself as a grief counselor and gave his name. He spoke just above a whisper in didactic cadence as if we might disturb the deceased. I grasped Jen's hand. It was damp and quivered slightly. I found myself hating this man for no other reason than that he was the one putting a part of my family in the ground.

He asked for decisions about headstones and obituary details. We perused a room full of caskets as if picking out a new car. The portly man explained features and benefits. I wanted to hold my palms to my ears and hum.

My sister wore a new black dress, that I assumed she would burn after this was all over. I wore jeans, boat shoes, and a clean shirt. I wasn't sure if I was appropriately dressed or not. My experience with shopping at a mortuary was limited; in fact, it was zero. Jen and I finally made decisions we didn't want to make.

Once outside, we held each other in the shade of a tree of

heaven and an acacia. Wetness soaked my shirt as she nuzzled in my shoulder. I leaned over her with intermittent dry sobs that popped spasms from my chest to my head. Jen held on to me as she would a life preserver in choppy water. My strength was chiseled away by emotions, while we ignored the world. All of the feelings swirling through my body made my knees weak. I wasn't sure if I was holding up Jen or she was holding up me.

After a time, I glanced toward feathery sounds from the sidewalk. A group of people glanced away, as if caught shoplifting. I pulled away from Jen as unnecessary embarrassment flooded through me. Roping my arm through hers, I led her to the car.

***

Days later, we stood to the left of the casket, our faces brimming with sorrow and disbelief. Crafted of highly polished cherry with curved edges, the casket refracted the window light from the south and continued to catch my eye as I shook hands and listened to innocuous condolences.

I'm well aware that we each have our final day; I just held too many undisclosed thoughts that I had believed could wait for another time. A better time. Somewhere in the future. And I assumed, as we all do, that life would continue to all those next days, even though death is imperative.

I couldn't seem to cry. The tears and feelings bunched up in my throat. My voice caught and squeaked as I uttered "thank you" to whatever well-wishers said. I wasn't listening. My mind was displaced somewhere in the distance, as if not a part of my body at all.

Amy leaned in to me from the left, Jen from my right. I spread my elbows out slightly, giving me breathing room. I listened to the rhythm of their voices as they held my hands, supposedly for support. I had none to give. I'm not sure I could even fog a mirror with each weak breath.

The craziness of the days before had sucked every morsel of energy and left me feeling like rotted fruit.

I glanced at the casket, remembering the insanity of picking it. Jen had held her lips tight, speaking in short, irritated sentences. "That's fine. Why would anyone want that? How much?"

The languorous mortuary man spoke in a soft, even voice, his jowls puffing with each word. "Perfect choice. Most people like the extra comfort for their beloved departed. We have wonderful finance terms."

Who the hell wanted to pick a casket at a time like this—or at any time, for that matter? I couldn't believe, now, that I had argued with my sister over the brass handles that would be used only once and would then be encased forever in a cement vault under bumpy grass and plastic flowers. I had finally seceded when Amy pinched my arm to get my attention and glared at me with the tightest face I'd ever endured. I had felt like an ass then, and now, remembering.

Jen let me have the closed casket. I'm not sure why anyone would ever want to see a puttied-up face, dead, with the façade of sleep seemingly making it all right. She hadn't argued; she simply started crying through closed eyes and nodded her head.

The picture of Dad, Mom, Jen, and me kept popping up in my mind. Family. It created a hollow space in my stomach.

The line kept coming. Dad made a lot of friends after losing the annoying bravado that fermented liquid previously allowed. His church seemed to send truckloads of people to pay their last respects and to remind me of the better place he was in. I wasn't sure. I needed more time with this man whom I hated and loved, this man who had been both devil and father.

Bowed heads that avoided eye contact streamed by me with similar rhetorics of sorrow. Most appeared genuinely distraught at his passing. It was etched into their faces and vocalized with quivering words. They seemed to truly love the man I had hated most of my life, the man who had caused knots to twist tightly in my stomach at his very mention. Now was a different time, though, and I felt far different emotions.

Jake came through with Rick. He grabbed me with those huge hands and pulled my shoulders toward him. He cried into my left ear while pulling me closer. His minty breath blew down my neck. I began bawling and held him back. We stayed that way for an eternity. There was a sense of fellowship and warmth in his grip. It felt right.

Jake finally backed up, putting his heavy paws on my shoulders. We stood with our eyes locked. "I knew I would catch you crying sooner or later," he tried to joke.

I wiped the wetness from my cheeks with my jacket sleeve. "It was the bear hug. Go a little easy on your old friend. I'm only mortal." I put my flat hand to his chest. "You'd cry too if your body was crushed by someone twice your size."

He squeezed me again. This time it really did hurt. "There is no one twice my size."

Jen gave a soft giggle.

The rest of the line was bunching up around Jen.

"We'd better move on. Come by the house before you leave."

"Okay," I said softly.

Aunt Velora was a couple of yards away. She was greeting people like it was a high school reunion. A faint smell of marijuana permeated her elegant black dress, as she shook hands and pointed in our direction. She talked about Dad's stroke as if it had been mild influenza.

"He had a little stroke thing while cooking up some bacon and eggs for breakfast. He was never that great of a cook, but he knew how to scramble eggs. They were always so fluffy, cooked to perfection. They practically melted in your mouth. No matter how many times I try, my eggs always have a hard brown side to them. I make rubber. Lawrence really knew his eggs." Her head nodded as if agreeing with herself.

Forty minutes later, the crowd moved into the main chapel. My family stopped behind, huddled together without any words. Aunt Velora, who had manned the greeting of Dad's friends at the entry, dropped down into a soft chair. She was pale and insignificant as she closed her eyes, breathing in as if trying to take in energy. She sat listless for fifteen minutes. The bishop signaled us twice that it was time. Both times, I shooed him out of the room with the back of my hand.

We waited patiently until Aunt Velora glanced up. Her eyes were sunken and red. I helped her up and walked her slowly out of the room and into the chapel. All heads turned our way.

We followed the pallbearers toward the pulpit. I glanced over at three rows left open for our family of five people. Somehow Albert was already seated in the middle.

My breath stopped, and my heart seemed to follow as I stared at the top of the casket between two colorful fans of flowers. How had I missed it before? It was smaller than I remember, but it had the same impact. A warm sensation spread through my chest as I finally took a breath. It was delightful. I couldn't take my eyes off the unfamiliar happiness of a family I once knew—a family I was once a part of.

There it was, the picture of Dad, Mom, me, and Jen, smiling as if we were the happiest family in the whole universe. At the time, I think we were.

I couldn't speak. My finger pointed with a shaky hand to the picture.

"I found the picture in my spare room. You must have left it when you stayed there for the night," Jen whispered. "It was under the bed. Obviously, cleaning down there wasn't a priority. I found it just after the call that Dad passed away. I'm not really sure why I went down there to clean. I was so upset. I needed to do something."

We all kept our eyes on the picture. I felt a smile spread across my face and knew the others shared the same feeling.

"Okay," I said, after a great deal of time passed.

"Okay," said Jen. She was bouncing her leg to the piano music coming from the left of the dais. It was an old show tune Aunt Velora requested. I caught myself tapping out the music with my fingers as I tried to recall the name.

My father's Mormon bishop, Lehi Orvin, stood and inched over to the podium. He raised the microphone closer to his mouth. His lanky build held his suit more like it was drying on a frame than fitted. He straightened his striped tie between the white collar, though it didn't need it. Bony hands held the sides of the podium as he spoke.

"Lawrence Parch was a wonderful human being, who took a long road to find God. I have known of him for years, but only enjoyed the pleasure of truly knowing him for the last six years, while he was finding his way into The Church of Jesus Christ of Latter Day Saints. I now think of him as a friend and a heartfelt addition to our church."

My eyebrows rose as I peeked at Jen. With a stern look, Aunt Velora waved a finger at me. As if I were six years old again, I straightened in my seat, her glare heating up the side of my face.

"We Mormons tend to use the surname 'brother' when talking about fellow male members of our church. He hated that and stopped me and many others after hearing that reference. I will respect his wishes and not refer to him as Brother Parch, even though I feel a great kinship to the man.

"As some of you know, Lawrence was a bit of a scoundrel when Todd and Arron, our local missionaries, first knocked on his door." The bishop glanced over at two baby-faced boys in the fourth row. They grinned, turning a slight shade of red.

Aunt Velora had told me earlier that Todd and Arron drove more than three hundred miles to be at Dad's funeral. That baffled me.

"They tell me Lawrence answered the door in a blue suit with a vest buttoned tightly, an undone tie, and a scowl on his face that took all the wind out of the two boys. After a full silent minute of eyeing the boys over, Lawrence boomed, 'WELL?'"

"Todd worked up enough nerve to ask, 'Do you want to be reunited with your family after death?'"

"Lawrence said, 'My family? They don't want me now, and I'm not so sure I want them either. You think they'd want to see this face in the hereafter?' I'm cutting out the colorful language he used at the time."

Everyone laughed.

"Todd replied, 'They might.' Lawrence thought about that for a few seconds then invited them in for what he termed as mediocre bourbon." The bishop grinned. "They declined the drink, but followed him in anyway. They gave him the first lesson. Drunk as he was, he listened and grilled them as if they were on a witness stand. He scared these two young boys to death, but they stayed for two and a half hours. Mr. Parch even fell asleep on them a couple times and then woke up with another question, as if he never left. The boys said they'd never met anyone like him before."

"As they left, Lawrence asked them to drop by anytime. They wondered if he would even remember them stopping by. They rang his doorbell again a week later. He invited them in, offered them a drink, which they declined again, and sat down to have another discussion with them.

"These boys slowly lost their fear and began to love their visits to Mr. Parch's home. I think he felt the same. I was a ward missionary leader at that time, and those boys were always coming to me with questions Lawrence asked that stumped them. They became excited to get back to him with answers. He taught them as much as they taught him."

Jen nudged my leg and whispered, "You think he's looking down on us now—you know, from heaven?"

I leaned over to her. "He's chuckling that his son actually shed tears for him."

"No, seriously," she said, "I feel like he's here somewhere. It's kind of comforting."

"That's a nice thought, Jen. You think Mom might be with him?"

Jen raised her chin and gazed up. "Yeah, I do." She squeezed my hand.

***

"The last time they visited him, I went with them," the bishop continued. "After an hour of teaching, with Lawrence giving alcohol-slurred responses, he folded down on the floor, quivering like a windblown tent, and passed out.

"I completely panicked. Todd and Arron were awestruck and speechless. I ended up calling an ambulance, dismissed the two boys, drove to the hospital, and waited by his side for several hours. Sometime during the wait, Jen was called by the hospital.

"That was the first time I met Lawrence's amazing daughter. She picked up Velora and they arrived to watch him detox. The two of them seemed pretty used to it. The doctor pumped his stomach, hooked him up to an IV, and let him sleep it off. It was just another day for the staff, but for me, watching an alcoholic detox was terrifying. Jen consoled me and told me to go home.

"For some reason, I felt somehow responsible and stayed throughout most of the night. When I arrived the next morning, Jen and Velora were there to find out when they could check Lawrence out. The doctor wanted to keep him for at least 48 hours. He was dehydrated and couldn't hold food down."

I remembered hearing an account of that day. Aunt Velora told me that Dad had appeared feral and disoriented. His hair was poking out in every direction. His hands were shaking, and he spent every shred of energy he possessed dry-heaving into a bed pan. Bishop Orvin had to hold Dad down to keep him from punching the nurses and Jen.

Aunt Velora said she sat in a corner and told her brother to behave. He traveled between fits and sleep. This went on until late afternoon, when he seemed to sober up. Dad had reluctantly agreed to stay another night, though according to Aunt Velora, his eyes had said he wanted another bottle.

Bishop Orvin continued, "He woke up late on the second day in the hospital with a more 'relaxed attitude,' as the nurses put it. He was smiling and hungry when I dropped by that morning on my way to work. He couldn't remember anything, but kept asking for Benjamin."

It seems he had wanted me to mow his lawn. I laughed at that and whispered to Jen, "At least he didn't want me for a Captain Morgan run."

"When I stopped over a few days after his release from the hospital," the bishop continued, "Lawrence was cleaning the house as if it had never been cleaned before. The place smelled of Lysol. The counter was lined with a hundred dollars' worth of cleaning supplies and rags everywhere. It was 40 degrees outside and the windows were open, but he seemed unconcerned."

I had heard earlier that dad was wearing a t-shirt with two frogs from a long-past vacation, camouflage boxers, and an old blue sports jacket, carrying a scrub brush on a long pole. The vision of it made me smile on the edge of a giggle. By the look on Jen's face, she was remembering the same story.

The bishop said, "He scrubbed the floor with soapy water and a new mop. Two trash cans in the front yard were filled with liquor bottles, Cheetos, candy wrappers, pieces of a wood chair, and over-ripe food from the fridge. I started to help him, but he told me to sit down—this was his mess and he needed to clean it. I felt thoroughly guilty."

"We talked about life and work and old times, until my phone rang. My wife had dinner ready. I returned an hour later with a plate of lasagna, salad, two rolls, and a root beer."

"Lawrence took a break and feasted. I recall him asking how many wives I had, and if he could maybe borrow the one that made the lasagna. I told him I only had one wife, but I'd ask her if she'd make extra the next time; I promised I'd drop it off.

"Before I left that day, Lawrence told me he'd had an epiphany—his word, not mine—that he would quit drinking. He went out the back door for a moment, returning with a box. He lined up four full bottles along the floor in front of him. He explained that he kept them on a high shelf in the shed . . . just in case."

Jen had told me earlier that the bishop didn't realize, until Dad told him months later, that all the bottles in the trash were empties. Dad had never thrown away partial or full bottles, just pretended to himself that they didn't exist when he was cleaning. Sometime after the bishop went home that day, Dad laid down in front of those bottles and fell asleep, exhausted from the cleaning.

Dad had woken up on the floor the next morning, sober. In front of him stood those four bottled devils; he decided his great manifestation of sobriety wasn't meant for that minute. He decided that a higher being must have put those out for him. He completely forgot about his great epiphany.

Velora had told me a couple of days ago, "I found my pathetic brother, your dad, laying on the floor and singing around noon. The four bottles were tipped over in a sticky mess." She wasn't sure how much he had drunk and how much he had spilled, but it was substantial on both counts.

Aunt Velora had immediately organized things, calling Jen and getting Dad's sponsor from AA—a guy named Frank Best—to help her sober him up. When Jen arrived, she went online to find a couple of rehab centers Frank suggested and about a thousand more. Jen sifted through the rehabs while Aunt Velora kept strong coffee brewing.

Frank held Dad's hand, kept him talking, and filled him up with black coffee. Jen picked a rehab place in Florida because it was a long way away and because I lived there.

I let out a tiny snort, remembering Velora telling me that—as if I might have done something to help at that time. People in the church turned my way. I must have made a louder sound than I thought.

They had sobered him up enough to sign papers and shipped him off to Florida. Interestingly, they had never even let me know he was there.

I raised my head back up as the bishop continued, "Before leaving, Lawrence promised me he would return sober as an angel and become a Mormon. I knew of his reputation and wasn't exactly expecting miracles. In fact, I wasn't entirely sure the promise would be remembered." The bishop grinned at that and held on to the podium with both hands.

"Lawrence came back sober months later and invited me over to his house one Saturday afternoon. He escorted me into his study and pointed to a section of bookcases.

"Lawrence told me he felt liberated. He held out the palms of his hands as he proudly showed me the destruction in the corner. He had thrown bottles at his bookcase. There was a shiny gloss of liquid and shards of glass everywhere. At first, I wondered if perhaps Lawrence was slightly off-kilter. He could see it in my eyes and my movements as I backed up. After some explanation, I realized Lawrence needed to physically rid himself of his addiction. This was his way of changing.

"My new friend, Lawrence Parch, began going to Sunday services and within a couple of months he became a baptized member of the Mormon Church." The bishop paused.

"He never drank again."

I repeated that in my mind several times. *He never drank again.* It was so incongruent and unlikely. The idea of him quitting actually irritated me. It was as if something was being taken away from me, and I wasn't comfortable with it. This whole sober thing was going to take a while for me to come to grips with. Even though I had seen him as a sober human being, I never quite believed it. I had expected him to screw up. Jen glanced over and patted me on the hand.

I would have thrown his bottles in the corner a long, long

time ago if I had thought it would work. Or would I?

"Lawrence became not just a Mormon, but a true Christian." The bishop's humble, soft voice began to thicken, and his eyes closed for a few seconds. "He helped a widow with the legalities on figuring out her husband's holographic will. He did it without charge and saved her a considerable amount of money, which she didn't have. He bought Christmas presents for several less fortunate children in the church, and he delivered them on Christmas Eve. Lawrence would ring the doorbell, then run away like a young boy. He never expected praise. If it weren't for a few next-door neighbors watching him, no one would have known."

The bishop told one story after another. My father sounded more like Mother Teresa than the drunken Eric the Red of my childhood.

Jen leaned over, saying, "I think we're at the wrong funeral." Her voice was thick and raspy from crying.

"It doesn't sound like anyone I know either," I said.

Amy put her finger to her lips and motioned with a tilt of her head.

Twisting my head around, I noticed the people directly behind me covering smiles. Perhaps we were talking a bit too loudly, again.

Forgiveness is a hard creature to swallow and harder to digest, I thought.

However, hearing about our Dad, Jen and I each had a grin on our faces, a pride we had never felt before. I put my arm around my sister. She cuddled into my chest, her body quivering uncontrollably. Amy and Aunt Velora joined in.

Chapter 26

Back in Florida, I kept myself busy with as much as I could pack into a day, but Dad's face kept creeping back into my mind. Sometimes he was the man in the family picture; other times he was that raging, unhappy drunk with crimson eyeballs that seemed to shoot fire.

I called Jen several times over a period of months, at times crying and telling her how much I missed our father. At others, ranting about his drunken meanness. A dichotomy always formed, creating a knot in my stomach with the tension of a tow rope.

When I phoned Aunt Velora, I would rant about the terrible man who fathered me, but not without the conviction I once held. She would listen and agree in her soothing voice that always made me aware of Dad's faults, without actually putting him down.

And Amy was always there for me, no matter how pathetic I felt. She was a trained listener when she needed to be and always seemed to know when we were in conversation, verses when I needed to expel childhood demons.

Amy and I found our flight pattern. There was something about the marital ceremony that left us with a tangible sensation. We had told each other "I love you" hundreds of times before, but we hadn't known until after how deep in our souls those feelings were rooted. We were not only physically, but emotionally compatible and connected.

Chapter 27

About four months after the funeral, Amy and I flew out to Utah again. We all met at Dad's gravesite. Amy and I pulled up in our Subaru rental. Jen parked her Explorer under a tree across from us. I watched as Albert and Aunt Velora got out of her back seat and ducked under a branch just before crossing the narrow road.

The pat of Amy's hand brought me out of a nostalgic stupor. Dad had asked me to go fishing after 36 years, and his hesitant request kept rolling around in my mind I wished we had gone. Of course, neither of us knew anything about fishing. I'd gone with friends a few times when I was in grade school, but we mostly waded in the creek and splashed each other. My throat hardened as I realized I didn't even know if Dad fished when he was younger. I knew so little of his history.

"Are you ready?" Amy asked.

"Yeah." My head rose.

"You're still coming to grips with this?"

"I'm sorting out all the things I missed and didn't realize I missed. Does that make sense?"

Amy nodded and squeezed my hand.

"Even when he was nice, he bugged the crap out of me."

She opened her door. "Let's go. Your sister is waiting."

I turned around. Jen was signaling me with her finger. I chuckled. She could make a government worker hop to it with her look of impatience.

Amy's hand passed warmth to mine as we approached the gravesite. Jen held the fishbowl to her chest.

"You ready?" asked Jen.

I stared at the grave site.

Lawrence Eugene Parch
1950–2013
"He learned how to change"

"You know the groundkeepers will think we're crazy," I said.

"Probably," Aunt Velora laughed.

"You gonna say something, big brother?"

"I thought we were just setting it down and running." I said.

Amy squeezed my hand. "You should say something."

My hands and neck were sweaty. I took in a deep breath. As I glanced around, all eyes were on me.

"It's okay," said Aunt Velora.

Jen nodded and wiped a stray tear from her eye. She handed me the fishbowl.

My lungs filled, and I began to speak on an exhale. "Here's to the father we didn't really know. And to the man who finally made himself a promise and kept his word—a promise that affected us all."

With that, I carefully put down the fishbowl, filled with shards of broken glass and discolored labels from the study, at the base of the headstone where my father now rested.

TATTERED PORTRAIT

Jef Huntsman

A glimpse into the new thriller:

Jamaica Rush

By: Jef Huntsman

Prologue

A turbulent shift as nine wheels banked off asphalt. Tia rolled unconscious, scraping off more layers of her soft skin. Her skull bounced off rough plywood, kicking her awake as slivers penetrated her bruised cheek. A muffled cry was heard to her left. Frantic sobbing, perhaps in the next room, came in stuttered and suppressed resonance. Her head throbbed, her body filled with lead. All around was darkness and a hard floor. Tia leaned towards the weeping, her legs catching on something. A numbing pain shot up her calf. With fading stamina, she kicked haphazardly, to no avail.

She could smell new pine and diesel fuel. Her delicate hands reached to untangle her ankles and there was a tug and slight burn on her thin wrists. Sitting, even partially up, caused a nauseous rise in her throat and her head pounded from inside. A burning gulp of bile. She rolled her tongue to find saliva. Her parched throat had the texture of pumice. Water and a couple of aspirin was all she could think about, between the throbbing and the bitter surge of vomit. Fatigue overwhelmed her and she lay back down on the rough floor. She tried curling up, but her ankles were gripped. Movement added to the other pains. Tears rolled down battered cheekbones.

She wondered if she had the flu and tried to think of yesterday, but the memory wasn't there. Dizziness enveloped her. She passed out for several hours.

Tia's eyes opened first to slits, then a touch wider. Her irises had adjusted to pitch blackness, but it didn't help. There was a jostling, like traveling on a train. As she began to sit up, a biting kink in her neck speared up through her skull. She reached to rub the muscles of her neck and realized her hands were somehow bound, so that as she moved her left hand, the right hand was pulled and followed about a foot behind. Her fingers felt a leather thin wrap tight to each wrist and strapped together with something that felt like a belt. She tried yanking them apart but their strength was greater than hers.

Panic struck. She screeched and tried biting through her bindings like a wild dog on a leash. The screaming and gnawing turned to heavy sobs. Her ankles were bound to the floor and her arms were bruised and sore.

Tia stretched out her arms and legs as far as the binds would allow. In burning agony, her surroundings formed from touch to mind. She was in a box. Tears welled up and her mouth quivered. She laid back at the edge of shock, listening to the biting murmurs nearby.

She felt the cries around her more than heard them, moaning animalistic, like cornered prey.

***

The car billowed clay dust in a hurried tail a half a mile long, coating the cedars. I sat lazily in my "office," with both feet propped up on the edge of an outdoor fire pit. Even with the blurred shape, I could tell it was a newer vehicle meant for roads with stoplights and street-sweepers. Where else could they be heading but right here? I wondered if they'd lose it over the cattle guard. A short sideways slide and the car found a furrow and locked in. The front end bounced out over the ridge, the driver over-compensating as sage brush scratched new paint. My cheeks puffed as a smile pasted to my face. Definitely, city. I turned and marked my place in Cervantes, Don Quixote with a Twix wrapper.

The shadows were lengthening off the Chinese elms and thick desert cedar gatherings. The late afternoon was calm in every direction but west. The car slid as it rounded the corner, bottomed the shocks over the culvert, forced its way down my rutted lane, and passed through the open gate.

Excerpt from: JAMAICA RUSH

Rocks spit from the tires. I imagined rabbits and lizards scurrying from the sound and coughing in the upheaval. The once shiny, gold Lexus stopped with a crunch of gravel and the settling of fine dirt on its professionally detailed surface. The car gasped twice before shutting down. A dry earthy taste filled my mouth.

Tan legs with chiseled calves stepped out of the car. My appreciation followed them. As I looked upward, I watched a tight face accentuated by black hair pulled back into a French braid. She seemed annoyed as she squinted down a thin nose. Her delicate hand snatched a tissue off from her dash and blew. Glancing around, she stood lost for a second, waving the tissue. Back in the car it went. A disgusted tightening of her mouth followed her strained neck, as she inspected the property.

"You Carson?" Her voice was demanding, but still soft. Feminine. Her eyes rolled over me as if I was green meat found hidden in the back of her fridge.

"Yes, ma'am." My hands grabbed the back of relaxed neck muscles, elbows out, as I stared up at the cloudless sky.

A canyon breeze torqued up and rippled her flowered skirt. Plump hips made her waist appear thinner than it was. "A Mister Calvin told me you could help me."

"The DA up in Salt Lake?" I asked. A squirrel ran up on the log pile, his head rotating in a jerky motion.

She eyed me with suspicion, keeping her distance as if a disease might strike her down. I ran my long fingers through matted blonde hair, watching powdered dirt feather out. I'd forgot about chasing Ernie's sheep that hid huddled inside my outhouse this morning. Those three damn ewes think the head is their bedroom. They snuggled so close last week they broke the mirror off the short wall.

"Yes, Roger Calvin. He's married to a friend of mine from college." She pulled her $300, pre-frayed, denim jacket closed.

I waited.

Her hands went to her sides as she looked me over, shifting her weight from one leg to another. She didn't seem all that impressed with me. Maybe, she wasn't all that perceptive, hadn't noticed my six-foot two-inch height or my BMI. I thought about standing up and flexing a few times, but thought better of it. A brief chortle erupted between my lips.

She raised her eyes. I'm pretty sure she was thinking of leaving. I tried smiling.

"Well, can you help me?"

"What's your name?"

"My name?" Two deep pressed lines formed between her eyebrows. She stood her ground for a moment, then with a loud exhale she dropped her shoulders slightly. "Annabelle Christina Linford. I go by Annie."

I nodded. I assumed she wanted me to stand at attention in recognition of her name. My grin seemed to have no effect on her.

Her throat cleared as if hearing was a problem for me. Waiting exasperated her and gave me a little pleasure. "Can you help me?" she repeated.

"Depends."

"Depends?"

I nodded my head and threw a log on the fire. It wasn't cold enough or dark enough for a campfire. I just liked the peacefulness it brought. "What is it you need help with?"

She looked at her heels covered in dust. "Is there somewhere we could talk?" Her eyes narrowed, glancing toward the cabin and then her feet. I think she wanted to buy new shoes shortly after this encounter.

"Sure, grab one of the camp chairs and have a seat." I pointed at a couple of Cabela's chairs folded and leaning against the picnic table.

She scrunched up her nose and coughed, as if having a hard time breathing.

Trying to be cordial, I stood up slowly, walked over, grabbed a chair, and unfolded it next to mine.

Annie brushed off the seat with a Wet Wipe from her brown leather purse and sat down. I watched her stare into the fire, perhaps organizing her thoughts. Maybe, wishing she could push me into it. The sun was about halfway dissolved into the Pavant mountain range, as the moon watched between clouds on the other side. She turned in the chair and glowered at my property in careful movements.

"My closest neighbor is three miles to the southeast and

unless you're afraid of a critter listening, you're probably safe telling me what you're here for."

Her face reddened. "Who the hell do you think you are?"

"I'm the one without a problem," I said. "I assume I'm not what you expected." Her red lips tightened together. "You know, handsome and brilliant and the owner of all this." I held my arms out. I swiped at some soot on my pant leg.

Her face softened and she let out a sound that could be construed as a chuckle.

"Well you're not what I expected either," I said. "Especially since I wasn't expecting any visitors today. You were a bonus. A pretty city girl driving all this way just to see me, makes me wonder about all the ones that don't make it this far."

"Don't flatter yourself," she said. "Didn't Roger Calvin call you? He promised me he'd tell you I was coming." A breeze kicked up, pushing the smoke south and into her face. She leaned to the left, then the right, trying to get out of it. Her hand fanned in front of her as she glared at me.

I ignored her disgust. "Roger could have left a message. I haven't checked my messages for a couple of days."

"This was a week ago."

"It's probably good you reminded me. I'll get to that tonight."

"Do you even have a cell phone?" She scrunched her nose again.

"Of course I have a cell phone. A good one. It's on the charger or in my glove box." I actually couldn't remember where I'd left it.

"What if I wanted to call you?" She was still leaning to the right as the smoke shifted.

"Just let me know when and I'll have it with me."

"That's preposterous. What if I hired you and wanted to get a hold of you?"

I gritted my teeth and took in a slow breath. "If I'm on a job, I carry the cell with me at all times. We are on my time now, so there's little need." My eyes had narrowed unconsciously.

"But . . . . Oh, never mind."

"Okay Annabelle Christina, what did you travel all this way

for? I assume Roger told you I find people and I'm not licensed." I tossed a couple more logs on the fire. She leaned way back in the chair as the smoke and ash billowed out. I folded my arms and waited.

"My sister . . . she's missing." She closed her eyes and I watched a single tear flow over her cheekbone.

Excerpt from: JAMAICA RUSH

Jef Huntsman

Acknowledgements

I would like to thank several writers, Jae, Marta, Catherine, Kathy, Vivian, Barry, and Nolyn for their dedication to the craft and jesting wit which helped to chisel another book from a pebbled brain. Thanks also, to the staff of Eschler Editing for their work on the manuscript. And a special clap of hands for Rachel Jensen who fastidiously attached and discarded thoughts and commas with the tuned mind of a teacher. Finally, to the lady whose presence always makes my day, Diana Huntsman, my wife and best friend.